The Two Pyramids

Donald C. Meyer

First Published June 2022
ISBN 9798824019001

Cover design by Books Covered (bookscovered.co.uk).

Acknowledgements:

Several friends and family members read earlier drafts of this novel and provided invaluable help: Janet Ashby, Liz Meyer, Steve Meyer, Michael Pickard, Margo Schroeder, and Ben Zeller. My wife, Liz, has been a sounding board for me ever since I first conceived of the novel in June 2018, listening to me recount ideas for the plot, adding clever bits of her own, and then reading the first draft carefully. She has been a support to me throughout this process. I am also grateful to Lake Forest College, where I have taught since 1995, and to the office of the Dean of Faculty for its support of my creative endeavors through the years and for providing funding for the recording of the forthcoming audiobook version of this novel. Lake Forest College students have been a consistent source of inspiration; in particular, I would like to single out Finn Kraker and Tom Mboya, summer research assistants in 2022, who helped me with the audiobook. Astute readers will notice my indebtedness to countless fantasy novels and movies, works of historical fiction, and popular history, too many to list here. And thanks to you, my unknown reader; I hope you enjoy this novel.

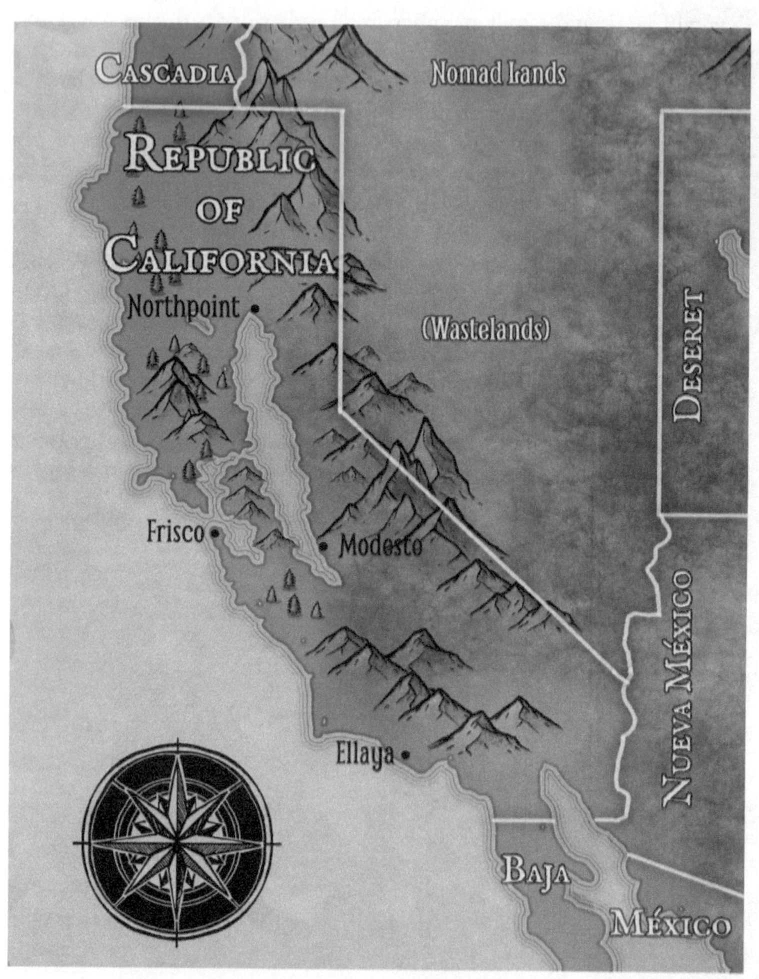

California in 2488

1

Benson City, Kingdom of the Great Lakes (KGL)
Monday, May 24, 2488 (High Solar Calendar Year 11)

Paul Girard stepped out of his wood-frame house early in the morning. He walked down the short pathway to the wooden sidewalk that ran along his street, carrying with him his academic robe, carefully folded inside his burlap carpetbag. He was leaving early enough so that he would have time to change into his academic robe before the Hearing. There was no way he was going to risk getting his finest robes dirty in these muddy streets on this important day. He passed his mother's vegetable garden in the front yard. Chickens clucked in the coop next door. Paul was both nervous and excited.

It was unusually warm for late May in Benson City. Paul worried about coming in sweaty and disheveled before the panel. He had considered riding in, but the stables near the capital were pricey. Even though they presented the image of a well-to-do Caste 3 family—the third of the Nine Castes—Paul and his mother had to watch their expenses carefully. It would be cheaper for him to take the omnibus uptown.

Paul was eager to get to the Hearing at the Black Pyramid on the north end of the city. After four years of study, he would finally receive his post-graduation appointment. He had reason to feel confident. Through diligent study, he'd become valedictorian of his class at the Seminary. It didn't hurt that he was well liked by his professors and his peers and came from a good family. But you never knew what the Elders would decide. They kept their cards close to their vests. There was an Assistant Pastor position open at Third Church, one of the greatest churches in the entire Kingdom, probably in all of Christendom. That was the position he wanted. From there, he could move up the ranks quickly to Associate Pastor or maybe a Pastor at one of the lesser churches in town or in the hinterlands. His goal was to make Assistant Elder by the age of thirty.

Paul crossed over to the shady side of the street and continued walking north. Traffic was light for a Monday morning, only a few one-horse delivery cabs and some boys running messages. The road was still muddy from the recent rains, causing the horses' hooves to make a sucking sound as they passed. A couple of large pigs waddled by him in the opposite direction, snuffling in the gutters for trash. The smell of horse dung was overpowering, but as usual, he got used to it.

Paul and his mother lived in a good district on the south side of Benson, not too close to the Inner Wall, where traffic was dense, nor too close to the south-side lakefront, where the stench from the tanners was overpowering. Paul turned right at the first intersection and headed east, toward the lake. After several blocks, he reached Lake Shore Drive, one of the grand boulevards that dated from the American Empire. Paul crossed the busy boulevard, weaving between the carriages and wagons, most of them horse-drawn but a few pulled by oxen. Directly across the boulevard was the bus stop for the north-bound omnibus. He found some shade and waited.

Not far from him stood another great relic of the past: Soldier Field, a huge stadium that once held athletic events in the Empire days—in fact, it might even date all the way back to the Republic. It was several stories tall, a strange blend of ancient Roman columns and what looked like a spaceship. The place was fenced off for safety reasons, which meant it was a very attractive place for Paul and his friends when they were teenagers. They would sneak in after dark through a hole in the fence and clamber around on the vast rows of seats, pretending to be gladiators in the long-forgotten contests once held there. It was hard to fathom a place like that filled with people. It could probably hold 50,000, far more than the entire population of Benson.

After a few minutes, Paul heard the familiar bells of the red city omnibus approaching behind him. He pulled his little calfskin purse out of his sleeve and fished around for a quarter-penny for the fare. When the bus stopped and the horses settled, he climbed aboard and dropped the coin in the till behind the driver. The driver cracked the whip; the horses jolted the wagon into motion. He had to grab the over-head bar to keep from falling. He settled himself into the bench on the side of the omnibus so that he could see the Lake as they headed north. The road veered to the right to run right along the waterfront. They passed more ruins from the past, including the vast Millennium Park. Paul saw that the Supreme Elder's sheep were grazing on the lawn.

The omnibus soon entered the heart of the city. More people were out and about here. Paul saw Church officials in their robes of brown or red on the sidewalks, depending on their rank, trailed by one or two serv-ants. Taxis trundled by him noisily, mostly two-horse cabs. Paul saw some city workers pushing a large wooden cart carrying a corpse, thank-fully covered with a white sheet. Like most citizens, Paul's first reaction was dread, that this was yet another pandemic sweeping through the city. Then he reminded himself that people also just died, every day.

As they trundled along, one of Paul's favorite sights came into view: the forest of masts and folded sails of the great ships moored in and around Navy Pier. Paul knew that there would be lots of activity on a Monday morning at the Pier as goods from hundreds of miles away came into Benson. Some of them would be ocean-going vessels, going out to the eastern seaboard, maybe as far as the remaining Caribbean islands. One or two might even be from Frisco, having sailed down through the Panama Canal and up through the Erie Canal.

The omnibus crossed the river, pulled over to stop for passengers, then continued north. In this part of the city there were more giant buildings remaining from the Empire, although not all were inhabitable. This was the heart of the administration of the city, the Church, and the Kingdom of the Great Lakes (known as the KGL). Paul felt his nervousness rise again like a worm wriggling in his stomach. He took several deep breaths to calm himself.

Even in this central part of the city, there were still vacant lots. Not far from the Pyramid, they passed an entire city block that was unused. Through the fence slats, Paul could just make out a giant hole in the ground, filled with water. This was once the base for a towering building, maybe even one as tall as the Black Pyramid. Like so much else, it had been destroyed in the Terrorist Raids of the last century. Scenes like this always made Paul contemplative. He had learned about the Fall of the American Empire in school, like every school kid, but the reasons for the Fall had never been adequately explained to him. "The Empire had become rotten," went the usual line. "Morality had degenerated, and more and more people had been tempted away from the Church, living lives of hedonism and excess. God saw that He needed to cleanse the world in order to build a new Church and create a new Heaven on Earth." *Talk about an incomplete explanation!* This question—why the great Empire actually fell—niggled at him like an itch he couldn't quite scratch. He was sure there was more to the story than he had been told. None of the books he read provided any more clarity. And every time he tried to ask somebody about this when he was growing up, he felt his questions being deflected. He suspected there was a dark secret that nobody wanted to admit. Was America conquered by a foreign foe? Were we too ashamed to admit this? If not, then what *did* happen? And how could the people have allowed it?

To his left, Paul saw the colossal statue of one of the 21st-century Presidents—Paul couldn't remember his name right now. The statue stood fifty feet tall. This President, wearing an old-fashioned suit and tie, stood with his arms folded, scowling down at the little people below. Paul remembered that this had been commissioned by the President himself and erected in the old capital city. When it became clear that the city could no longer hold back the floodwaters, his descendants had the statue moved to Benson just before Washington, D.C. was inundated by the rising ocean. This was one of the Presidents who slowly inched the Republic toward authoritarianism, a process finally completed by the end of the 21st century. Most people who thought about history longed for the days of the Empire, but for Paul, the Republic was the true golden age of America. As the bus passed below the statue, the President seemed to be saying, *I don't give a damn what happens to you people of the future.*

After turning westward, then north again, the bus pulled up a couple of blocks away from the Black Pyramid. Paul stepped out and reflexively looked up. Here it was, the center of both the government of the Kingdom of the Great Lakes and the Evangelical Church of America. The size of the building was staggering. It was a hundred stories tall, full of expensive windows that reflected the city. Each side of the building featured steel beams running lengthwise and crosswise like the letter X in the old English alphabet, one on top of the other, stretching up beyond his sight. How the builders of the Republic managed this was beyond comprehension. Paul had heard that back in those days, there was a second Black Pyramid on the other side of the city, even taller than this one, but it had been destroyed during the Years of Terror along with most of the other great towers of the period.

The Supreme Elder and his family lived here, somewhere up high in the tower. Rumor had it that he never left. Paul knew that the building had running water, pumped all the way up to the top by servants and oxen in the basement. Paul had only been in the building once, on a school trip when he was a child, but he still remembered the opulence of the place. Paul took a deep breath and pressed his way through the rotating glass door into the building. Inside the lobby, lined with marble on the floors and walls, Paul saw Church officials in red robes moving here and there. This was the epicenter of everything.

Paul first went to the restroom. He tested the faucet, just like he did when he was here as a little kid. Fresh water came pouring out, without him having to pump. He cupped his hand and took a drink, but quickly turned it off before he got into trouble. His own house was considered fancy for having a pump for well water indoors. This kind of plumbing was a luxury indeed.

He went into a stall to change into his formal school robes. As he came out, he looked at himself in the mirror. He looked good. Really good. He always got a little charge of pleasure on those rare occasions when he saw himself in a mirror. His mother always reminded him that vanity is unbecoming, but what could he do? If he was honest with himself, he knew he was good looking—tall, with curly brown hair, well-built, with deep brown eyes. He had full lips, strong cheekbones, thick eyebrows, and had made sure he was clean-shaven for this day. Women passing him in the streets sometimes looked at him surreptitiously from beneath their head scarves. He liked that.

Paul exited the bathroom and walked to the main reception desk. A middle-aged man in servant's livery sat behind it. "How may I direct you, sir?"

Paul was sure the man could tell from his clothes what the answer was, but he went through the formal motions. "I am here for the Seminary Graduation Hearing."

The servant made a show of looking down at a sheet. Paul was doubtful he could actually read; very few lower-Caste people could. "Very good, sir. You will find the Hearing Rooms on the twentieth floor."

Twentieth floor! Paul was glad he left early; this was going to take a while to climb. He thanked the servant and slid a hay-penny across the desk. A look of mild disgust passed quickly over the servant's face then disappeared. He pushed the coin back across the surface. "That won't be necessary, sir. Best of luck in your Hearing." Paul quickly took back the coin, looked around for the stairway, then began the long climb up. He remembered from his field trip back in grade school that these super-tall buildings once had special little rooms that whisked passengers up to any floor they desired at the touch of a button. Alas, along with the other magical conveniences from the past, this technology was lost when the Empire fell.

Paul was in good shape but still took a breather after every five floors. His heart was pounding by the time he reached Floor 20. He wondered fleetingly if this was deliberate on the part of the Elders, to exhaust the students before they were told their fate. He entered another marbled lobby area, smaller than the first, with church pews along three sides. One of his classmates was waiting in one. Paul sat next to him.

"What's the news, Thomas?"

"Edmund's in there now. He's been in for ages."

Thomas was a small guy with wispy brown hair that was already thinning. He was unconsciously cleaning his fingernails with his thumb while staring apprehensively at the big double doors.

"Have you heard about any appointments yet?"

"Jeremy got Third Church."

Paul felt his stomach clench. *That's the best posting!* he thought. *That was supposed to be mine!*

He quickly pulled himself together. "Good for Jeremy. He'll do well there."

Thomas nodded absently, still staring at the door. As though he had willed it, the doors opened. Edmund, a tall student Paul knew from several classes, stumbled out. Edmund was very devout but not terribly bright. He glanced at Paul and Thomas without acknowledgement and then rushed out of the room and down the stairs.

Thomas stood up as though pulled by a string. He walked slowly and steadily to the doors, which were being held open for him by two servants. Paul could just barely make out the Hearing chambers, another vast room with five old men sitting behind a high table. Then Thomas crossed the threshold, and the doors were shut.

Paul stood up and walked over to the window. He had never been this high up before. The view was magnificent. The Black Pyramid was less than a mile from the North Wall, which Paul could see clearly from here. Paul thought he could even see the Outer Wall, another mile or two beyond that, the space in between mostly filled with farmland and pastures for grazing. Beyond the Outer Wall lay dangerous territory. Only well-armed merchants and messengers braved the journey between the far-flung cities of the Kingdom of the Great Lakes. Old people loved scaring children with tales of unwary youths who ventured beyond the Outer Walls and never returned…

He could hardly concentrate. *What the hell is happening here? Why didn't I get the Third Church position? No offense to Jeremy, but I can think circles around him.* Paul knew he was a better public speaker, too; he had won the all-campus Sermon Award two years running. Hell, Paul could think circles around most of his professors, truth be told. *Are they going to stick me out in some hinterland assignment? Are they feeling threatened by me? Or did I slip up somehow?*

A cold chill ran through Paul's body. *What if the Elders know?* Paul had been careful to hide his lack of faith—he was pretty sure only his mother knew the extent of his skepticism—but he knew the Church had spies everywhere. Maybe they had sent someone to listen to his dinner-table conversations. Maybe one of their servants told a servant in another household. Or maybe he let something slip with his friends and word got back to the Elders….

This could be bad. Everything Paul and his mom had been working for could go up in flames. It hadn't been easy for them after his father died, back when Paul was four. Even getting into the Seminary was no guarantee, despite his top performance on the entrance exams. But he had made it, and he had done exceedingly well. He had already sketched out his future in his mind, working his way up the administrative ranks in government, maybe even becoming a part of the Supreme Elder's Council someday. He daydreamed of being promoted to Caste 2, even though that almost never happened. Obviously, his interests were much more aligned with politics than religion, but in the KGL, you couldn't have one without the other.

And more importantly, a good position in the hierarchy would make him eligible to begin courting women. He wanted this almost as badly as he wanted a secure position.

I've been able to pull the wool over the eyes of the faculty, but maybe this is where it stops.

"Mr. Girard."

The doors were open. Paul saw Thomas hurrying across the lobby to the stairs, with not even a glance at Paul. The servants manning the doors were waiting expectantly for him. Paul took a deep breath, swallowed, and walked into the Hearing Chamber.

The Hearing Chamber was a large, windowless room. The room was well-lit, though, with oil lamps hung on the walls every five feet. Under each lamp was a bust of an American President, each one on a column to make them about normal height. They were made from plastic, that ubiquitous material from the late Republic and early Empire, through a long-forgotten process called "3D Printing." Paul knew about this because there was a replica of the bust of President Benson at various places in the city, including the Seminary. Apparently, these busts were extremely true-to-life, created from precise measurements of the living President's features. Unfortunately, there was something about the procedure that required the person's eyes to be closed. And thus, Paul had the impression of two dozen Presidents asleep on their feet as they listened to the proceedings of the Hearing Chamber. Back at the Seminary, a common freshman prank had been to paint eyeballs on the sleeping President Benson. Every year, the officials had to clean off the offending graffiti, and thus, the President's eyes had become worn down by years of scrubbing.

Paul walked toward the dais where the five older men awaited him. The Elder in the middle was one of the High Elders. Paul had heard him give a sermon at church. The Seminary's Headmaster was there, just to the left of the High Elder, his bald head glistening in the torchlight. To the far left was a foppish younger man wearing Imperial purple and an extravagant hat with a yellow plume. Paul recognized him as a member of the Supreme Elder's family, perhaps a cousin. It was rare to encounter anybody from the First Caste in person, and Paul had to force himself not to gawk. On the other side of the High Elder was seated two more high-ranking Church officials, both quite elderly. One seemed to be fast asleep.

"Please step forward, Mr. Girard," said the High Elder. He spoke in English rather than Merican, very formal and old-fashioned. Paul could speak English, of course—they made sure of this in the Seminary, since it's the language of the Three Testaments of the Bible. The language was the parent of the Merican dialect, but there were a lot more consonants in English ("going to" rather than "gon'," for example). Paul moved to the little rug that lay about ten feet from the Elders and kneeled in supplication. "I greet you, Elders," he said in the ritual language, "and await your wisdom."

The headmaster spoke first. "Mr. Girard, we have taken careful note of your progress at the Seminary and have been most pleased with your academic performance." Paul wondered if he should respond, but his throat felt constricted, and he didn't dare try to speak. "You have won several awards, have earned top marks in your courses, and are spoken of highly by your professors and peers." Paul swallowed and nodded mutely.

The young man in purple spoke next. "Look, you seem like an impressive student. But look at your shoes! They're covered in filth. Is that any way to present yourself at your Hearing? Honestly, I don't understand the morals of these students these days." He turned to the headmaster. "Don't you discuss these matters in your classes?"

The High Elder cut him off impatiently. "Mr. Girard, as we were saying, we have been watching you closely, and we believe you are the right candidate for the most important posting of this graduating class." Paul looked up expectantly. "Are you familiar with chapter three of the Book of Edgar in the Third Testament?"

Paul felt a single trickle of sweat roll down his back. *Think quickly, Paul!* "If I remember correctly, this is one of the passages that discusses the return of our Most Blessed Savior."

"Correct. I am referring to chapter three, verses one through four: 'In the presence of God and of Christ Jesus, I tell you truly: the day of Christ's return is at hand. As the calendar makes a momentous turn, He shall make His Presence known to us, in the blessed land of the United States. Prepare the way; sew up the torn fabric; cleanse the land of all wickedness and waywardness. For He shall only come when the land is ready.'"

Like all Seminary students, Paul had to memorize the entirety of the Third Testament, and now the next lines came to him. "Whoever has ears to hear, listen to what I say: victory is at hand, but only if you prepare the way."

The High Elder smiled, and Paul could see the headmaster nodding. The High Elder lowered his bushy eyebrows. "Do you understand what it means?"

"I have studied the passage several times," Paul lied, "but I will admit its true meaning has always eluded me."

"The Elders have been studying the signs closely, and we are becoming increasingly certain that the Second Coming is at hand. Another key passage is in Second Benjamin, chapter 19: 'Christ says, I have kept you waiting hundreds of years. You will have to wait longer. Even if it be twenty-five times a hundred years, you must not lose faith.' Do you understand?"

"Yes, sir."

"We are less than twelve years away from the year 2500. If we are going to sew up the torn fabric, we must move quickly."

Paul couldn't figure out where this was going, so he just repeated, "yes, sir," which seemed safe.

Another Elder picked up the thread, speaking in a whispery voice. "We have been hearing troubling reports from our brethren in the Republic of California. A strange new cult has arisen there. They call themselves the Children of the Sun. It has been growing rapidly, and the donations from the churches out there have been falling rapidly. We are at risk of losing that entire region for Christ."

The Children of the Sun? They sound like morons to me, thought Paul. *The great Evangelical Church of America is threatened by a bunch of pagans?*

The High Elder coughed. "We are sending you there, young man."

Paul's heart started thumping in his chest. More sweat trickled down his back. *This can't be happening to me. They can't really mean to send me away like that.*

"Because of your extraordinary promise, we are promoting you to Assistant Elder."

Paul's head was spinning. Becoming an Elder was what he had always wanted—but not like this. He had no qualifications for this job. He was no great adventurer. He only ventured outside with his books. The notion of the dangers of the unknown terrified him.

"You will be accompanied on this important journey by Associate Elder Simon Eastman, who will be in charge. You are to assist him in any way he requires. Also travelling with you will be three members of the Imperial Guard, to provide protection and assistance. One of these, Echleph Domain, has much experience traveling in these lands."

Paul tried to recover quickly. "When do we sail?"

The High Elder smiled. "You won't be. You'll be traveling there by land."

"By land?" *Are these people insane? Are they trying to kill me?*

"Yes. We have some important messages for you to deliver to the faithful along the way. We also think it will provide you with an important perspective on the Church's strength on your journey to California."

Paul swallowed. He wanted to tell them *Thanks anyway! I'll just take a quiet church job in Benson where it's safe!* But you didn't talk back to the Elders. "Yes, sir," he croaked.

"I don't need to tell you how important this mission is, young Elder. If you confirm the rumors—that is, if you find that the Church has lost its grip on this region—we will have to act quickly. If the situation is as bleak as it seems, our Most Supreme Elder is ready to authorize a holy crusade for the restoration of American Christendom. You and Elder Eastman will be the instruments of the Lord. You will surely be recognized by the Returning Christ as he returns to cleanse us of our Original Sin and begins the prophesied Thousand Year Reign."

Paul swallowed again. "Thy will be done, Elders."

I am a dead man.

"No!" cried Paul's mother.

Paul was sitting at the long wooden kitchen table with his mother. He had just returned from the Hearing and told her the news. As he feared, she wasn't taking it well.

His mother was a tall woman with straight brown hair, now turning to gray. She was dressed casually since they were indoors. Around Paul and the servants, she didn't need to keep her head covered, but of course she would have to if she went outdoors, like all women and girls did. Paul thought of his mother as strong, a real fighter, but he could see that tears had sprung up in her eyes.

"I'm sorry, Mother. I know this is not what either of us wanted."

"It's a death sentence. That's what it is."

"I wouldn't go that far."

She stood up and walked briskly to the hearth, her back turned to him. He could hear the tears in her voice. "You don't know what it's like out there. You've never left Benson."

"I thought you said we did leave, back in the pandemic of 2470."

"You were just four years old. That hardly counts."

Paul knew that this was a sensitive topic. It was during the pandemic that his father sent them away, to a little village up north, to escape the danger. He hadn't survived.

"Mother, it's okay. We're traveling with three Imperial Guards."

"Three guards! You think that'll be enough?"

"I'm sure they're well-trained."

"You would need a hundred men. Do you have any idea what's out there? Highwaymen. Indians. Cyclops. Dwarves and Elves. Sirens who will try to seduce you and prevent you from leaving them. Hermits who live in trees and kidnap people who trespass on their lands. Strange demi-gods who have made a deal with the Devil and cheated death…"

"Okay, now you're being ridiculous. Do you even hear what you're saying?"

Paul's mother would not be mollified. "That's the whole point! You just don't know. There's a reason we stay behind the city walls and don't venture out. The Years of Terror were not that long ago. People still get murdered out there. If it were safe, we would tear down the walls and travel all over the place."

Although he couldn't admit this out loud, Paul agreed with her. The prospect of leaving the safety of the city terrified him. "What do you propose I do?"

"Tell them thanks, but no thanks."

"I can't do that."

"Why not?"

"I can't just say 'no' to the Elders."

"Sure, you can. Just tell them you've thought about it, but that the Lord is calling you to do something else. They'll buy that."

"You don't understand, Mother. If I say no, it can mean the end of my career. I would be sent off to a terrible position and would never be able to advance in the Church hierarchy."

"So what? You don't even believe in this stuff."

"Mother! Shh!" Paul knew that the servants were right upstairs, probably listening closely to every word that was being said.

"Well, it's true. And anyway, who says you have to be a part of the Church hierarchy?"

"You do if you want to have any sort of meaningful career. You do if you want to stay in the Third Caste."

"None of that matters. Not when your life is at stake."

Paul shook his head. "Mother, I understand your worries. I have them too. But I don't have a choice."

"You always have choices."

Paul felt tears in his own eyes now. His mother had turned to him with a pleading look in her eyes. There was a part of him—close to 50%, if he was honest—that wanted to acquiesce. Just stay home, give up, drop out of the system, find another way. And yet, he knew this wasn't the right answer. In a way, fighting with his mother strengthened his resolve. If he did this—if he gave up—there would be a cloud over his head for the rest of his life. In fact, there would be suspicions about him, that he wasn't sufficiently faithful to accept his calling—or worse, that he was too timid. No, he had to do this.

"I'm sorry, Mom."

Paul's mother closed her eyes, then hugged herself, rocking back and forth slightly. After several moments, she spoke again without opening her eyes. "When do you leave?"

"This Sunday, after church."

"Lord, have mercy."

2

Northpoint, Republic of California
Sunday, May 30

Alex was awakened by noise in the courtyard well before dawn. It was Sun'sday, departure day for the tour group, the day he had been looking forward to for years. He couldn't wait to get going.

His cousins were all asleep still, lying around him in vague lumps in the common room. He quietly stood up, rolled up his sleeping mat, slipped into his sandals, and tiptoed carefully between the sleeping bodies. But he accidentally kicked his sister, Jasmine, on the way out. "Damn it, Alex," she growled. "Go back to sleep!" He muttered an apology but kept moving. There was no way he was going back to sleep now.

He walked up the half flight of stairs out of the room and padded through the dirt courtyard. He could just make out the shadowy silhouettes of his aunts and uncles carrying crates and musical instruments to the front of the Taiyo Clan compound, putting the last few items into the ox cart for the journey down to the pier. The last few days had been filled with trips to the boat—as always, Alex had helped out, even though at the age of eleven he was not able to do much heavy lifting. Most of these crates this morning contained perishables from the cellars. Alex couldn't make out which family members were there, but he could guess that Charles would be one of them. As Clan Leader, Charles typically supervised the loading of supplies.

Alex turned around and walked through the hallway between two of the buildings, then to the outhouse 200 feet to the back of the compound. As he peed, he thought, *where do people go to the bathroom on the boat?* For some reason, in all these years, he had never thought about this. *Did they, like, just go over the side?* Would he have to go to the bathroom in front of the *girls? Ugh!*

Who cares? I'm going on Summer Tour! Like some other clans, Alex's family took advantage of the Fairdays around the Inland Sea to barter and earn cash to sustain them through the long winter months. Some families had homemade goods to sell—pottery, baskets, quilts, and so forth—but some, like Alex's, made their money by providing entertainment. The Taiyo Clan had been doing so for at least three generations. The family also had a good-sized farm, but it was hard to raise crops in the depleted soil around there. Alex had been told that California had once been overflowing with good crops, but that was back in the Olden Times, before the climate changed, before the waters rose, and the Central Valley became the Great Inland Sea.

Alex had grown up playing music. It was part of the atmosphere at the compound. Family members played music several times each week. Music was natural for him, but he had never performed in front of strangers before. He felt like a snake was wriggling in his tummy at the thought of performing on the Tour.

He ran out of the outhouse and into the courtyard. He found his Uncle Evan carrying two canvas bags of food across the courtyard.

"Hi, Uncle Evan! Can I help?"

Uncle Evan was Alex's favorite uncle, tall and thin, with a funny little gray goatee. "Hey there, Alex! You must be excited for your first Tour."

"Maybe just a little." Alex followed him to the oxcart out front, filled with provisions.

"Why don't you go back to the sleeping room and rouse your cousins? It's almost Sunrise."

Alex turned and ran across the courtyard back to the room. Like most of the rooms in the compound, the sleeping chambers were half a story underground, where the natural cooling offered some relief from the California sun. Alex ran down the stairs and shouted, "Everybody up! Evan says it's time to go!"

There was a chorus of groans from the bodies sprawled out on the ground, but Alex saw a couple of cousins sit up and rub their eyes. It was gratifying to be able to give them orders and see them obey, even though he was the youngest in the Clan to be going on the tour this year. Jasmine didn't stir, however. He went over to her and shook her shoulder. "Jasmine! It's time to get up!"

"I heard you the first time, pipsqueak."

She had been up super late last night—doing *what*, Alex had no idea. He was asleep before she came in. He loved his sister deeply, his only direct kin since their parents were both long gone, but she remained a mystery to him in many ways. She was 17, six years older than him, old enough that she didn't want him around much. He also thought she was the prettiest person in the world. Of course, he realized he was biased.

Alex stepped carefully over the cousins lying on the floor and pulled aside the curtains so that the sun would come in when it rose. He then ran up the half-flight of stairs, across the courtyard and into the front of the compound, where Grandma Meta, Aunt Rosa, and Uncle Carlos were putting out food for breakfast on the big picnic table. His stomach grumbled in anticipation—he smelled the eggs and tapas and fresh baked bread from here. He could just eat and eat and eat these days, but he knew he had to wait for the rest of the Clan. Food had been running low recently. Nobody was allowed to be a pig.

Grandma Meta noticed Alex and smiled broadly. "Good morning, young sir! Are you excited for the tour?"

Alex shrugged, then nodded his head. Seeing Grandma Meta made his stomach flip. He realized for the first time that he was going to be away from her for three whole months. Aside from Jasmine, Grandma Meta was the person he loved the best in the whole world. She was short and plump and incredibly old, but she was the real boss of the place. Even Charles listened to her. She was like the mom to the whole Clan. She took special care of Alex and Jasmine since they had no mom and dad of their own.

She seemed to understand what he was thinking, as she often did. She opened up her arms and said, "Come here." He buried himself in her ample flesh. "It's gonna be fine, Alex. You'll have a grand ol' time."

"I'm just worried about you, managing here without me."

He could hear her chuckling softly. "Don't you worry 'bout me. I'm a tough ol' bird. We'll keep the farm goin' 'til you get back."

Alex heard some cousins coming down the hill and quickly pulled away. He didn't want to look like a baby. Jordan and Chi joked with each other and sat down together at the long wooden table in the middle of the dusty yard, in the shade of the big valley oak tree. Alex quickly sat down on the other side of Jordan, his favorite cousin, and was about to stick the wooden spoon into the dish of eggs when Jordan spoke.

"Can we dig in, Grandma?" Jordan was 18, just like Chi. He and Chi could almost have been twins, but they were just first cousins. And best friends.

"Well, let's say grace first. Would you like to lead us, Jordan?"

Jordan rolled his eyes at Chi, but he went through the formula anyway. "We thank the chickens for giving us these eggs to eat. We thank the fields for their bounty of grain. We thank our family for the labor that made this food. And we thank the Sungod and Mother Earth for sustaining us all."

Before Jordan was finished, Alex had scooped up a heaping pile of eggs for himself. And soon, the entire table was filled with the thirteen Clan members who were leaving. By unspoken agreement, the tour group got to eat first on Departure Day. Alex remembered watching enviously last year. He still couldn't believe that he was now one of them.

After breakfast, Alex helped carry the plates back to the kitchen building, then gathered with the rest of the Clan at the gate of the compound. Every year, the whole Clan made this journey down to the pier to send off the tour group. By tradition, it was always the last Sun'sday in May, just in time for the first Fairdays on their tour. The Clan would be attending something like a dozen fairs in the towns and cities around the Sea over the course of the summer, entertaining the people with their music and stories. Every year, the tour group came back talking about their adventures.

Uncle Evan was sitting in the driver's seat in the oxcart. He spotted Alex and waved him over.

"Wanna ride shotgun?"

Boy, do I! This was a special treat. Alex ran over and stepped on the big wooden wheel to clamor aboard. Usually, the oxcart was filled with people, but today, they used the space for the boxes going on the boat. This meant Alex and Uncle Evan were the only ones who got to ride down to the pier. Evan pushed down the brake to release the wheels, and the oxen started moving without having to be told. They knew the sound of the brake and had made the journey down to the pier countless times. Some of the younger cousins let out a cheer and then ran on ahead in their excitement.

The entire Clan moved together down the hill and into the village of Northpoint, so called because it was the northernmost town on the Great Inland Sea of California. The entire town consisted of about twenty buildings clustered near the waterfront. The compound's driveway connected with the main street, which ran right through the town to the waterfront. As they rolled through the village, Alex could see the Clan's big boat tied up at the pier along with a handful of fishing boats. It was a familiar sight; he had made this trip at least once a day over the past week, helping to load up tour supplies. It was hard to believe the moment had finally come. When the cart came to a stop, Alex jumped out and ran down the pier. It was about twenty feet wide, built with long wide planks, and probably extended a hundred feet into the Sea.

He was the first one to the boat. Then he hesitated. Should he just climb on board? How would this work? There was so much he didn't know about the Summer Tour.

Then he remembered that the oxcart couldn't go on the pier—it wasn't strong enough to hold that much weight—and the Clan was loading up supplies onto wheelbarrows. So, he ran back and helped with the loading. He carried the lighter bags and musical instruments down to the hold on the big boat. He was surprised how much stuff they were taking with them.

He was sweating when he finished making the trips and breathing heavily. Jasmine sometimes made fun of him because he was a little plump. He hoped that working on the boat this summer would work off some of his baby fat.

The Sun had come up, and a light fog drifted up from the Sea, glowing pinkish in the early light. By tradition, the Clan gathered together in a circle at the end of the pier, and everybody held hands. Alex was relieved he didn't have to hold hands with any of his girl cousins; instead, he was next to one of his aunties, Grandma Meta's little sister Bella. She was the oldest Clan member who was still making the journey each summer.

Grandma Meta closed her eyes and said a prayer for the group. "Blessed Sungod, blessed Mother Earth, we are gathered here to wish our travelers well as they embark on their journey. Look over them, keep them safe from harm, and let your bounty shine upon them. We know we are but spirits in the material world that have chosen to incarnate in this time and place. Help us to remember that all we encounter are infused with your divine spirit, and let our souls vibrate in harmony with everyone we meet. Let our lifestreams flow gently.

"We ask a special blessing on young Alex as he begins his first journey this summer." Alex felt his face go red and hoped everybody was keeping their eyes closed just like he was.

Alex felt a little squeeze in his hand from his Aunt Bella when Grandma Meta finished, and he let go of her hand. He followed the members of the Clan that were boarding the ship up the short ladder and over the side. Grandma Meta untied the ropes holding the boat in place, and Alex felt a little shudder as the sails came down. Just like that, the boat slipped away, and Alex waved at Grandma Meta as they headed out to sea. His heart seemed to skip a beat as she waved back, growing smaller and smaller.

The Clan's boat was about ten meters long. Some of his aunts had festooned the railings with garlands of wildflowers for good luck. The boat had a big mast in the middle holding up two large sails, plus a smaller sail that connected to the front. The boat was mostly made of wood but some parts of it were plastic, remnants from the Olden Times. There was a level down below that ran through most of the length of the boat, divided up into three cabins. The main room was in the center, where a circular table surrounded the mast. Then there was the Captain's Cabin up front and the head in the back. Alex thought that was a funny name for a bathroom. Why wasn't it at the head of the boat?

Alex and his cousins swam in the sea every summer, and he even went out on a little raft last year that he made with Jordan and Chi, but this was his first time on a big boat like this one. They were moving southward at what seemed to Alex like a good speed. There was a rolling quality to the motion of the boat. It was smoother than the feeling he had on that little raft. Alex held on to the side rail. It was exciting but made him a little dizzy. Alex turned and saw Uncle Evan at the back holding on to the big ship's wheel, with spokes coming out at regular intervals, like the Sun symbol. Alex hoped that someday, he could be at the helm of the boat like this.

Jordan walked over to him. He seemed perfectly at ease with the motion of the boat. "What do you think, Alex?"

"It's awesome!"

Jordan smiled. Like the rest of the Clan, Jordan had curly dark hair, dark eyes, and light brown skin. Grandma Meta always said, "We're the mutts of the world; that's our secret weapon." Alex didn't really know what she meant by that. It just seemed normal to him. Alex himself was a little weird looking, the only one in the whole Clan who had blue eyes. He didn't like it, but Grandma Meta said her father had also had blue eyes, so it wasn't so strange.

Jordan said, "There are three rules you need to know about life on the boat, for now. Are you listening?"

Alex looked up at Jordan and nodded his head solemnly.

"First, if somebody asks you to grab a rope, or lean one way or another, or do anything—just do it. Don't ask questions. Don't think about it. Do it right away."

"Okay."

"Second, you can go anywhere on the boat except for Charles' cabin. That's the one up front. Stay out of there."

"Okay."

"Finally, when we go into the towns, it's exciting and fun. But stick with somebody else when we're ashore. Every town is different. Some are friendlier than others. And at some point, Charles will blow his conch shell. This means we're leaving in ten minutes, no matter what. If you're not on board, you'll be left behind. Got it?"

Alex swallowed and nodded.

"Do you have any questions?"

"Yeah! Where are we going to today?"

"Our first stop is always at the Buttes. Do you know what those are?"

"Sure, I do. You can see them from Northpoint sometimes. They're the islands that jut out from the middle of the Sea."

Jordan laughed. "They're nowhere near the middle. They're actually a marker for sailors, showing them that they've reached the northern end of the waters. Not many people live there, but we do have some friends on the islands. We'll dock and pitch our tents on the nearest island."

As the morning turned to early afternoon, the Buttes grew in size, but it seemed to Alex like they were never going to arrive. As they got closer, he could see that there was really one big island with several peaks plus a few smaller islands scattered nearby. Finally, the boat pulled up to the big island, around the east side, to a little inlet in the shade of the hill. It made sense that the settlement was there, away from the hot afternoon sun.

The Clan pulled up to a short pier. Alex was told to stay on the boat while Charles, Uncle Evan, and Charles' son (who was also named Charles but whom everyone called "Junior") went ashore to talk to the villagers. Alex could see them talking with four white-haired people, but he couldn't hear what they were saying. It seemed like they were talking forever. Alex was getting hungry. He saw Jasmine talking with some cousins at the back of the boat. He walked over to them. Jasmine looked up.

"What's up, Squirt?"

"Why are they taking so long?"

"Who?"

"Charles and Evan and Junior."

Jasmine squinted at the shore. "Oh, I don't know. That's what they do when we encounter people on the tour. You don't just barge in. You have to ease people into things."

"Jordan told me these were friendly people."

"They are."

"So, what's the problem?"

Jasmine rolled her eyes. "There's no problem. That's just the way things are done. Why don't you go find Jordan and see if you can help bring things up from the hold? We'll be spending the night here, in tents on the shore."

Alex knew that meant she wanted to get rid of him, so he left her and climbed down the ladder to the hold below. Sure enough, Jordan and Chi were moving boxes around, making a pile of items they would need that evening. Alex felt a little twinge of excitement when he saw the musical instruments among them.

"Are we gonna be playing music tonight?"

Chi was standing closest to Alex. "Sure. We have to keep our chops up, don't we?"

"Oh boy!"

"Here, Alex: why don't you stand at the bottom of the ladder and help hoist things up to me?"

Alex eagerly took his position. Most of the instruments were light but some were too heavy for him to lift that high. He didn't like to admit he was a weakling, but there was no hiding it sometimes. Fortunately, Jordan was nearby. He helped him lift the heavier items without saying anything, such as the bass. Also moving along the line were guitars, a mandolin, fiddles, pennywhistles, congas, some hand percussion, and smaller strummed instruments like the ukulele Alex sometimes played. By the time they finished, and Alex had climbed up to the deck, the three Clansmen had returned from the shore. Without anybody giving directions, the family formed a line to move their materials off the boat and onto the little beach. It went quickly. Before they had even finished bringing their things ashore, some of the family had started putting up their tents on a grassy area just beyond the beach. It was a little like the clan's compound at home, even down to the ring of stones to form a fire pit. When Alex stepped off the pier, he lost his balance and stepped knee deep in the cold water. Jasmine, standing nearby, laughed at him. He could feel his face turning red.

One of the old people from the island walked over and reached out a hand to help Alex to the shore. Alex thought about refusing, just to prove that he wasn't a complete baby, but then thought that might be rude. Alex took his hand. The skin felt papery.

"Welcome to the Buttes! People call me Friendly Fox." He was surprisingly strong for an old guy.

"I'm Alex." He stepped onto the beach and bent over to wring the water out of his pants.

"Come, have something to eat."

The very thought of this made Alex's mouth water. The fire was already crackling, and Alex could smell some peppers and nuts being roasted. He also could smell fish, which made his stomach turn. The Clan was all vegetarian, but he knew most people around the Sea lived on seafood. The Clan had brought plenty of its own stores: pickles, peaches from last summer, cornbread left over from one of Grandma Meta's big feasts. He sat down on a log next to Jasmine and ate his fill.

After the big meal, Alex began to get sleepy. He thought he was dreaming at first when he noticed one of the old people was now sitting next to him. She was really old, older than Grandma Meta, even, and her eyes looked cloudy. Still, she seemed to notice him noticing her.

"You're the young one, aren't you?" Her voice was crackly. Alex found her a little scary.

"Yeah, I'm Alex."

She reached over and put a bony hand over his. "You're a special boy, aren't you?"

Alex felt uncomfortable. He wished she would move her hand away. "Nah, I'm just a regular kid."

The old woman looked him up and down, but it seemed like she was looking through him to something on the other side. "No, you're a special boy. You're going to be an important person someday. That's all there is to it."

Alex blushed. He hoped she couldn't see him. After a long moment, she sighed, pulled her hand away, and used a walking stick to hoist herself up. She shuffled away without looking back.

By this point, Jordan and some of the other cousins were getting instruments out and tuning them up. Alex jumped up in anticipation. There was nothing better than playing with the tour group. Oh, they played most nights back at home during the summer, but Grandma Meta had her favorite five or six songs, and she always called those. When the tour group came back, it was like riding a fast horse after sitting on a donkey for weeks and weeks. They played hard tunes, and they played them fast. Alex could never keep up.

Like most in the Clan, Alex had learned several instruments. He liked playing bass the best, but Uncle Evan usually played bass and already had it in his hands. Jordan and Chi played fiddle, and *man, could they play!* They competed when they took breaks, and Alex couldn't tell who was better. He thought maybe Jordan, but they were so far out of his league, he didn't feel qualified to judge. Junior and Jasmine both played the guitar. Other members rotated among the various instruments, including a number of djembes. The only member of the group who didn't play was Charles; he was the chief storyteller, and that was enough for him to do.

Eventually, Alex chose a little four-string cavaquinho. It was pretty easy to play. Alex knew most of the chords, and it was quiet. He could hide his mistakes better. Everybody was noodling and tuning, but then a tune started to emerge from Junior. Alex thought it might be "The Girl That Got Away," but he wasn't sure. Suddenly, everybody was playing it, and Alex couldn't keep up. He tried watching Jasmine's fingers—he could sort of translate the chord shapes to the cavaquinho—but it went too fast. After the verse was repeated, they launched into a chorus. Alex was pretty sure they were in minor now, but he couldn't find the new key. He quietly tested chords. Just as he figured it was in E Minor, they were back in the verse, back in G Major, and Alex was fumbling through the chord changes once again. Chi took a breath-taking solo, perfectly phrased, ending on an impossibly high note. Then Jordan took over, copying some of Chi's phrases but extending them, turning little melodies upside down, darting like a bird. Alex forgot to play. He was too busy listening.

Then the ensemble returned to the chorus one last time to finish it off, and Alex joined back in. By unspoken agreement, the group decided to ratchet up the tempo another notch. Alex's heart raced as he desperately tried to keep up. Just before they played the chorus pattern for the last time, Alex felt something click inside his brain. He never got the changes, not completely, but he somehow knew how it went.

The next time they played, he knew he'd be able to keep up.

3

Benson City

Sunday, May 30

"Wake up, Paul. It's time to go to church."

Paul moaned and rolled over in bed. He had been out late the night before—his friends had insisted they spend one more night at their favorite tavern—and he had just woken up to the worst hangover of his life. His mother stepped around his bed to the small window and pulled aside the curtains. Sunlight cut like daggers into his eyes. He moaned and rolled over again.

"Come on. We have to go."

Paul felt like his mother was shrieking at him, even though he knew she wasn't. Reluctantly, he pulled back the quilt and sat up in bed. A wave of nausea washed over him. He put a fist to his mouth. His mother left the room and came back with one of their large ceramic mugs filled with water.

"Here, drink this. Slowly."

Paul obeyed. It helped.

"I'll leave you now to get dressed. I've laid out your dress robes for you."

After Paul's mother left the room, he allowed himself a few minutes before getting up, gently rubbing his temples. He needed to go to the outhouse pretty badly, and this, more than anything, finally motivated him to get moving. His body felt stiff and wobbly as he stood up, like he was an old man, not a healthy 22-year-old. He put on his robes then moved slowly down the hall with his eyes closed, touching the wall for reference, through the kitchen, where their servant Helen was preparing breakfast, by the sound of the pots and pans she was moving. His stomach gurgled at the thought of food.

Paul went through the back door of the kitchen, down the wooden steps, then onto the pathway to the outhouse. The air was crisp and cool for late May. This was something older people talked about a lot, the weather. Each year seemed to be getting colder and colder, the growing season shorter. People were worried about the food supply. Right now, Paul just worried about not throwing up.

The outhouse stunk, as all outhouses do. Paul's mother had been talking about building a new one, something that was long overdue, but this cost a lot of money. Paul finished his business and poured a spoonful of lime into the privy hole, as he had been trained to do since childhood.

Once Paul got inside, Helen pumped water for him at the big kitchen sink. He washed his face and hands, then sat down at the big family table across from his mother. Helen placed the thick ceramic plate in front of him and gave him a heaping serving of scrambled eggs, ham, and toast. He had no appetite but knew he had to eat anyway. Helen had been with the family since before Paul was born. The last thing he would want to do is insult her on his last day at home. She patted his shoulder as she left the table. He took a tentative bite of the eggs then quickly washed it down with water.

"Did you have a good time last night?" his mother asked in a neutral tone. She spoke in Merican, the dialect of the streets, even though she could also pull off the more formal High English when the situation called for it.

"A little too good, perhaps," Paul replied raspily, also using Merican.

His mother forced a half smile. Paul looked at her for the first time this morning. He could tell by the puffiness around her eyes that she had been crying. He also knew that she would not want him to call attention to this fact, so he kept the conversation's focus away from his departure.

"Each of the guys insisted on buying me a drink. I lost track of the count after five or six. We sang every bawdy song we knew, then some we didn't. Beyond that, I'm afraid I can't recall."

"Well," she began, then didn't finish the thought. After a moment, she seemed to rally her strength. "Eat up. We need to get to Church. And you have a big journey ahead of you."

Paul had hoped that his mother would have become reconciled to his departure over the past week, but she hadn't. She had given up trying to convince him after that first day, but a chill had come between them. Paul regretted this, but he didn't regret his decision. In fact, he had begun to grow a little excited about the journey, along with his increasing nervousness. He had long wished he knew more about the world outside Benson. Maybe he would finally come to understand what really happened to America, how the Empire had fallen from such heights.

He still felt apprehensive, however. His friend Corbin had heard some gossip about Paul's travel companion, Simon Eastman, that had made him uncomfortable.

"He's a fairy," Corbin had said last night at the tavern. Paul laughed this off. There was no way a homosexual could have been made an Elder in the Church. Paul said as much, but Corbin just shrugged.

"That's what they say. He's never been married, for one. And he's got some unusual habits, if you know what I mean. I'd watch your back if I were you."

"Especially at night," someone jeered, and everyone laughed. Now, in the cold light of morning, those words didn't seem so funny.

Homosexuality was strictly forbidden in the KGL, of course. There was apparently an underground world of these kinds of people, right there in Benson, but Paul tried not to think about this. Those who were caught were arrested and sent to "re-education camps" somewhere out west. Certainly, this would spell the end of any sort of career in the Church hierarchy, so Paul couldn't imagine that Elder Eastman was actually a homosexual. Still, he did find it a little strange that Eastman hadn't tried to contact him during this week. Paul thought they would at least have a meeting to discuss the trip. He felt like he was flying blind.

Beyond this gossip, Paul knew very little about Simon Eastman. He was from the Fifth Caste, he knew, right in the middle of the Nine Castes. He was a mid-ranked Church official, highly respected. Paul worried about how he would be able to conceal his lack of faith on this long journey.

Paul had been packing and repacking for much of the week. He had noticed that his travelling trunks were no longer in his room; his mother must have had Ben put them in the carriage already. Ben was the other family servant; he also dated back to Paul's father's time. Ben was long past his best years, but Paul's mom would never turn him out. Others would have.

Paul took his half-eaten breakfast to the sink for Helen to clean up. She was already washing a pan. He bent down to kiss her cheek, knowing this would be their goodbye. They would be going directly from Church to the point of departure on the south side of the city. Paul tasted tears on her cheek. She turned around and gave him a long hug.

"You take care of yourself, now," she said in her rough Merican tongue.

"I will. And you take care of yourself, and my mother."

"Yes, sir."

Ben had already pulled the family carriage around the front of the house, so there was nothing left to do but head out. He took one final look at his childhood home and stepped into the blinding sun.

The First Church of the KGL stood several blocks south of the Black Pyramid, another old structure that dated from the Empire. It was built of white stone and could hold a thousand parishioners, but it was rarely full, even though attendance at Church was compulsory. Paul and his mother usually attended a service closer to their home, a much smaller church with less pomp and ritual. First Church was the official Church of the Supreme Elder (although he himself rarely attended in person). It was made known to Paul that he was expected to be there this Sunday. As members of the Third Caste, Paul and his mother had relatively comfortable seats near the front of the sanctuary, with cushions on the pews. The parishioners from the lower Castes had to sit on the hard wood. If any were from the Ninth Caste, they were required to stand through the service at the back of the sanctuary. Paul and his mother settled into their pew and waited for the service to begin.

Paul's hangover was getting worse, not better. The light from the stained-glass window seemed to be slicing directly into his eyes. The service was given in English, which Paul knew fluently, of course, but which was probably difficult for most of the congregation to understand. They weren't missing much. Most of the words were the same every Sunday. Even the sermon was essentially the same, a tribute to the virtue and excellence of the Supreme Elder, anointed by God to lead the Church and the nation to new heights of glory in anticipation of Jesus' imminent return, *blah blah blah*. Something about the routine irritated him.

"Today is the day that the Lord hath made," the officiating Elder intoned. "Let us rejoice and be glad in it. Almighty God, to you all hearts are open, all desires known. And from you, no secrets are hidden. Cleanse the thoughts from our hearts by the inspiration of your Holy Spirit..."

Paul shut his eyes to block out the sun and soon fell asleep. His mother nudged him awake when it was time for Communion. The idea of eating the stale bread—*sorry, the "Body of Christ"*—made Paul's stomach churn, even with the reassurance that the pastor's blessings had removed all possibility of infection from the epidemics that periodically swept over the country. Still, he knew he had to follow the ritual. He stood up with his mother and waited in line for the bread and wine and the pastor's blessing.

This was the first time he was wearing the robes of an Assistant Elder in public, with its thick, red woolen material with one white stripe circling each sleeve up near the shoulder. The pastor offering Communion was one of the High Elders, indicated by a purple robe and four stripes. Paul recognized him from other services but couldn't remember his name. He worried a little about being exposed as a fraud; he was awfully young to be appointed Assistant Elder. He was also sure his hangover was apparent to everyone. When he got to the front and knelt in front of the Elder, the old man didn't show any particular reaction to Paul's robes. He placed his hand on Paul's head, went through the ritual words—*in the name of the Father, the Son, and the Holy Spirit*— and placed the square of bread on Paul's outstretched tongue. Paul received the wine, and then returned to his pew.

The best part of the service was always the music. The church had two choir lofts high above both sides of the sanctuary. The musicians took advantage of this feature by using split ensembles, trading lines back and forth across the sanctuary. They were playing brass instruments, some of which probably dated from the Empire, gleaming beautifully in the morning sun. The music was designed to expand or contract based on the number of parishioners taking communion on that particular Sunday; Paul was impressed that they could communicate this wordlessly across the sanctuary. The space was big, so the sounds echoed across the walls, creating a serene, calming atmosphere, but constantly shifting in a subtle way. It was in these moments that Paul felt closest to the Divine, like there really was something beyond his everyday knowledge. Then, the presiding pastor would speak, and the spell would be broken.

As the service wound its way, slowly, to the end, Paul's apprehension started to grow. By the time it ended, Paul struggled to control his breathing. The parishioners filed out from the front of the church to the back, caste by caste, so Paul and his mother were among the first out. The sun once again caused Paul to wince in pain, but his headache might have been getting better. They wended their way around the building to a side street where old Ben was waiting with the family carriage. He had fallen asleep but woke up when they approached. He jumped down, opened the door, and put down the wooden steps for Paul's mother to help her climb into the carriage cab. The family owned a fairly nice vehicle, a two-horse Rockford model with an enclosed cabin and suspensions, the back wheels larger than the front. Paul knew that he wouldn't have this kind of luxury on the journey ahead. Ben closed the door behind them, placed the steps back on top of the cab, sat down in front, clicked his tongue, and the horses clopped forward.

Paul and his mother rode in silence to the river dock, southwest of the church. Paul stared out the window at the familiar sights of the city, wondering when or if he would see them again. Black metal poles rose up from the ground, then curved overhead, mysterious remnants from the Empire days, now repurposed as the anchors for clotheslines. Ninth-caste beggars sat on the wooden sidewalks, their hands outstretched in supplication. A pack of wild dogs ran down a side street.

They reached the departure point in good time. It was a small park at the juncture where the Chicago River split into the North and South branches. There was a packet boat docked there, presumably the vessel they would be taking on the first leg of their journey. Paul had never been on one. They were frequently seen in Benson, typically one-sail vessels, long and low, about sixty feet long and maybe fifteen feet wide with an enclosed cabin, designed specifically for rivers and canals. A series of windows ran along both sides of the cabin. This one was painted white along the top.

Ben pulled up to a hitching rail, climbed down from the carriage bench, and tied up the horses. Paul reached through the open window, unlatched the door, and jumped down. He could see a group of men near the dock in conversation. One of them was dressed in a red robe, like Paul's. *That must be Simon Eastman,* thought Paul. He was wearing an Associate Elder's red robe with two stripes instead of one. He was also holding a large map, presumably discussing the route with the ship's captain, identifiable by his white cap, and a man in his mid-thirties wearing the homespun brown of the worker castes, but no clear identifier that could help Paul place him in a specific one. He could be Caste 6, 7, or 8. He wore the broad-brimmed felt hat of a frontiersman. Lying next to him was a big German Shepherd.

Paul approached the group, his heart thumping in his chest. Elder Eastman flicked a glance in his direction, then continued his discussion with the other two men. Paul felt affronted. Someone from Caste 5 would be expected to doff his hat to someone in Paul's position. Of course, Eastman was one rank higher in the Church hierarchy, and perhaps he was trying to underline his position of authority. Paul waited patiently.

Eastman looked to be in his mid-forties, tall and thin, with hair cut nearly to his scalp in the manner of many churchmen. His hair was gray and thinning. He wore square glasses with metal frames. He seemed to be having trouble focusing his vision. He kept readjusting his glasses and trying different angles to view the map. His face was squarish, with a sharp jawline and high cheekbones, his nose slightly hooked. Paul had trouble imagining the rumors of impropriety surrounding the Elder.

At last, Eastman finished his business with his fellow travelers, then meticulously folded his map and tucked it into his robes. He then looked at Paul appraisingly. "You must be Paul Girard," he observed drily. His High English was impeccable.

Paul decided to treat him deferentially. "I am at your service, sir."

Eastman paused, pursed his lips inscrutably, then looked over Paul's shoulder. "I hope you are not intending to transport all that luggage."

Paul turned around. Ben was just bringing Paul's second chest down the hill, visibly laboring under the weight, stacking it on top of the first. The truth was, Paul was indeed intending to bring both trunks.

"We do not have the luxury of servants on this journey. You will be responsible for carrying your own gear. Even one of these trunks is too much. At the very least, you must consolidate your belongings."

Paul swallowed. "I was given no instructions on . . ."

"Do it quickly. We're already late." Eastman turned briskly and walked up the plank to the boat.

Paul stood dumbfounded for a moment. He was not used to being treated this way. He squeezed his eyes shut. The headache seemed to be returning. He gathered his resolve, then walked up the hill a short distance, to where the two trunks sat. Ben was waiting there. Paul's mother was just making her way down the hill, lifting her hem as she walked.

Paul explained the situation to Ben, then opened his two trunks and quickly made decisions about what to keep and what to send back. It pained him to do this, but he could see that he would have to part with most of his books. These were some of his most prized possessions. They kept boredom at bay, and he presumed there would be many boring days ahead. But these were also heavy, and books were rare and expensive. Did he really want to have this liability? He also got rid of most of his nicer, tailored clothes. He could see already that he would have no need for them. He closed the trunk lid and sent Ben back with the heavier one, feeling a little bad for the weight he made the old servant lift.

His mother had just arrived as Ben left with the trunk. Paul noticed her lower lip was quivering.

"I'm not going to embarrass you by making a scene. Give me a hug and promise me you'll come back safe and sound."

"I promise."

Tears welled up in Paul's eyes as he hugged her. And then, without another word, his mother broke away, turned, and marched up the hill without looking back. Paul wanted more time with her, but perhaps this was best. He saw Ben hoist the trunk onto the back of the carriage, then he quickly opened the door for Paul's mother. Then Ben turned around to look at Paul. Paul held up his hand in farewell. Ben paused, bowed to Paul, then climbed up to the driver's bench and drove off.

Paul watched them leave. He stood there past the time they were out of sight. *What the hell am I doing? This is insane.*

The sound of activity around the boat broke his reverie. He shook his head, then bent down to lift his trunk. He was relieved to find he could lift it easily. He would not give Eastman the satisfaction of seeing him act like a pampered Third Caster.

When he got to the boat, Eastman was just emerging from the cabin. Paul was surprised to see that he had changed clothes, exchanging his dress robes for a travel outfit. *Did he simply wear his dress robes for my benefit, to emphasize his Church rank?* Eastman strode quickly down the plank and signaled to a couple of men who were smoking down by the river. Paul hadn't noticed them before. They snuffed out their pipes and walked over to the boat. The man with the dog also appeared.

Eastman made quick introductions, reverting to Merican. "Elder Girard, these are our travel companions from the Imperial Guards. This is Captain Echleph Domain"—the man with the dog closed his eyes and inclined his head slightly— "and Corporals Archibald Rayphe and Turgin Broadstreet."

"Sargent, actually," said Broadstreet. He was a large man, about as tall as Paul but a good fifty pounds heavier, mostly muscle but with a hefty gut. He looked like he would be good to have on your side in a fight. He was wearing the casual version of the Guards' uniform, but Paul guessed from the shape of his hat that he was in Caste Seven. He had a luxurious beard at least six inches long, and his brown hair was thinning on top. He was probably in his late twenties or early thirties.

Rayphe was much smaller, probably only five foot seven, with a wiry build. He wore a similar uniform but carried a bow on his back with a quiver of arrows. He had long, stringy, dirty blonde hair and a spotty attempt at a beard and moustache. He had a furtive, calculating look to his eyes, which were blue and bulged slightly.

The captain was a different story. He also had long hair, pulled back in a ponytail, and a three-day old beard. He was dressed shabbily, not in uniform, the rough homespun fabric of a frontiersman. He was probably in his late thirties, his face tanned and lined from the sun. Something about him seemed utterly self-assured. *Probably Sixth Caste,* Paul thought.

Elder Eastman continued. "As you all know, this journey is of utmost importance to the Church. We are the Supreme Elder's representatives at every stop. I expect all of us to behave accordingly. I will make all the broad-range decisions for this group, although in matters regarding navigation in the hinterlands, I will of course defer to Captain

Domain's judgment." Domain acknowledged this with another slight bow of the head. "We will do our best to avoid conflict," Eastman continued, "but we will also not be deterred from our mission. Understood?" Paul nodded, along with the others.

"And now, let us pray."

Paul automatically closed his eyes and bowed his head.

"Heavenly Father, bless our journey. Keep us safe from harm, let us be an instrument of Thy will, and let us bring the Good News to all who need to hear it. Let our journey bring faith to the faithless and hope to the hopeless. In the name of the Supreme Elder, amen."

"Amen," Paul repeated. One or two of the others might have repeated it with him, but he couldn't be sure.

"And now, let us depart."

The men quickly followed Eastman up the ramp onto the boat. Paul noticed that Captain Domain's dog followed him without any commands. Paul lifted his trunk onto one shoulder and followed the rest of the group onto the boat. There were three crewmembers getting ready for departure. Two of them pulled up the plank as soon as Paul was aboard.

"Store your trunk in the main cabin," one of them said, nodding toward the rear of the boat. Paul followed the narrow pathway between the cabin and the railing to a door at the back, facing the rear of the boat. He opened it up, then ducked his head to go inside. There were stairs leading down about half a level below.

He paused at the top of the stairs to get his eyes adjusted. This was a long, narrow room, a bench running beneath the windows on each side and a big mast in the middle. Paul saw a pile of trunks to his right, then continued down the stairs and settled his belongings with the other trunks. To his irritation, he saw more than a dozen trunks back there, held behind a rope netting. He was hardly over-packed with two trunks! But maybe some of these belonged to the ship's crew.

"You won't be needing them fancy robes, where we're going," said a voice behind him, startling him. Paul turned to see Sargent Broadstreet, wiggling his bushy eyebrows in an attempt at humor. He smiled at Paul and ran up the steep staircase, surprisingly agile for such a big man. Paul suddenly felt foolish, wearing his formal robes. He opened his trunk, pulled out some travel clothes, and quickly changed.

With a shudder, the boat jolted into motion. Paul lost his balance and sat down abruptly onto the bench. He looked out the window and watched the city slowly slip away. The river marked a boundary between the inner city and outer city. Soon, he would be leaving everything he had ever known behind. More than anything, he wanted to jump off the boat and swim back home.

He sighed and stayed where he was.

4

The Inland Sea of California
Monday, May 31

Alex felt his foot being gently kicked.

"Hey Squirt! Get up!"

It was Jasmine's voice. Alex was lying in a pup tent on the beach at the Buttes, trying to get in just a little more sleep. They had stayed up late playing music the night before.

Jasmine nudged him again. "Get up. We have to get going before we have the Delta Breeze in our faces. We've got a long way to go today."

Alex rolled over. Now that he was awake, he could hear the sounds of the Clan getting things packed up. He sat up, his head brushing the top of the canvas tent, then started gathering his clothes. By the time he emerged from the tent, Jasmine was nowhere in sight.

The sun was well up now, high above the Sierras to the east. Alex broke down his tent, as he had been taught by Uncle Evan, and headed down to the inlet. To his embarrassment, he saw that he was the last one up. Everyone else had already gotten their things to the ship.

"There he is!" said Uncle Evan. "You ready to go?"

"Oh, lemme go pee first," said Alex. He ran off to some bushes behind the beach to relieve himself. When he got back to the beach, Charles was saying his goodbyes and bowing to Friendly Fox and the other folks from the Buttes. Alex was a little relieved that the weird old lady wasn't there. When Alex reached the water's edge, Evan silently pointed to the boat. Alex took this to mean he should get in, so he did, carrying his bedroll with him.

He saw Charles give a little package to Friendly Fox, wrapped in woolen cloth, and the old man gave Charles a hug. Then Charles came aboard, and they were ready to go.

"Weigh anchor!" yelled Charles, and soon, as if by magic, Alex could feel the boat start to pull away. He could see Evan and Junior and Chi using long poles to push off from the sandbank. He wished he knew how he could help, but everybody seemed to know what to do, and he was too embarrassed to ask. Then he remembered he had missed breakfast. He climbed down the stairs to the cabin to see if he could find any food.

An hour later, Alex was full and sleepy. It was a beautiful day, clear and warm. He was sitting out of the way, toward the back of the boat, in the shade of the main sail. The Buttes were slipping farther away in the distance as they continued south down the length of the Inland Sea. He hoped they would stop there again on this trip.

Alex looked down into the water. What he saw made his heart leap into his throat. He didn't know what he was seeing at first, and then he realized what it was. *These are the roofs of houses! All underwater!* The houses were huge, all lined up along a paved road, which he could just barely make out (it got murky the farther down he looked). He looked around and saw Jordan sitting on the other side of the boat, playing cards with Chi, and rushed over to them.

"Jordan! Chi! Look down there! Quickly!"

Jordan and Chi both set down their cards and peered over the side of the boat. "Oh yeah," said Jordan. "Houses. I can't remember which city we're over right now. You'll see a lot of these on this trip."

"Why did people build houses underwater?"

Jordan and Chi laughed. "They didn't, kiddo. These are from the Olden Times. All this used to be regular land here, before the floods."

Alex blushed. He felt ignorant. "Did they all drown?"

Jordan stared at his hand then played a card. "I seriously doubt it. I think it all came on pretty gradually. I'm sure everybody had time to get to higher ground."

"But why would they build houses there, if they knew they could be underwater?"

Jordan looked up at Alex and paused. "You know, I don't know. I assume they didn't think it could happen. We do know that the oceans and all the waters were much lower back then. This was before the Fall, of course."

Alex nodded. He had learned about the Fall in his lessons, but it had always been an abstraction before now, something that had happened long, long ago. This was the first time he really thought about what it must have been like to have lived through that time. It must have been scary, watching the climate change from year to year and the most powerful nation in the world crumble and break apart.

Alex walked back over to his side of the boat and looked down at the houses again. It was mesmerizing. Then, something strange happened to him. He felt himself go into a kind of trance, a little like he was dreaming, but not quite. He felt his mind float down to the streets below, and then he saw the neighborhood as it was, way back then, hundreds of years ago. He saw blue skies, kids like him, riding bicycles down the street—he was envious; bikes were very expensive and rare in his world—wearing weird clothes with colorful images and strange writing on them. And then he saw *a car drive by!* He knew about cars, of course; there were some rusted old vehicles on the family compound. But this one was shiny and new, rolling by him with a loud, annoying sound. It left a huge stink.

Alex floated along the street. He saw more people, including an older couple with a funny-looking small white dog on a leash. On the next street, there was a man with a strange machine, a little like the car but much smaller. He had to push it; the thing didn't go on its own. He was making lines in a rectangle of grass. Alex realized he was cutting it down. *Why did people want to do that?*

Alex didn't want this to end, but he began to get a little worried that he wouldn't be able to get back to his real world. He squeezed his eyes tight, gripped the railing of the boat to help ground him, then slowly reopened his eyes. He was back on the boat, in his normal time.

That was weird. Was I really there, or just imagining it? He wanted to talk to Jasmine about it, to see if she ever experienced anything like that, but she'd probably just make fun of him. He decided he would keep this to himself, for now.

The boat docked at the town of Lincoln for lunch on the east side of the Inland Sea. Alex was very curious to see the town but was told that only Charles and Aunt Rosa would be leaving the boat. The main town was up the hill a little way; the part that Alex could see was just a few old wooden buildings for the town's fishermen. Alex grew bored waiting for them.

After a while, Charles and Rosa strode back to the boat quickly. "We're going," said Charles brusquely, and the Clan sprang into motion to get ready to leave.

"What? What happened?" Alex asked Jasmine.

She shrugged. "Sometimes, towns become less friendly to our kind, so we move on. It's okay. There are plenty of towns on the Sea."

Alex worried that this meant they wouldn't be receiving lunch, but soon, some of his cousins brought up trays of fruit and nuts from their stores down below. Alex ate ravenously and then helped Jasmine and the others clean up, using seawater to wash their plates and bowls.

He was just finishing up when Jordan tapped him on the shoulder. "Hey, Alex—I've got something to show you. Come here."

Alex followed Jordan up to the top of the poop deck in back. Jordan pointed to a landmark some distance away over the right-hand side of the ship. "Do you see that?"

Alex squinted. It looked like square mountains coming out of the water.

Jordan handed him one of the Clan's prized possessions: a pair of binoculars. "You were asking me earlier about the underwater buildings. Well, those are some buildings from before the Fall, but they were so tall, they're not all the way underwater."

"Wow! People actually lived in those things?"

"They weren't all for living in. People also worked there. This used to be a big city called Sacramento. It was the capital of California back then."

Alex turned the little dial in between the lenses and brought the buildings into focus. He saw several ships docked around the tallest building. He also saw that some of the buildings were connected by rope bridges. It looked like it would great fun to climb around on.

"Can we go over and climb around in the buildings?"

"No, we steer clear of Sacramento. Pirates live in those buildings now."

Alex's heart started beating a little faster. "Really? Pirates! What can you tell me about them?"

"They're awful. They attack ships that are passing by, steal their goods, sometimes murder the people and take their boats. These are not the swashbuckling heroes you may be dreaming about. You don't want to mess with pirates. Trust me."

"Okay."

Jordan gently took the binoculars out of Alex's hands and returned them to the storage box near the back of the ship.

A little while later, the ship docked at another town. This one looked a little larger, with several buildings surrounding the pier, all of them painted in bright colors. A dark-skinned man in a wide-brimmed hat came out to meet them when they pulled up. Charles spoke to the man in a different language while remaining on the boat.

Alex whispered to Jordan, "What are they saying?"

"I don't know. They're speaking in Spanglish. This is a Mexican town."

After a few more words exchanged, the man smiled and bowed. Charles turned toward the family. "He says we can fill our casks with water, but it's not a trading day. We can come back later for that."

The Clan members seemed to know exactly what to do. Several cousins went down to the hold, and soon, three water casks were being rolled to the side of the boat. Emma—another cousin, but a generation older than Alex, so he called her "Aunt Emma"—Junior, and Evan each picked one up and carried the casks on one shoulder off the boat, down the pier, and into the town. Alex wished he could go with them. Then, Alex saw some village women come down to the pier, spread out a blanket, and unwrap some food. Even though he had just eaten, Alex's stomach rumbled.

"Is that food for us?" he asked Jordan hopefully.

"It is, if we pay for it."

"How much do you think it would cost?"

"Well, this town trades in Pesos, not Frisco Dollars or Sovereigns. I don't know—maybe a few Pesos?"

"Do we have some Pesos? I'm getting hungry."

Jordan leaned down and spoke softly to him. "We do, but don't ask. The Clan has been short of cash lately. We're trying to not spend where we don't have to."

Alex sighed and turned away so he wouldn't have to look at the food anymore.

The Clan continued sailing south. The shoreline of the Sea was very irregular here, going in and out. Sometimes they had to steer out toward the middle to avoid marshy areas that were shallow, where reeds were poking up out of the water. It smelled saltier here than up north. They passed several villages and even some larger towns, but they didn't stop. When he asked, his Aunt Emma told him they were heading to a town called Lockeford, which was situated in the southern half of the Sea, on the eastern shore. This was the first Fairday town on their itinerary.

One of the towns they passed had a big flag up by the dock, a red flag with a diagonal blue cross filled with stars. Alex asked Emma about that.

"That's the White Ethnostate. The flag shows their allegiance to the New Confederacy."

"What's that?"

"It's a country far away from here, on the other side of the continent. It used to be powerful, but now a lot of it is underwater."

"Why do people in California want to be a part of that country?"

"Well, it's hard to say. We try to keep away from them. They're not friendly to outsiders."

Alex was holding the binoculars. He peered through them at the dock. There were a couple of children standing there, looking back at him. They had skinny arms and big bellies, like they were pregnant. They had a hollow look in their eyes. Alex felt like they were looking right at him.

Please, help us, Alex felt them saying. *We're really, really hungry. The grown-ups beat us all the time.*

Alex shuddered, put down the binoculars, and closed his eyes to shut out their voices.

They arrived at Lockeford in the late afternoon. This was a real city, with a big dock. Thirteen boats were tied up already, and there was room for more. Alex felt his heart beating rapidly with excitement. Charles took the wheel to steer the boat to their designated spot, and Junior and Jasmine leapt onto the pier to secure the line. Alex moved to the side of the boat, eager to get on land and go explore the city. Yet again, he was held back.

Emma put her hand on his shoulder. "Hold your horses, Alex. We're not going in until tomorrow morning. The city doesn't allow us to set up yet."

Alex rolled his eyes. *Wait, wait, wait!*

Once again, Charles and two other adults went into town to talk with the locals. While they were gone, Alex and the others put together dinner. The whole Clan ate together on deck. Alex could hear musicians on other boats practicing, their music sounding weird, very different from the Clan's music. He hadn't realized that there would be other musicians at the Fairdays. Alex could hear music and raucous laughter all through the night as he tried to sleep in his hammock below decks.

The next morning, he awoke to the sound of activity on the deck above him. He rolled out of the hammock and climbed up the ladder. Most of the Clan was already up, carrying supplies off the boat to a stack on the pier. Alex was starving, as usual, but ignored his hunger and helped out.

Evan gave him a box to carry. It was a little heavy, but Alex didn't complain. He followed his Clan members down the pier and into the city.

Lockeford was probably as big as Chico, the only other big city Alex had ever been to. The buildings were huge, some of them even three stories tall, and they went on for block after block. Alex thought for a moment about the ruins of Sacramento, so much taller than these, but those were from a different time. After a while, they came to the opposite side of the town where there was a big fenced-off field. People were coming and going through a wooden gate, as tall as two men, getting ready for the Fair. Alex followed his family through the gate and around the left-hand side of the field for maybe 500 meters. Then they all stopped, without anybody saying anything.

"This is our place, every year," Evan explained. "You can put the box down over there. Then go back and see if you can bring something else."

Alex was relieved to set the box down. It had been starting to hurt his arms. Still, he ran—literally, ran—back to the pier to bring more. On his way he saw Jasmine and his sixteen-year-old cousin Ellie carrying some planks of wood. He didn't even know these had been stowed on the boat. On his next trip, he brought a chair, and then he went back and helped with other planks, which he carried with Chi. When they got back, he discovered that the Clan was putting together a little wooden stage for their performances. All the planks slotted in neatly together. It was all assembled within an hour. Alex pitched in and felt good about being able to help. The stage was flanked by two larger tents that Alex had never seen before, both of them six-sided with thick fabric in dark green and orange, maybe four meters in diameter. A full-grown man could stand up straight in the middle of these.

"Wanna get something to eat?" asked Jasmine. Alex suddenly remembered his hunger. He nodded eagerly. He followed Jasmine and two girl cousins into the center of the fair.

The fairgrounds were filling up quickly. Alex saw all sorts of goods for sale. One vender had wooden cages filled with chickens, squawking and clucking. They passed a shepherd leading three sheep, tied with ropes, one after another. One vendor was selling only olives. Alex couldn't believe how many varieties there were. He only had ever tried two, black and green, but there were red ones and different shaped black ones and all sorts of shades of green. Another vendor had bins full of spices. Alex inhaled deeply then sneezed. Jasmine laughed.

Jasmine bought them all artichokes with butter. They were expensive! But boy, were they good! They all sat together on a wooden bench. Alex wanted another one but didn't dare ask. When they walked back, they passed by another clan, this one an acrobatic group currently performing on a stage like theirs. Alex wanted to join the crowd and watch but Jasmine said they had to get back. But then *she* and the *girls* had to stop at a merchant selling fabric, even though that had to be the most boring of all the vendors in the entire fair. They held up bolts of colorful weave and talked about the kinds of dresses they would make with them, but they didn't buy anything. Alex couldn't believe how long they stood there, talking about *fabric!* It was crazy. He thought he might die of boredom.

Alex's job for the afternoon was to carry a sign advertising their performances that evening, to be held at supper time and at sundown. Alex couldn't read very well, so he had to ask Jasmine what it said, just to be sure. He made one circuit of the fairgrounds, then his arms got tired from carrying the sign. Most people ignored him, but some seemed to notice and point it out to their companions. When Alex got back, he went into one of the tents, where the family was getting ready for the performance, and fell asleep.

He awoke to the sound of his family tuning up their instruments. He quickly got up and went outside. He ran up to Jordan, who sat at the front of the stage with his fiddle up to his ear, trying to get it in tune.

"Jordan! Can I play with the band tonight?"

Jordan plucked his strings a couple more times, then looked up at Alex. "Sorry kiddo. Not this time. We need you to collect money in the hat."

"Aw!"

"Hey, this is important. This is how we eat. Try to look cute as you go around. Alika will go with you."

Not Alika! She was another girl cousin, the one closest to his age. She was always flaunting how much older she was—even though she was only 13—making fun of Alex's childishness. Alex could see that this was the way it was—the youngest Clan members on the tour had to do the least fun kind of work. *It's not fair!*

Nevertheless, he left the stage without any more complaining. After a little bit of hunting, he found Alika. She ignored him. Within a few minutes, the band was ready to go.

The band started in with a familiar tune, called "Hope." Like a lot of their tunes, this one started off with guitars and bass, a simple two-chord progression in an AABB form. R.J., one of the cousins from his Great Aunt Rosa's line, took the lead on pennywhistle, keeping it simple at first, just a few turns and ornaments. Jordan and Chi then came in on the fiddles, just sustained notes at first, but then starting to get more complicated. It was slowly accumulating energy, and Alex was excited, anticipating the break. Every time they played the melody, it was different. Alex never knew who cued the switch to the break, but they always did it right in synch. And it happened perfectly this time, a sudden doubling of tempo. Alex was satisfied to hear the audience gasp. Four people got up and started to dance, and the band seemed to feed off their energy.

There was good applause at the end. Some audience members left but more came. After two more tunes, the band played "Sultan," one of Alex's favorites. To his surprise, Jasmine came out of one of the tents right after the intro and performed a dance at the front of the stage. She was wearing a revealing costume, dancing in a "sexy" manner that Alex found disgusting. Some of the men in the audience whooped and whistled. It made Alex uncomfortable.

At the end of it, Alika nudged him. "C'mon. This is where we make our first round. You start over there, and I'll do this side."

Alex picked up the black velvet hat. He was unsure of what to do. Alika went up to one of the men in the audience who had been cheering and said, "If you want more of that, put some coins in the hat!" Alex was too embarrassed to say that about his sister, so he just offered the hat to people silently. Most made a show of pretending he wasn't there, even though Alex knew they knew he was. He came back with just a handful of pennies and hay-pennies.

Alika peered inside his hat. "I got twice as much as you did," she observed piously.

"When do we go around again?" asked Alex, now flushed with competitive spirit.

"After Charles. Shush now."

Alex hated when Alika treated him like a baby, but he shushed anyway. Charles was striding up to the center of the stage to recite one of his epic poems. Alex had heard some of these before—Charles practiced them a lot over the winter—but there was something exciting about seeing him perform in front of an audience for the first time. Charles was wearing his fanciest robe, and with his long hair and thick black beard with strands of white, he seemed to be channeling the voices of the past. The sun was getting low, shining right on Charles, like the Sun God was smiling upon him—Alex realized that they planned this when they planned their set. Alex always liked the epic stories Charles told—*The Tale of Harry Potter,* for example, or *The Saga of Luke Skywalker*—but unfortunately this time Charles did one of his history talks. Oh well. It was still interesting to watch Charles deliver the poem in front of strangers. Alex wondered if he might someday become the Clan's Storyteller...

5

Charles' Tale

Gentle souls, I beg you to attend
The words I speak upon this barren stage
And coax your ears listen, and suspend
The here and now, our rigid mental cage

And permit your rich imagination
To smooth out imperfections in my tale
Your scope enlarged, encompassing a nation
Whose story is concealed behind a veil

How could our distant relatives destroy
This country? And then leave us so bereft?
It still affects us, every girl and boy
We wonder at the wreckage that they left

We take a break from Springtime's gracious flowers
And turn the wheel of time now in reverse
The dial speeds past seconds, minutes, hours,

Increasing speed, while current cares disperse…

Our story starts four hundred years ago,
The nation filled with famine, floods, and fear.
The leaders, ancient, baffled, scared, and slow,
Could not decide which way the ship should steer

The President who finally put to rest
The fiction of democracy and choice
Was not the one that hist'ry deems the best
But rather one who had the loudest voice

Arising at a time of great discord,
Of rising tides, increasing heat and storms
The rich indulged their tendency to hoard
The poor's despair assumed more violent forms

By stoking fear and strife, he rose the ranks
And surprised observers with his new techniques
Curtailed free speech, controlled the wayward banks,
Derided all his enemies as freaks

And though the deeper source of all this strife
Might fairly be ascribed to his own faction
He claimed the threats to property and life
Demanded swift response, and violent action

"The deeper problem here is not internal,"

He told the people hiding in their houses.
"The threat is from the foreigner, infernal,
Who's out to steal our jobs, our homes, our spouses."

He claimed he could restore our missing glory
But only by suppressing all dissent.
With only one official, sanctioned story
The truth was soon distorted, curved, and bent

Emergency declared, he then postponed
The coming re-election to his post
"Only temporary," he intoned
While troops took charge, in cities coast to coast

His critics were harassed, and some imprisoned
And then, he urged his followers to fight
And silence them by force. And thus, the schism
Turned deadly, and the ones who could, took flight.

And when he said his son would now succeed him
A timid, passive Congress just agreed
Some told themselves the crisis made us need him
And justified their weakness and their greed

For underneath the table, each was paid,
And promised riches for their acquiescence.
They told themselves this bargain, quickly made
Could be reversed. It would not spoil our essence

Of course, it never was. And after years,
The son took power, indolent and rash
Continued stoking anger, lies, and fears
Just less discreet. More bullying and brash.

When Congress finally woke to this great danger
The ones who spoke were quickly put to death
People soon mistrusted every stranger
And watched the words that rode on every breath

The nation somehow lived through this undoing
And lingered on a hundred years, and more
But slowly, it began a long ungluing
As region after region closed its door

Many of the presidents who followed
Would try to reunite the fractious nation
But what success they had would just seem hollow
And lost upon the next assassination

A hundred years along, it seemed we might
At last restore stability and calm:
Jack Benson took the crown, and with his light
It seemed like all our wounds received a balm

The nation, reunited for a while,
Enjoyed a golden age of arts and glory.

If only this did not become defiled!

But this, my friends, begins another story…

6

The Outskirts of Benson City
Sunday, May 30

After some time below decks, Paul decided to get some fresh air. He also wanted to get a better view of the city. The boat was heading due south right now, probably passing by his house (although he knew he wouldn't be able to see it). Still, he wanted to catch one more glimpse of his hometown. By the time he got up to the deck, his part of the city had passed, replaced by a district crowded with stockyards and tanneries. The smell was acrid. When Paul got to the railing, he saw a reddish greasy smear on the river, effluvia from the slaughterhouses.

Paul noticed Elder Eastman standing nearby, hands on the railing, staring intently away from the city. Paul felt an instinctive dislike for the man but decided he would try to get along. They would be together for a long time, after all, and might as well be cordial. Paul walked over to stand with him.

"It's a beautiful day, Elder Eastman."

Eastman didn't look at Paul. He paused for an uncomfortable length of time before finally saying, "Yes, it is. Propitious for our journey, I should think."

"I agree."

Paul ignored the stench rising from the river. "I would welcome any information about our journey you might want to share," he ventured.

Eastman continued avoiding eye contact. "We will be taking this boat to LaSalle. Our first stop is the church there. We have pamphlets and missives to deliver to all the major churches on our itinerary."

"I see."

"Then tomorrow, we continue by land. Hopefully we will be able to cross the Mississippi by mid-week."

This was the famous border of the KGL. "Have you ever left the Kingdom?"

Again, there was an uncomfortably long pause. "I have not."

"Nor have I," Paul replied.

Paul waited for Elder Eastman to offer more information, or even ask him some questions, but he remained silent. Paul couldn't figure out this man. He acted as though Paul had offended him somehow, which made him worried that Eastman somehow knew of his lack of faith. Yet this was all conjecture. It felt like talking to a brick wall.

After a few minutes, the river turned more toward the southwest and Paul could see the Outer Wall of Benson coming into view. It was a large structure, built into one of the ruins of the Empire, made of big chunks of concrete left over from the olden days. Paul had been told that it was originally a massive, raised roadway, but he had a hard time believing so many vehicles would be coming and going into what was then old Chicago. It stood maybe 40 or 50 feet tall and was even wider than it was tall. Watchtowers stood on the wall on either side of the river to guard the city. Paul felt a little tremor of excitement and nerves as they inched closer to leaving Benson.

There was a line-up of boats as they approached the border of the city. Paul could see Imperial Guards boarding each vessel before passing them through. There was probably an exchange of coins, too. When their boat reached the giant bridge, however, the guard simply made a circular motion with his hands, sending them through. Paul wondered why they were so privileged, then remembered the Imperial flag flying from the back—red and white horizontal stripes with a rectangle of blue in the corner, in which sat an ornate golden cross. Only official KGL vehicles were allowed to fly this flag.

They glided smoothly under the bridge, held up by decaying concrete pillars and jerry-rigged wooden braces. And just like that, Paul was out of the city. On the other side of the wall, he saw some ramshackle wooden buildings clustered together, almost on top of one another.

"What are those?" he asked Eastman.

"The homes of the Outcastes," he replied with a disgusted look on his face. Paul was intrigued. He had never seen Outcastes in Benson and wondered what they might look like. Unfortunately, none of them was in sight.

The shantytown quickly faded into the distance as they rolled on. Replacing it was a strange landscape. It was mostly forested, but Paul could see the ruins of old buildings on both sides of the river and what looked to be ancient roads. Their boat passed through a set of rusted pilings in the river that must have been the support for a bridge from the olden days, now long fallen away. And then, a few minutes later, another set of pilings, and then another set. *How many bridges did these people need?* Paul wondered. Occasionally they would pass by the ruins of a larger building, trees growing out of a broken roof. A branch of the river split off to the south, and Paul saw another packet boat coming up from that river into theirs, heading into Benson. Then more ruins, and still more. It went on, and on, and on.

"Good lord! How many people lived here back then?" he muttered to himself.

"Way too many," said Echleph, startling Paul. He hadn't noticed him coming up behind them. The man moved quietly.

After maybe an hour, the ruins slowly began to disappear, the forest reclaiming the land. They passed through another massive bridge-like structure from the Empire—*another roadway? Really?*—and then they were deep in the woods, stretching for as far as Paul could see. Even here, artifacts from the Empire remained. Intriguing to Paul were some massive metal towers, looking like mechanical men, lined up in a row, marching out into the distance. They were mostly evenly spaced, although Paul could see that some had fallen over. They were covered in ivy to varying heights. They must have been a hundred feet tall, or more.

"What are those?" he asked Eastman.

"Idols," he replied quickly. "When the people started losing sight of God back in those days, they ended up venerating machines instead. I'm afraid you will see more examples of this kind of thing the farther we go." Eastman abruptly turned away from Paul and walked toward the back of the boat. *Did I say something offensive? Or is he just wearying of my questions?*

Echleph, now standing on Paul's right and looking at the towers, spoke in a whisper to Paul: "They're electrical towers."

"Electrical towers?"

"Yeah. There used to be wires hung 'tween these towers, bringing electricity to the cities."

"What's electricity?"

"It's a kind of power source. Like lightning. People back then figured out how to grab it and use it to light their houses and run their machines."

Paul had to take a moment to digest this. The electrical towers slipped behind them as they sailed on. Paul stared after them.

"I'm having trouble imagining how they captured lightning."

"They didn't. The people back then had ways of generating it. They were willing to wreck the planet to have as much power as possible."

After a lunch of cornmeal and beans, Paul walked down below to rest. He still hadn't fully recovered from his late night, and soon, he had fallen asleep. He was awakened by the boatmen singing a work song above decks:

Every day I'm workin' on the Illinois River
Get half a day off with pay
Oh, a tow boat picking up barges,
On a long, hot summer day

Paul shook off his sleepiness and climbed up the stairs to the main deck. The sun was now getting low on the horizon. They were sailing directly into it. Paul could see the walls of what he presumed was LaSalle coming up, made up of what seemed to be huge boulders of rusted metal, mostly covered in grape vines. He saw Echleph sitting with his dog at the front of the boat and walked up to join him.

"What's that wall made of? It's massive."

"Those are 'cars' from the olden times."

"I've heard of those. That was their main form of transit, right?"

"That's right. A man could get up one morning, get in his car, and go all the way across the continent in a few days. They were lightning fast, but they spewed waste into the air that we still have with us."

"Did these 'cars' use electricity, too?"

"Not at first. Later, they did. By that point, it was too late."

Paul wondered if Echleph was telling him the truth about these things. Perhaps he thought Paul was gullible enough to believe in such wizardry. Or maybe these things were true. Paul had no way of knowing.

Unlike Benson, the walls of LaSalle did not extend across the river. Paul could see up ahead that the dock for the city lay some distance outside the city walls. The packet boat slowed down to pass by a long, narrow island in the river on their left. Then they slipped into a small harbor that looked man-made rather than natural, on the north side of the river. There were four other boats moored there.

The boatmen had already hoisted their trunks up to the deck—*when did that happen?* Paul lifted his trunk up onto his shoulders and saw that the three soldiers travelling with them carried all their belongings in big packs. Paul was grateful now that he only had one trunk to carry. He took it off the boat and set it down with the other items from his group piled up on the shore.

Paul saw Eastman pull out some coins from a purse and drop them into the hands of the ship's captain, who bowed and tipped his hat to the Elder. Eastman was once again dressed in his Elder's robes. *I wish he would communicate with me!* He strode quickly past Paul to a stone building at the end of the dock. Paul didn't know if he should follow him. Paul was standing next to Sargent Broadstreet, but the latter was looking at Echleph Domain for guidance. When Echleph started following Eastman, the rest of them followed as well.

Eastman had paused at the stone building, waiting for them. "They've given us a carriage from the church," he told Echleph. "You'll find it around back of this building."

Broadstreet looked at Echleph as if to say, *Is this part of our job?* Echleph paused then nodded almost imperceptibly. Broadstreet and Archer Rayphe headed off together to the back of the building. After a moment, Paul decided to help them. He liked horses and already missed his own. When he got to the stables, he discovered that the soldiers had already gotten the two horses into position, but he was still able to help with the harnesses. Broadstreet's bushy eyebrows rose in surprise when he saw Paul come in to help, but he didn't say anything.

The carriage was a small one, with just one bench inside, so the five of them wouldn't all be able to ride. Paul was fine with walking, but when they pulled the horses around to the others, Eastman looked at Paul and pointed to the carriage. *Maybe the guards can better protect us if they're not sitting in a carriage.*

The three soldiers heaved the luggage onto the back. Broadstreet took the driver's seat, Paul and Eastman rode in the carriage, and Echleph and Archer walked along side. Paul was fascinated by the city walls made from stacked up cars. The sheer number of them was staggering. It must have been hundreds of vehicles, stacked up five or six cars tall, but squished down as though by a giant's hand. And how did the people lift them up to that height? There was a two-story metal gate in the wall not far down the road. When they got there, the guards looked at the papers provided by Eastman, opened the gates and let them through.

The city was much smaller than Benson, of course. They entered it on a narrow dirt road lined with two-story wooden buildings fronted by wooden planked sidewalks. Paul didn't see any remnants from the Empire days, but that didn't mean there wasn't a town here back then. There seemed to have been towns *everywhere* in those days. Paul had trouble imagining what it must have been like to share the planet with so many other human beings.

The main street led right up to the church, an eclectic structure made of stone and brick. As Paul got closer, he could see that it was built of reclaimed materials from other buildings. There were buildings like that in Benson, too. It was a natural thing to do, with so much leftover material from the olden days. The church had some bigger yellow stonework at the base, followed by a hodge-podge of yellow, red, and blackened bricks (presumably from some fire) as the walls rose to the roof. It was topped with a three-story belltower, also ramshackle. The mortar was sloppily applied and needed tuck-pointing. Paul was not impressed.

As they pulled up to the front of the church, the double doors opened and two pastors strode out to greet them, wearing the traditional brown robes of their rank. They bowed deeply as Eastman stepped out of the carriage. Paul followed behind him.

"Welcome to LaSalle, Elder! We are most grateful for your visit." They spoke in perfect Church English.

Eastman bowed back perfunctorily. "Thank you. This is my associate, Assistant Elder Paul Girard."

Paul bowed politely. Their attention was fixed on Eastman, however. "You must be tired from your long journey," said one of them. "We have prepared the second parsonage for the two of you to stay in tonight. We will take you there now, let you rest, and then we'll have a dinner with Elder Andrews in the chancel room in an hour or so."

Paul wondered briefly where the three soldiers would be staying, but quickly put them out of his mind. He was eager to change out of his travel clothes and eat a good meal. Their hosts gestured politely, and Paul followed them with Eastman to the back of the church. The parsonage was a small brick building set not far behind the chapel, one room, crowded with furniture. Paul saw that there was only one bed. *Maybe I'll sleep on the floor tonight.* The pastors quietly closed the door behind them after Paul entered the room.

Eastman placed his bag by the bed and pulled out a well-thumbed copy of The Three Testaments. He lay on the bed and began to read. I guess we will not be having a conversation, thought Paul. He pulled out his own book, one of his favorite historical treatises about Emperor Benson, one of the last emperors of the olden times. Before Paul knew it, the hour had flown by, and it was time for him to change into his formal robes for dinner.

Eastman was waiting for him outside. Paul sensed disapproval in his glance but couldn't quite decide if he was reading him accurately. Without a word, Eastman started walking toward another outbuilding behind the church. This one was also built from discarded material, in this case, chunks of old concrete. There was a lot of concrete left over from the Empire.

Inside the building was one large room, clearly used for social gatherings and meetings. In the center was a long wooden table with a white tablecloth, and piles and piles of food. Paul was a little stunned. How many would be joining them? He could see a boar's head as the centerpiece, plus various roasted small birds and about a dozen loaves of bread. Each seat had a porcelain plate and gleaming silverware, freshly polished.

The two pastors in brown were talking near the back of the room. When they saw Paul and Eastman enter the room, they quickly walked over to greet them.

"Elders! Welcome to the chancelry! I trust you are well-rested? Come with us, we must introduce you to the High Elder of this region, Elder Andrews."

Eastman bowed politely. They followed the pastors to the back of the room, where a boy sat with an elaborate wooden train set. A finely dressed woman with a colorful headscarf stood next to him. Paul found it strange that this boy—presumably the Elder's son—would be permitted at the banquet. When they reached the back of the room, the pastors bowed deeply to the boy.

"Elder Andrews, please allow me to introduce Elders Eastman and Girard from the capital."

The boy looked up blandly, then turned to the woman. "Can I go outside and play now?"

"Yes, my prince," she replied. *This child is the High Elder?!*

Paul had heard of this sort of thing before—the children of the rich and powerful being appointed to high positions—but he didn't expect to encounter it at their first stop, nor with an Elder quite this... young.

Paul took a closer look at the Elder's mother. After a moment, he recognized her from some illustrations in the newspaper: she was the

Supreme Elder's fourth wife, and this must be his fifth child—Paul thought his name was Henry-John-James (the hyphenated first names so typical of the First Caste). The High Elder's mother was dressed elegantly and carried herself with that ineffable quality of confidence of the First Caste—not that Paul had met very many of them. She had rich brown eyes, the fine bones of the upper castes, and just the hint of faint wrinkles forming around her eyes and mouth. Ten or fifteen years earlier, she must have been one of the most beautiful women in the world. Paul had trouble taking his eyes off her.

"Gentlemen, I am Elder Andrews' mother. On behalf of the Elder, I welcome you most warmly to our diocese. I will leave you now to your business. Please send my warmest greetings to the officials in the central office." She bowed gracefully and followed her son out of the room. Paul watched her move with barely concealed lust.

He remembered hearing this story a few years ago, probably from his mother, who took some interest in celebrity gossip. The Supreme Elder was now on his fifth wife; this was probably the mechanism for him to get rid of Wife No. 4, appointing his son to this position, so that she would follow and leave him free to pursue the next wife. Paul couldn't imagine anybody rejecting this woman. *Down, boy!* Paul said to himself. *She's out of your league, quite literally.*

The two pastors led the way to the table. Paul saw that the head of the table was set for the High Elder, probably out of courtesy, and the two pastors took the two seats on the right-hand side. Paul and Simon Eastman sat on the other side. The head of the table would remain empty. *I wonder which one of you is really running this church,* Paul thought as he sat down. *Or maybe, it's the mother…*

The dinner began with venison soup, served by two male servants also wearing brown robes. Paul dug in with relish. The bread was warm and flavorful, and there were flagons full of white wine. Remembering his night of debauchery, Paul kept his drinking in check.

If Paul had been expecting anything of substance to be discussed at the table, he would have been disappointed. The group discussed the weather, some arcane points of church doctrine, and the prospects for the economy for the rest of the year. Not until the end of the dinner did Eastman pull out a thick envelope from the folds of his robes and hand this to one of the Pastors.

"I would like to give you these greetings from the Supreme Elder, plus some of his most recent thoughts about changes to the recommended liturgy for your services."

"We thank you most kindly, Elder."

"Please make sure the High Elder receives this and let me know if he—or you—have any questions before we leave tomorrow morning."

"We will."

⁂

The next morning, Paul and Eastman met the soldiers in front of the church. They had procured a covered wagon for the next leg of their journey, with two stout mares who looked like they were accustomed to working together. Echleph and Archer were holding two other horses, presumably for them to ride. Paul would have preferred riding his own mount, but this was clearly not going to be discussed. Paul didn't recall Eastman giving them any instructions. In so many ways, Paul felt like an outsider.

The two pastors met them outside to see them off. They handed them each a warm fruit tart, a rare treat, by way of breakfast, wished them Godspeed, then walked back into the building. Eastman conferred quietly with Sgt. Broadstreet, then climbed into the wagon, where there was a bench along each side. Paul followed him. Broadstreet took the front bench, outside the tarp covering, gave the reins a little flick, and the wagon creaked into motion.

The wagon was filled with all their bags and trunks, stacked up neatly between the two benches. *The soldiers were busy while we slept.* There was also a little space carved out for a small bed, with a cotton mattress and a quilt. *Is that for one of us, or the dog?* Paul leaned over and looked at Echleph, riding to the right of the wagon; his dog was trotting happily beside him, no problem keeping up with the horses.

The group was heading north, through what remained of the city, only five or six blocks. They paused at the gate in the wall made of cars, but this time the guard just waved them through. Unlike Benson, there were no Outcaste buildings beyond the gates. Instead, fields of young corn stretched out as far as Paul could see.

Paul turned to Eastman, sitting on the other bench across from him in the wagon. "I was surprised to find that the leader of this church is a little boy," he ventured.

Eastman frowned at him. "Are you questioning the wisdom of his appointment?"

Well, yes—I am.

"No, of course not," he replied.

"Good," said Eastman. He pointedly looked away from Paul and out the front of the wagon.

After a moment, Paul decided to try to converse with Sgt. Broad-street instead. He climbed up and sat next to him on the bench. The big man glanced sidelong at Paul when he sat down, with a half-smile. He had clearly heard the conversation.

"Good morning, Sargent."

Broadstreet, now looking back at the road, grunted a response. "You can call me Turge."

"Thank you. And you can call me Paul."

"No, I don't think so."

Paul decided not to press the matter. "I was wondering where you and your companions spent the night last night."

"Oh, we's got ourselves a nice little tavern—good beer, plenty of grub. And a sweet young waitress to keep me warm last night, if you know what I mean." Turge chuckled in satisfaction, which Paul felt more than heard, a kind of rumbling in the bench.

Paul smiled. He didn't admit to Turge how inexperienced he was in these matters. People in Paul's caste were wary of casual sexual en-counters, given the prevalence of lethal diseases that were transmitted—or so they were told. The expectation was strong that young men and women would save sex for marriage. Paul was not alone in remaining a virgin at 22.

Turge pulled the horses abruptly to the left to avoid a large pot-hole in the middle of the dirt road.

"Are all the roads going to be this rough?" asked Paul.

"Oh no. We're coming up to an old Empire road. It's just up ahead. Then, your pretty little bum can get more pampering."

Paul looked up and saw that they were already climbing up a very gradual slope. When they got to the top, the road became paved. Paul realized they were on top of one of those bridges from the Empire days, one of the few that had managed to stay intact. After they crossed the bridge, they veered to the right, making a long, slow turn onto the roadway below. Finally, they reached the massive roadway, wide enough for three, maybe four vehicles. Then Paul realized there was a second roadway to their left. This roadway was all for vehicles going in one direction! *Amazing!*

The roadway had held up remarkably well over the centuries. The concrete had webs of cracks in it with grasses growing out, but steady traffic probably kept the weeds in check. Paul saw a caravan of merchants riding the opposite way, two wagons surrounded by guards on horseback, not unlike their own situation. It was probably the only way to be sure you and your goods would arrive safely, given all the criminals and highwaymen roaming the countryside. Not too long after this, a solo rider on horseback passed them at a gallop. *Probably a messenger,* Paul thought.

Still, Paul's group was also moving along at a good clip. The road was paved and almost perfectly straight, and if they didn't have to rest and water the horses, Paul could see them reaching the edge of the Kingdom very quickly.

"There's a jug of water under the seat," said Turge, as though reading Paul's mind. Paul reached under, found a big ceramic jug, pulled out the cork and took a long drink. He offered it to Turge, who lifted it easily with one hand, keeping the other holding the reins, and seemed to chug half the remainder. Droplets of water glistened in his reddish-brown beard.

Paul fell into a kind of trance, watching the flat fields roll by. After an hour or so, the farmland gave way to pastureland, and then gradually to forest, thick and dark. These were dangerous; every child knew cautionary tales about the forests. Occasionally, Paul would see the ruins of a building among the trees, indicating that the forest had grown here after the Fall. It looked like the forest could have stood for millennia, though, it was so thick and tall. The trees were a mix of deciduous and pine, giving off a rich fragrance.

Around midday, they stopped at a roadside tavern for lunch. Paul was surprised that there was enough traffic to support such an establishment this far from any city. Turge took the horses around back for hay and water while the rest of them went inside the dark building for beer and mutton. The soldiers took turns guarding their wagon. The clientele seemed rough and uncouth, their country accents strong and sometimes incomprehensible. Paul felt vulnerable. He noticed Echleph quietly scanning the room for trouble as they sat, ever on the alert. They made it through their meal in one piece.

In the middle of the afternoon, Turge abruptly pulled off the main road to follow a dirt path, mostly northward. "Where are we going?" Paul asked him.

By way of response, Turge pointed to a large sign, where the words *Big Rock Candy Mountain* were written in Mojies. Paul was confused. "Why are we stopping here?"

"Elder's orders," said Turge.

Paul looked back at Eastman, but the latter was staring off into the distance serenely. Paul decided to just wait and find out.

He didn't have long to wait. A huge mound of dirt—several mounds, actually—came up over the horizon. They were bigger than any hill he had seen in Benson, maybe up to half the height of the Black Pyramid. As they got closer, Paul could see a strange mist or fog emanating from the hills, as though they were smoldering. The hills were located behind a wooden palisade. They had to pass through a gate, a log on a hinge blocking their path. A strange-looking little man was sitting on a high chair.

"That'll be two shekels," he said in a squeaky voice. Eastman was ready with the coins. He reached forward and handed these to Turge to hand to the dwarf. The little man tucked the coins into a pocket, turned a crank next to him, and the log slowly lifted. They passed through the gate and into a large parking area. Paul thought there must have been two dozen horses feeding at the trough. Carriages and wagons lined the perimeter.

"What is this place?" asked Paul as they climbed down from the carriage.

"It's basically a trash heap from the olden days," said Turge. "The dwarves mine it for goods from the past. People come from all over the Kingdom for these things."

Paul still didn't understand why they were stopped here, but he did find it interesting. There was a footpath leading out of the parking area toward the hills. Along both sides of the path were numerous little stalls, each one manned by one or two dwarves.

"Why dwarves?" Paul asked Turge.

He shrugged. "They make for good miners, I hear. And the ground inside the tunnels is unstable, so their light weight is an advantage."

Paul followed Eastman and Echleph into the compound. As they got closer, the stench of garbage grew stronger and more acrid. Paul wondered how the dwarves could stand it. He could also see that the hills, which from a distance seemed a kind of dull grayish brown, were actually multicolored. Most of these consisted of bags of plastic, that ubiquitous material from the Empire. Something about plastic made Paul's skin crawl.

And yet, he was also fascinated. There was a small field filled with colorful toys for children, most of them in the shape of cars. Some of these were broken and jury-rigged, and most were faded in color, but a surprising number were intact. *This plastic stuff sure is durable. But where on Earth did they extract this?* Once again, Paul was struck by the sheer number of toys. The children of the American Empire must have been spoiled and coddled, and clearly encouraged to practice operating their cars from a very young age. *Cars seem to have been a fetish with those people.*

Paul was astounded by the amount of trash there. In his world, you rarely threw anything away. There was always an opportunity to reuse that scrap of wood or that piece of fabric, unless it was so threadbare it just blew away or crumbled in your hand. Paul was envious at the obvious wealth of the citizens of the American Empire.

One table that caught his attention contained strips of paper with words in English written on them. These were also coated in plastic, preserving them. Paul couldn't understand what these were used for, or even what some of them meant, despite his fluency in English. One of them read, "Warning: the closer you get, the slower I drive." Another one read "KZAP 98.5 FM." Paul frowned, trying to figure out the purpose of these things.

Paul noticed that Eastman and Echleph had moved on, and so he rushed to catch up. Eastman was now stopped at a table a little distance away. When Paul caught up, he found out what had made him want to stop at the trash heap.

Eyeglasses.

On the table were hundreds of glasses from the Empire days, of all sorts of shapes and, presumably, strengths. Behind the dwarf at the table was a chart of Mojies, each line getting progressively smaller, so that a customer could test the prescriptions. Eastman looked over the selection, gingerly picked up a pair, wiped it thoroughly with a handkerchief, then tried it on. He squinted at the sign, put the glasses down, and ran his finger down the row of glasses, searching for another pair.

Paul could see that Echleph and his dog had moved on. Was he searching for more interesting trinkets? Paul jogged to catch up. He passed table after table of goods, many of them completely incomprehensible to Paul. *What was that chunk of plastic used for?* He had no idea. He also saw a table piled high with shoes. Even these looked like they were made out of plastic. These were tempting for Paul—he only owned two pairs of shoes, and he worried that his current pair wouldn't last this entire journey. The prices, alas, were too rich for him. And once again, Echleph had moved on. Paul didn't want to lose sight of him in this maze.

The soldier turned down a narrow side alley, then through a hidden passageway that was not easily seen from the main pathway. Paul followed.

Paul understood why this passageway was hidden. Spread out here was material that the Church would deem unacceptable. On one table there were colorful printed materials with photographs of totally nude women on the covers. Paul was shocked, a little short of breath. He had seen photographs before—yet another example of a magical technology now lost—but never any like this. He couldn't believe women would willingly take off their clothes and let themselves be seen like that. What on Earth would make them agree to debase themselves? Paul was intrigued, despite himself, tempted to look more. But Echleph passed these by and went to another stall. Paul reluctantly pulled away and followed.

When he caught up with them, he saw that Echleph had stopped at a stall selling maps. Most were ancient and brittle, but some were preserved in little plastic sleeves that seemed to have helped keep them intact. A piece of wood with Mojies written on it advertised then as costing a tenth of a Sovereign each, which was big money. Echleph browsed quickly through them, selected one, then slipped the dwarf a coin. The merchant accepted it with a bow. Echleph gave Paul a small nod as he tucked the map into his pack and walked out.

They ended up spending the rest of the day at the Big Rock Candy Mountain. Next to the compound was an inn, also run by dwarves, and they spent the night there. It served a hearty meal, with good singing around the hearth. All five of them were put in one room, with two beds. Paul was designated to share a bed with Turge, but quickly discovered he snored loudly, so Paul retreated to the floor again. It was not a restful night. Paul dozed in the back of the wagon after they departed for the day.

By mid-morning, they had reached the border of the KGL. A little unwalled town held about ten ramshackle buildings and a marketplace. The Mississippi, which Paul had heard about his entire life, was not visible from the town; a two-story ridge of earth ran the entire length of the river, as far as the eye could see. The dirt road that ran through the center of the town went up a slope to the top of the ridge. The group passed straight through the town and up the banks.

When they crested, Paul was astounded by the breadth of the river. It reminded him of Lake Michigan. There was a large island in the middle, big enough for a small settlement, and then the water just seemed to go on and on. There was a faint mist drifting up from it. Down at the bottom of the levee was a little dock for ferryboats.

Ferries were shallow and maybe 25 feet wide, carrying two horses. These were tethered to the opposite sides of the boat, facing opposite directions, both with blinders over their eyes. Paul could see that the horses would be walking on a circular wooden platform on the floor of the boat that turned the paddle in the back. It was still wide enough that their entire wagon could board on either side of the paddle, with all four horses.

The ferryman was a tall, taciturn man named Mr. Sharon. He held out his hand for the passage fee before they boarded, in silence. Once they were all secure, he lifted the ramp up behind them, untied the mooring rope, then walked to the steering wheel at the front. He spoke an inaudible word to the horses, and they began to move lethargically. The boat slowly eased out into the river. Paul swallowed nervously at the prospect of leaving the Kingdom behind.

The boat slowly but steadily headed across the river, through the mists, toward the wilderness beyond.

7

The Inland Sea of California
Tuesday, June 1

The next night, Alex had a dream:

I am wandering through the Fairday alone. It's exciting at first but then it begins to get scary. I can't find anybody in my family. I see Alika from a distance, but she only laughs at me and says, "You're too much of a baby to be on the tour!" When I try to catch up with her, she disappears into a crowd. I start to cry. Then I see Grandma Meta sitting behind a booth.

"What are you doing here, Grandma?" I say to her. "Aren't you supposed to be back home?"

She says, "I can be in two places at once if I want to, can't I?"

"I guess so," I say.

Then she says, "Come here. I want to tell you something."

I walk over to the booth, and I sit down on the bench next to her. She says, "I thought you should know that it's time I left the material plane."

I say, "What do you mean?" even though in my heart, I know.

She looks at me sadly and opens her arms to give me a hug.

"No!!"

Alex woke up, with Jasmine shaking him. "Alex! You're having a nightmare!"

It took him a moment to shake off the reality of the dream, then he fell into her arms, crying. The noise he was making woke up some of the others in the Clan (but thankfully not everybody). Aunt Rosa and Aunt Emma came up from the cabin below, where they preferred to sleep. Aunt Rosa was Grandma Meta's little sister, not quite as old and round as Grandma Meta but similar looking. She was kind of like the second in command of the Clan, and Emma was her daughter. These two also looked alike. Emma had a kid on the tour, R.J., but they were still asleep on the deck.

Rosa knelt next to Alex and whispered, "What did you dream?"

Alex was a little shaky and now a little self-conscious. "It was just a weird dream."

"Tell us your dream," she said with a serious tone in her voice.

Alex recounted the dream. He left out the part about Alika laughing at him; he didn't want to admit how much she irritates him in real life. He was still in Jasmine's arms, a little sweaty, but she was stroking his hair and he liked it. She rarely did that.

When he finished, Emma turned to her mother. "What do you think?"

"I don't know. It worries me. It has some of the earmarks of a True Dream."

"What's that?" asked Alex.

"Well, first, you know that dreaming is important, right? We need to dream each night, to shut out the energy influx of the material world and turn inward. Some of the dreams are about understanding our world better, putting some order on things. But other dreams give us access to the Spirit World, where we can have contact with a different level of information."

"Do you… Do you mean…" Alex felt like he was going to start crying again, and he really, really didn't want to.

"Hush. We don't know anything. I'll bring it up with Charles to-morrow morning. He's in charge of the tour. If he thinks we should skip the next stop and go check on her, we'll do it."

Alex now felt even more self-conscious, now that she said she would tell Charles about it. "I don't want us to miss out on the Fairdays. We need that money, right?"

"We do, but family is more important than money. Go back to sleep. We'll discuss it in the morning."

Alex didn't have any more dreams that night, at least not that he could remember. While he was eating breakfast at the big table in the main cabin down below, Alika came down and said to him, "Charles wants to talk with you as soon as you are ready." She said it in a tone that implied she had insider knowledge, which meant Alex was in trouble. He rarely talked with Charles. He kind of scared him.

Alex quickly shoved the rest of his breakfast bread into his mouth, wiped his mouth with the back of his hand, and climbed upstairs. Charles was at the front of the boat, scanning the horizon. Alex crept up to him but didn't know what to say. He didn't want to interrupt him. So, he stood quietly about a meter away and waited. He was there quite some time before Emma approached the two of them, cleared her throat, and Charles turned around.

"Oh. There you are. I didn't see you."

Alex swallowed and said, "Good morning," self-consciously.

"Good morning. Emma tells me you had quite a dream last night."

Alex was now thoroughly embarrassed by this whole episode and wished it would go away. "Yeah, I guess so."

"I want you to tell it to me. The whole thing."

Alex recounted it, but again left out the part about Alika. That was private, anyway. Charles listened without interrupting, staring out into the Inland Sea.

When Alex finished, Charles remained quiet. After a few moments, Emma said, "What do you think, Charles?"

"That sounds like a powerful dream."

"Do you think we should go back and check on your mom?"

"I'm not sure. This next Fairday is usually one of the best ones for us, as you know. If we leave now, we'll miss it."

"Yes, but maybe Aunt Meta was trying to reach out to us."

"Could be. I wonder why she would choose Alex for this, and not, say, your mother."

"Or you, her oldest son."

Charles shrugged. Then he fixed his gaze on Alex. "Tell me—have you had any other powerful dreams like this? Or any waking visions?"

The truth was, Alex had. But he didn't know if these counted. Maybe he was just having one of his daydreams. Jasmine always said he spent half his life in a fantasy world. He didn't want to tell Charles about these.

"I don't want us to go back," said Alex. "I really think it was just a dream. I think I've just been missing her. Maybe I'm a little homesick. I don't know! I'm sorry I've caused all this…"

Charles knelt so that he was more on Alex's level. "Listen: you're not causing any trouble. We just take dreams very seriously. Here's what we'll do. We'll continue for now, but if any of us has a similar dream about your grandma, we'll reconsider and head home. That way, it won't all be on you."

Alex nodded, relieved. He was imagining the whole Clan sailing home, finding Grandma laughing at them, and then everyone would hate him and call him a baby even more than they already did.

Charles stood up. "Emma, can you spread the word about this? I want everyone to report their dreams tomorrow morning, if anybody dreams of Meta. In the meantime, we're heading to our next stop."

Emma stood there for a while, like she was considering arguing with him, then nodded quickly and headed off to the cabin below.

Nobody reported any Grandma Meta dreams the next morning—including Alex, thankfully—and so they sailed on to their next stop. Now that they had crossed into the month of June, the days getting longer, with more time to travel. By the evening, they were already at Havenport and had tied their line to a dock in the harbor with the other boats. Alex couldn't count the number of boats in the harbor—it must have been over a hundred. This one was going to be even bigger than the first Fairday, Alex could tell.

He slept restlessly that night, as he had the night before. It was partly because he was excited about the Fair, but he was also a little scared that he would dream of Grandma Meta again. He would fall asleep, start to dream, then startle himself awake. He did sleep, but when the Sun rose early, he was already awake.

This was a good thing, though: The Clan was already stirring so that they could get ready for the day. Just like in the last town, they all helped carry their instruments, stage boards, and tents off the boat then into town. This city had a very different look to it, though. The first thing Alex saw was a big plaza at the seaside, already filled with people getting ready for the day. The ground of the plaza was made up of different colored stones put together in an intricate design, blue wave-like shapes. Alex couldn't believe people would put that much effort into artwork you would just be *walking* on. In the plaza, there were also benches built in, just for anybody to sit on. Palm trees were growing here, too, set very deliberately into circular dirt areas. This city seemed to be rich. Alex liked it! *No wonder Charles was eager to make this stop.*

As they walked through the city itself, Alex was surprised how many buildings were made of stone and brick. They looked old. He wondered if they dated back from before the Great Earthquake that happened about a hundred years ago. There was nothing that old up where he lived. Some seagulls scattered and flew off as the Clan walked through the city.

After about a kilometer they came to another plaza, much, much bigger than the one by the sea. There was a church at the far end with a steeple as tall as four or five houses. This would be where the fair would happen—also different from the last Fair Day, in that it would be held in the middle of a city rather than on the outskirts. There were already at least a hundred tents and booths already set up. The center of the plaza was also paved with a beautiful mosaic, a giant square design, with a real, working fountain in the middle. Along the edges, where the tents and booths were set up, it was just dirt. Still, this was the fanciest city Alex had ever seen.

At the entrance to the plaza there was a woman sitting behind a desk. Charles talked with her. She gave him a lanyard to wear around his neck and a piece of paper with a map of the exhibitors, pointing to the spot they would be occupying. This seemed much more official than the first Fairday.

The Clan's place was marked with a sign. Charles frowned for a moment. He said to Aunt Rosa, "Not as much space as last year, I don't think."

"We can make this work. Remember, we don't actually need to set up to play here. We've got a slot on the Main Stage. Why don't we take the stage back to the boat?" Alex looked around behind her and saw, underneath the church steeple, a big platform for the musicians, a meter tall and maybe fifteen meters wide. He felt a little tremor of excitement. *Maybe they'll let me play up there this time!*

Charles nodded. He got right to work setting up one of their tents. Alex wondered how he could help. Then he saw that Jordan and Chi were carrying some of the stage materials back to the boat and ran to catch up with them.

After they set up the tents, Alex went out with Jordan and Chi to get some lunch. And then, once again, he fell asleep inside one of the tents, where it was cool and quiet. After some time, he woke up to the voices of some people coming into the tent. One of them was his Aunt Mary. She was not his blood aunt—she was married to his Aunt Betta, who always stayed behind with the farm. Aunt Betta was the youngest sister of Charles, as well as Alex's dad, Erik, who had died not long after Alex was born. Aunt Mary was young and pretty and was always very nice to Alex. One of her daughters, though, was the awful, awful Alika.

Alex knew he should get up and leave as soon as he heard people coming into the tent where he lay, but he was embarrassed. He was also well-hidden, almost completely covered in cotton blankets and clothes. It didn't seem like Mary noticed him.

She was there with a woman. Mary sat down at the table in the middle of the tent, and the woman sat down opposite her. Mary lit two candles with a little flint she always carried with her. Mary's back was to Alex and his view of the woman was partially blocked by a screen they used when changing clothes, but he could hear everything. He tried to make sure he was breathing quietly.

The woman said, "How much does this cost, again?" She had the accent of the people from the south part of the Inland Sea, just a little different from the northern speech, the vowels more in her throat.

"Five shekels for a five-card reading, one silver dollar for a full spread."

"Give me the full spread."

Alex could hear the jingling of coins in a purse and saw the woman smack a coin down on the table, rather forcefully. Mary quietly slipped the coin into the folds of her dress then reached down and pulled out the nicer deck of Tarot cards she liked to use. Alex had seen this before. He liked to flip through the cards when nobody was around, even though he didn't understand what the pictures meant.

"Think about your question while you shuffle these." She placed the deck in front of the woman, who took the cards and made a quick gesture of reordering them. When she handed them back, Mary did her own shuffling, neatly and quietly. She had the woman cut the deck, and then laid out the spread, card by card.

Alex couldn't see the cards from where he was lying. He wanted to stand up and look but of course that would be even more embarrassing than if he had gotten up earlier. So, he just listened to their conversation. He heard Mary flip over the first card. He then heard a sharp intake of breath from the woman.

Mary said, "Your Signifier is the Three of Swords."

"That's bad, isn't it?"

"There are no bad cards. There aren't even really any completely good cards. Some are happier than others, it's true. But they all tell us something."

"This one looks awful."

"It's a challenging card, I will admit that. It suggests that someone's been keeping a secret from you, and it's about to come out."

"I knew it," the woman whispered. Alex could hear that she was starting to get choked up.

"People usually do know, at least on some level. Whatever it is, though, it's better to have it out in the open, even if it's hurtful when you hear it."

The reading continued for at least an hour. All through that time, the woman was either crying or seemingly on the verge of crying. Alex got bored after a while and wanted to get up and find something else to eat, but he stayed in his hiding place.

Finally, they finished. They stood up and the woman gave Aunt Mary a long hug. She told Mary she was going to send all her friends to her. Mary thanked her sincerely then came back to the middle of the tent. "Hello, Alex," she said quietly.

Alex could feel himself blushing. He pulled off the blanket, gratefully. It was getting hot under there. "How did you know I was there?"

"You have a distinct way of breathing."

"Sorry, Aunt Mary."

"It's okay. But these sessions are best kept private."

"I'm sorry," he repeated, even more sincerely. She smiled at him, and so he felt brave enough to ask her about her reading.

"Are those cards magical?"

Mary laughed. "No, not really. They're simply a tool we use to gain access to your higher self and the spiritual world, to get you out of your mental ruts for a brief time."

"That seems like magic to me."

"Well, they're not, not any more than anything is magical. They're a tool. It's actually a kind of three-way collaboration between me, the cards, and the customer. Sometimes, one of the three isn't in synch, and then it doesn't work so well. And it's never perfect, because we're still material beings, not entirely spiritual. But they can help."

"How do they work?"

She laughed again. "It's not that the cards 'work.' It's that I understand the stories and myths and deeper truths that the cards are pointing to. I can help draw these stories out of the customer, and hopefully they see their lives from a different angle. If I'm doing it right, I feel like

I can just get out of the way and let the spirit world speak through the cards to the customer."

"Wow."

"And now, you need to leave, because I think I have another customer."

In the later afternoon, Alex was bored. He was anxious for the music-making to begin, but for some reason, they had to wait until after dinner. He had walked around the fair with his cousins twice and had seen everything he wanted to see. There were some good bands playing music very different from the Clan's, but that was pretty much the only thing of interest to him. He kind of wanted to listen in on another Tarot reading, but he knew better than to push his luck. So, he sat in the dirt between their two tents in the shade of a palm tree, next to Jordan, who was lying down face up, with his eyes closed. Charles stood up in front, greeting people and handing out little slips of paper advertising the Clan's music-making and one of his story sessions.

At one point, Alex noticed Charles talking to a local man. Their conversation went on for a long time, not like the others where Charles was promoting their shows. While they were talking, Charles took the long stick he was holding and drew the Sun symbol in the dirt. He did it casually, not even looking at it, keeping his eyes on the man he was talking to. After a few more minutes, the man picked up a stick of his own and drew the Moon symbol next to it, then two arrows. Like Charles, he didn't look at what he was drawing. The man wished him well, tipped his hat, and walked off. After he left, Charles kicked dirt over their little drawings, then came back to where they were sitting. Jordan seemed to wake up out of a deep sleep to full alertness when Charles approached.

"Jordan, take over for me," he said, handing the fliers to him. Charles walked off in the same direction as the man. Jordan got up and stood at the front of the tents to hand out the fliers.

Alex followed him. "What's happening? Where's Charles going?"

Jordan turned around and shushed him angrily. "We can talk about this later," he said under his breath. Alex turned around, kicked the dirt a couple of times, and went back to the shady spot. After a few minutes, Charles came back, took over for Jordan, and Jordan returned to his lying-down position, eyes closed again.

Alex waited patiently, but it looked like Jordan wasn't going to say anything. Finally, he said, "Well?"

Jordan put a hand up to block the sun and squinted at Alex. "Well, what?"

"Are you gonna tell me what that was about?"

Jordan held his gaze for a little while, then said, "Okay, but you mustn't blab about it."

"I don't blab," Alex said defensively.

"I'm serious. It's a matter of life and death."

"Okay, okay."

Jordan looked around to make sure no one was listening. "The Children of the Sun are not exactly welcome everywhere. Charles was trying to find out who's a part of the tribe and who isn't. If he can find a local group, we can gather on Sun'sday. Most often, there's an outdoor place in the woods where we meet, near the town."

"Oh."

"It's good to make these connections, because the People of the Tribe look out for each other. But we have to be careful."

"Why is that?"

"Because there are people out there who don't want us to worship whomever we choose. They want to make sure everybody believes the same way they do."

"That's so weird. Why would it matter to them?"

Jordan looked at him with a slight furrow between his brows. "That's a really good question."

After dinner, the Clan took their instruments to the main stage for their performance. A band opened for them with all the members dressed in black playing instruments made from different animal skulls. The music was horrible. It didn't even sound like music to Alex. Fortunately, they didn't play for long. The Clan set up quickly after they finished. Alex wasn't sure whether he would get to play or not, but at the last minute, Jordan handed him a ukulele. This was it! He would be playing in front of a real audience!

Uncle Evan was the leader for the music-making. He had Emma play an A on her accordion, and everyone tuned quickly. The instruments were in pretty good shape. Then they waited. Alex was wondering what they would be playing, hoping he could keep up. Then, a local man in a big hat jumped onto the stage. He lifted up a big cone-shaped thing to project his voice and called for the audience's attention.

"Hey, everybody! Guess who's back this year? That's right: it's the Taiyo Clan! Get yourselves into two lines, and we'll start the dance."

The man turned back to face the band and said to Evan, "Let's start with a medium tempo, four-four. As usual, I don't care what you do as long as you keep a steady beat and follow my signals"

Evan nodded, then turned around to address the band. "We'll start with 'Ice and Stone,' then see what's next." Alex knew that one! He could definitely play along.

They waited for the dancers to assemble, then waited some more. Finally, the man with the hat held up a fist. Evan called out, "one-two-three-four" and they kicked off the song. The man called out instructions to the audience for their dancing, but Alex didn't pay any attention. He concentrated on the chord changes to make sure he didn't mess up. The ukulele was a quiet instrument, but the Clan would probably notice if he missed a chord. He did make some mistakes, but he covered them up quickly. When they circled around for the second verse and second chorus, Alex felt solid.

And then they kept going. They went through the song, the entire song again, then a *third* time. Alex started getting bored. For the next song, a faster one in triple meter, he saw Jordan and Emma trade instruments. Now he understood why they were trained to play several instruments. These dances could be really boring. For the third song, a couple of people in the Clan left the stage to go get something to drink. No one in the audience seemed to notice; they were busy laughing and twirling around. As the evening wore on, Jordan and Chi took more and more daring solos on the fiddle, egging each other on to top what the other one had just done. It was fun to listen to them.

At about the sixth song, Evan took his bass back to the rear of the stage, where Alex was sitting. "Want to have a turn at big Bertha?" he asked him. *Boy, do I!* He loved playing bass most of all. It was like the rudder of the ship. It really controlled where things were going. He pulled over a little step stool so that he could reach the neck, and then started playing with the group when the next song kicked off. He concentrated extra hard so that he didn't mess it up. Uncle Evan came back after that song and took his bass back, but he winked at Alex. That made him feel good.

After a couple of hours, Alex began to get sleepy, and decided to take a break himself. He found Jordan and Chi drinking some water off to the side and joined them. Alex said to them, "How do you guys know what to do when you're improvising?"

Chi pointed to the dancers, twirling about. "Do you see those dancers? The rhythm of the music is like the legs, the harmony is like the dancer's body. The melody is the dress, the frills and the lace. As long as the body is moving in the right direction, and you stay attached to it, you'll be fine."

Alex didn't fully understand. Maybe this was another thing that would make more sense later.

Then it was time for their last song. Anyone who had heard the Clan perform could predict they would finish off their set with the old, old folk song called "Going to California." Nobody knew who wrote it, but it had been around for hundreds of years. Alex and Jordan and Chi climbed back up on stage. The whole band always played the last song.

Alex had played this song with the Clan at home over the winter many times, but he was surprised to see the audience's reaction. As if they had all talked beforehand, they all stopped dancing and pulled out little candles, lit them, then waved them in the air as the band went through the song. Alex could hear them singing along, too. It was beautiful.

Alex had never paid much attention to the lyrics before, partly because the language was so archaic and fancy-sounding. But this night, with all the candles lit in front of him, he finally understood that there was a kind of secret message embedded in the middle of the song. He wondered if the song was written by someone in the Tribe, addressing other members, informing them of the secret powers they possessed:

The mountains and the canyons start to tremble and shake

As the Children of the Sun begin to awake

When Alex reached that part of the song, he felt chills running up and down his spine.

8

The Duchy of Iowa
Tuesday, June 1

The ferry dropped them off at a little dock near one of those tall electrical towers from the Empire days. The dock looked more like a wooden sidewalk in Benson, lying next to a graded slope to the shore. Turge carefully walked the wagon horses off the ferry and onto the narrow dock. Just beyond the shoreline stood a village with shops aimed at travelers heading into the Kingdom. Paul saw several signs written in Mojies: *Last-Stop Shopping Before the Kingdom! Adult Gifts and More!* He had a hunch about what this might mean.

What was most striking was the architecture. All the buildings were built on stilts about six feet high, with wooden stairs leading to the front doors. Paul asked Turge about them.

"Yeah, the river floods in most years. The KGL has levees on their side so that when the floodwaters come, they always flow over here. The Iowans got tired of rebuilding, so they just gave in and put their houses up higher."

"Why don't they just build levees, too?"

"They did. Your kingdom just built them higher." *My kingdom? Aren't you a part of the KGL too?*

When they reached a dirt road, they mounted their horses and the wagon and headed north. The street was rutted and muddy, the houses much more dilapidated than the ones Paul had seen just on the other side of the border. After a half hour or so, they reached the continuation of the wide roadway they had been on in the KGL and they were able to pick up speed, to a trot. Paul saw a rusty metal sign on the side of the road, bent nearly to the ground. He could just barely make out the English words "Hwy 80." *Does that mean there were 79 other roads this big back in those days?*

Paul didn't know much about the Duchy of Iowa, just that it was a quasi-independent client state of the KGL, along with the Duchies of Kentucky and Minnesota. In the past, they each had been a part of the Kingdom but were now more or less separated from the political apparatus of the Church, although all were officially allied and loyal. Thus, it was a surprise to see, painted on a wall on an abandoned building, *"KGL can go to hell."* He glanced over at Elder Eastman, sitting next to him on the wagon bench. If he noticed it, he didn't reveal anything. Paul felt a chill go up his spine. They were clearly in more dangerous territory now. Paul felt his stomach muscles tighten.

They stopped for lunch just off the roadway, eating from their stores. They took an extra-long break so that the horses would be well rested. Paul decided to take advantage of this quiet moment to add some notes to his journal. His mother had given him a beautiful blank book as a departure present. He was hoping to document his impressions of the world beyond the KGL, if only for his mother to read when he returned. He found a shady tree to lean up against, added ink to his pen from the bottle he had brought, and started to write.

After about a quarter of an hour, Archer interrupted him. "Whatcha got there?"

Before Paul could respond, Archer grabbed it out of his hands and darted away. Paul was shocked. *Are we children, playing keep-away on the playground?* He stood up and strode toward the wiry little man.

Paul tried to grab the book from Archer, but he pulled it away. Archer was small and quick on his feet. Paul now started to get worried. He had already written some unflattering things in the journal about his travel companions. He didn't want anybody to read its contents.

Archer, now walking backwards, was flipping through the pages. Paul hoped he would trip on a tree root and fall.

"Do you people actually read this stuff? I always thought it was all for show. What's wrong with writing in plain old Mojies? Are you too good for that?"

Paul could think of a thousand reasons why he didn't write in Mojies, starting with the fact that they used symbols rather than letters, and each symbol represented a whole word. A Mojie could mean one word in one town and an entirely different word somewhere else. It was imprecise, crude, and childlike. English was nuanced, sophisticated, and had something like ten times the number of words. If you cared at all about depth of thought, you wrote in English.

Archer put on a fake upper-crust accent, rather badly. "Oh, my delicate sensibilities are too disturbed by the common writing you animals indulge in! Why don't you just go back to the pigsty where the rest of your kin live?"

This didn't warrant a response. Archer had, in effect, acknowledged that he couldn't read what Paul had written. *Of course, he can't! People like him are completely illiterate.* Paul shrugged and went back to his tree, sat down, and closed his eyes, determined to wait him out. A minute or two later he felt his journal land in his lap.

This is going to be a long trip.

⋅┼──── ☀ ────┼⋅

When they got back on the road, Paul sat up front with Turge again. He preferred the view from the driver's bench, and Elder Eastman wasn't much of a conversationalist. Paul was still seething from the child-like behavior of Archer. Turge seemed to sense it.

"Don't pay Archer no mind. He just got a chip on his shoulder."

"I can't see what I might have done to offend him."

"You didn't. Or maybe I should say, you just being *you* offends him."

"I don't understand."

"People like him—and like me, the seventh-casters—well, it's easy for us to look at people like you and think your path through life is pretty easy, with your fancy schools and whatnot."

"That would imply I haven't worked for what I've got. The Seminary only admits twenty students per year, with over a hundred applicants. I worked hard for my grades to get in, and I worked hard all the way through the last four years."

"Yeah, but how did you get your grammar school education, and your high school education? Did you see any people like me in your schools?"

Paul looked away. It was true. Everyone in his schools was either Caste 3, 4, or 5. *Still…*

"And why do you think that is?" Turge continued. "Is it because we're all natural-born morons? Or is there something built into the system that keeps us locked out?"

Paul had to admit, to himself at least, that he had never been impressed with the intellectual firepower of the lower castes. Instead of saying this out loud, he turned the question back on Turge. "Would you have wanted to go to school, if you had been given the opportunity?"

Turge chuckled. "And miss the chance to bash some heads in? Naw, that wouldn't've worked for me. But it might've been nice to've been given the option."

"Okay, I get that. But clearly, you must understand that it isn't my fault, right? I didn't set this system up. This has been the way of the world for hundreds of years, if not thousands."

"I gotta correct you there, kid. It hasn't always been this way. In fact, it used to be that America was the place people went to in order to *avoid* the caste system in their home countries."

"How do you know that?" Paul demanded. He wasn't about to accept on face value some sort of history lesson from some unschooled seventh-caste soldier.

"Some knowledge is passed down through the generations. Let's just say we have different lore in Caste 7 than you do in your more lofty realms."

Paul sat quietly after that. The road was getting less interesting the farther they travelled. The land was lightly forested, giving way to prairie grasses here and there. Paul realized with a start that they hadn't seen any other people on the roadway for miles. Nor had they passed any cities or towns. It was getting less and less densely populated the farther they got from the KGL.

Now that they had turned the calendar into June, the days were getting longer, enabling longer stints of safe travel. Paul was starting to get hungry and ready to be off the road, but they kept going. Finally, Echleph trotted next to the wagon and said to Turge, "Follow me."

Echleph moved into the front and took a curving road off the main roadway, heading north. They were now on another paved road but narrower, more broken up, with tall grasses growing up through the cracks. They were travelling through what was once a large city, now completely deserted as far as he could tell. The street had boarded-up shop windows and trash piled up in the streets. After a mile or so, they passed by the remains of a sports stadium, easily as large as the one Paul knew back in Benson. This one was more ruined, though.

Echleph led them through a couple of side streets where the pavement disintegrated completely into rocks and occasional remnants of gray asphalt, the ride now rough and jolting. Turge had to keep a close eye on the horses to make sure they avoided the biggest holes and rocks. After nearly an hour, they came to a long building surrounded by a sea of old asphalt, cracked with tall weeds and trees growing out of it. The building looked to be only two stories tall, but it covered what would be at least ten city blocks in Benson. There were poles placed evenly throughout this expanse of asphalt, poking above the weeds and trees;

Paul knew that they once contained lighting apparatuses—probably powered by electricity, he realized.

Echleph led them through the weeds, around to the back of this big building, then down a concrete ramp. There was a wide, rusty metal door that looked like it opened from the ground up, presumably leading into the basement of the building. Echleph dismounted, handed his reins to Archer, pulled some pieces of wire out of a satchel, then proceeded to pick the lock on the door. He made quick work of it. The gate lifted creakily, but it still opened. It was wide and tall enough for them to ride through. After they got in, Echleph pulled a torch out of the back of the wagon, placed it under his arm, held a piece of flint against the jute top, flicked a piece of steel against it, and lit the torch in one try. He gave it to Turge to hold while he closed the gate behind them. Then he walked back to the wagon and removed an old lock—again, probably from the Empire days—and locked them in.

"Time to get out of the wagon," said Turge. "We're walking from here."

"What is this place?" Paul asked him.

Echleph answered for Turge. "It's called a mall. These were kind of like marketplaces back in the old days. Most of them have been plundered in the years since, but this one is in pretty good shape. Still, we should give the place the once-over before we settle for the night. If you feel like being useful, you can set the horses up in that room over there."

Paul welcomed the opportunity. He missed his horse, Shadow, and enjoyed the ritual of setting him up for the night even though it was considered servants' work. Echleph lit a second torch from the first and handed it to Paul. He had pointed to a room to the right of the ramp with a wide door, easy to bring the horses through with the wagon. The horses followed Paul willingly, perhaps knowing this meant they would be done for the day.

The room had a concrete floor. Paul had no notion of what it might have been used for in centuries past, but now it was clearly a stable. There was hay on the floor, and nobody had cleaned it out for ages. Paul was too tired to take that job on himself. He released the mares from the wagon, tied them to a piece of rusted steel that ran along the wall, and gave them some oats and water they kept in buckets in the back of the wagon. He gave all four of them a quick brushing.

Paul and Elder Eastman had to wait quite some time before the soldiers came back. Finally, Turge appeared at the bottom of some concrete stairs and gave the "all clear" whistle. The two elders followed him up. They then had to walk down another dark corridor before entering an astonishing space. It was a vast, open area, two stories high, with glass panes along all the walls. There must have been fifty store fronts in Paul's immediate vicinity, and the mall continued out of sight around bends in both directions, and onto a second floor. The roof had dirty glass windows in it, letting in the waning light of the evening.

"This space is amazing," said Paul, speaking in English to his fellow Elder.

"Hardly," said Eastman derisively. "It was nothing but a temple for shopping."

To Paul, 'shopping' meant food. Surely this entire building wasn't meant for food. "I don't understand."

"Before the founding of the Church, people worshipped money. They spent all their time buying things, adorning themselves with trinkets to distract themselves from their lack of spiritual direction. This building is a monument to their decadence."

In this case, Paul thought Elder Eastman might be right. Paul walked over and tried one of the glass doors to see if he could get inside of one of these shops, but it was locked. He cupped his hands to peer through the glass into the darkened room beyond. He could barely make out what looked like racks for clothing. Any goods that might have been there had long since been carried off.

They found the soldiers building a fire in an abandoned fountain and joined them for dinner. That night, they each had their own stuffed couch to sleep on, more comfortable, even after all these years since the mall was in use, than the bed Paul slept in at home.

The next day, they left the mall, retraced their path through the ghost town to the main roadway, then continued west. The landscape remained unchanging. No other humans crossed their paths, although Paul did see a pack of wild dogs roaming across the roadway. Echleph's dog Rex was asleep in the wagon at the time, fortunately. Wisps of cottony tree pollen floated through the air like light snow.

Late in the afternoon, they turned off the main road and headed to the north along a straight road. Paul was curious where they were heading but didn't bother asking. After a few miles, a handful of older buildings came into view. There was a large brick building—two towers side-by-side, actually—with a big archway in the middle. To either side of these towers stretched two long buildings with a similar pattern of arches. They rode through the main arch into a big grassy area, a large square surrounded by buildings that must have been five hundred years old at least.

They rode up to what seemed to be the main building, five stories tall and built of gray stone. About twenty monks filed out of the building to meet them. *So, this is a monastery!* Paul had never been to one. He was surprised to see Eastman leap down from the wagon and greet one of these monks warmly with a fond embrace. The two men looked to be about the same age. Paul had never seen Eastman so animated.

"Welcome, Simon!" the man was saying, in English. "How long has it been?"

"Too long, Torval!"

Paul approached and waited to be introduced. After a few moments, Eastman remembered his duty. Torval Edmonds was an old friend from Seminary, the abbot of this monastery, Eastman told him. He shook Paul's hand warmly and invited him in. To Paul's surprise, four of the monks stepped forward to take care of the horses. Paul and the soldiers followed the old friends inside.

The building was as beautiful inside as it was out, with broad passageways of clean, polished stone and leaded windows in a diamond pattern. "This was once a liberal arts college," Edmonds was saying to Eastman. "It was founded by Christians, abandoned its church affiliation as the late-Republic decadence set in, and now we've reclaimed it for the Lord!" Eastman nodded approvingly.

The travelers were taken directly to a large wood-paneled hall for a rich meal of various meats, dark breads, and darker ale. The soldiers joined them this time, sitting in among the monks. Only the abbot held a position of authority, sitting at the end of the long table. To his right was Eastman, the two engaged in a private, jovial conversation. It was like Eastman had been kidnapped and replaced by another man. Paul shook his head in disbelief and took a long drink of the rich ale.

Paul was seated next to a monk who didn't seem that much older than Paul but whose head was completely bald except for a fringe of dark brown over his ears. He introduced himself as Brother Bryce.

"So, what's your role on this expedition?" he asked Paul while handing him a basket of bread. He spoke in perfect English.

Paul thought about giving the monk a bland answer but decided to be blunt instead. "To be honest with you, I haven't the foggiest idea."

Brother Bryce laughed heartily at that, as though it was the best joke he had heard in years. "I have often found myself in that situation," he replied. Paul found his heart lifting a little, for the first time since he left Benson.

"Please don't tell Elder Eastman I said this," Paul whispered to him.

Bryce looked him straight in the eyes and turned serious. "I think you'll find that this is a place where privacy is respected, if not treasured."

Paul felt uncomfortably exposed. He decided to redirect the conversation. "And you? What's your role at the monastery?"

"We try not to specialize too much, but I've found a particular niche in our bookmaking department."

"You make books here?" Paul couldn't contain his excitement.

"Oh yes. This is one of our main sources of income. Would you like to see our operation?"

"Very much!"

"I would be delighted to take you there after we eat."

The rest of the conversation flowed easily and comfortably. Paul didn't realize how much he missed this—good conversation with someone sympathetic and intelligent. He wondered what Bryce's story was, and specifically, what caste he might be in. All the monks dressed the same way here, perhaps deliberately. At the risk of invading his privacy, Paul asked him if he had gone to Benson Seminary, but Bryce shook his head. "No, most of us here went to the Iowa Seminary in Des Moines." Paul had no idea where that city was, if it even was a city.

After dinner, Bryce helped clean up the plates (Paul offered to help but was told to just relax). Then, Bryce took him out of the back of the building toward another, smaller one, some distance away. The monastery was peaceful, green, quiet, with monks walking together and talking avidly on the pathways. Paul had always imagined monasteries as places of silence.

The building they entered had a large, open space inside, an atrium that extended up two floors. It reminded Paul of the shopping mall they had stayed in the night before, even to the extent that this also had windows in the ceiling to let in extra light. Most exciting, however, was the array of books. Two vast walls were entirely covered with bookshelves. Paul had never seen so many books in one place before, not even at the Seminary. Several monks were sitting in comfortable chairs by the windows, reading and taking notes.

In the middle of the room were long wooden tables, sturdily built. Five monks were working there with piles of little pieces of wood, trays, and big sheets of paper. And next to them was a large piece of black machinery that looked like it dated from the Republic.

"This is the heart of the monastery," said Bryce. "Let me show you our pride and joy. I think you'll find it interesting."

They walked to the machine. Paul had never seen anything like it before. It was almost as tall as he was, made of black iron, a jumble of cylinders and platforms at different levels. Gears of various sizes interlocked on the side of the machine, performing functions Paul couldn't quite understand. There was a big black crank on one side of the machine. Paul felt the urge to turn it.

"This is a printing press," said Bryce proudly. "We found the specifications in a particularly rare book. This design dates from over seven hundred years ago, but it works—more or less! It's quite remarkable. We can make numerous copies of a single page, just by setting the type and making sure we have enough paper and ink. Which is easier said than done, these days, but we have our connections."

Paul was awestruck. He knew about printing, of course, as a passionate booklover, but had no idea who was still making them.

"What kinds of things do you print?"

Bryce looked away. "Oh, this and that," he said evasively. "We have a long list of titles my brothers are eager to print, but we have only one printing press. Probably our most successful book has been a translation of the *Three Testaments* into Merican, written in Mojies."

"How is it even possible to use Mojies for that?"

Bryce laughed. "It's not easy, let me tell you. We had to invent several new symbols, for certain words only found in the sacred texts. We like to think of it as a linguistic challenge."

Paul wondered how this could possibly work, given the fluidity of the meaning of Mojies, but decided it would be impolite to bring this up. Instead, he walked over to the table and ran his fingers over the tray of type. He noticed that it was placed backwards. This made sense, given the way it would come out when run through the machine.

"How do you make these little wooden pieces with the Mojies?"

"Well, we have to carve them. It requires a lot of very close, detailed work. We've had to have our smith develop new tools. And they eventually wear out. What we'd love to do, eventually, is to move to metal type. That's what they did back then. We can't quite figure out how they created the molds for the type, but we're working on it."

"This is all so amazing. Do you think there are enough people out there who read Mojies to make this worthwhile?"

"Most of our books are still in English. Based on our sales, though, it seems that there are more and more people out there who find reading Mojies easier."

Next to the trays of type were stacks of big sheets of paper with Mojies printed. Another monk was folding these with a ruler and passing them down to another monk, who was sewing them into folios. "I hope this doesn't portend the end of English as the standard language of scholarship and literature," Paul commented.

Bryce laughed again. "I don't think we have to worry about that just yet. Merican isn't spoken much beyond these borders. English is still the universal language, thanks to the vast reach of the American Empire."

"Speaking of which—do you happen to have any books about the history of the Empire?" Paul asked in an undertone.

"Plenty. Here, let me show you some." Bryce led the way to the wall of books, shelves that stood taller than the two men. "These are, shall we say, not officially sanctioned by the Church, just so you know."

Paul's heart was beating faster. Bryce ran his finger along the spines of books, then spotted one, pulled it out, and handed it to Paul. "Here, you can start with this one. It's pretty good. Why don't you sit over there? I'll give you a little time and come check on you in a bit."

Paul sat down with the book by a bright window with diamond panes. He flipped it open to a random page toward the beginning and began reading hungrily. As he read, a wave of disorientation came over him. This section was about the founding of the American colonies back in the 1600s. He had been taught that the colonies had been established by pious churchgoers, but this book suggested that this was only true of the Pilgrims in New England, and that the first English colony that lasted, in Jamestown, had very little to do with religion. And this was just the beginning. He uncovered stories about slavery and the treatment of the native people that had been glossed over in his school. Possibly the most scandalous of all was the news that the so-called Founding Fathers were not religious men, overall, and that they believed strongly that church and state must be kept separate. The story he had been told was one of a devout founding of the American nation followed by a falling-off of faith, and that when the Church was reconnected with the government, this was a restoration of the natural order. If this book was to be believed, the truth was very different. It made Paul feel positively giddy.

Paul walked back and picked up another history book from the same shelf, this one about the Roman Empire. And again, he found the information radically different from what he'd learned in school. He had been taught that the Roman Empire, like America, was founded by devout people of faith, became decadent and pagan over time, as it grew, until Emperor Constantine reunited Church and State in around the year 300 and set things to rights. Instead, this book argued that Constantine's reign was actually near the end of the Empire's glory days. When Rome fell, there ensued a thousand-year period of chaos. This was lifted not—as Paul had been taught—by Martin Luther, but rather by a group of secular humanists. It wasn't religion that saved them; it was learning and questioning and reasoning…

Paul sat back in his chair, flooded with emotions. He didn't know whether he could trust these books. What they said was so different from the stories he had been told; it was hard to digest it all. On the other hand, all his life, he had been questioning these stories and was never given a satisfactory response. Questioning authority could land you in serious trouble. All this made him suspicious he wasn't being given the truth, or at least the complete truth. He just never knew where to go to find it. It was both exhilarating and nauseating, as though he had discovered that gravity wasn't working anymore, and he was likely to float up into the air.

And why aren't these monks being burned at the stake for printing these things?

He stood up again and went back to the shelves, moving now to a different section. Here were works of fiction that looked to be ancient, very brittle. He didn't want to accidentally destroy them, so he just read the titles on the spines: *A Handmaid's Tale, The Collected Poems of Emily Dickenson,* Frank Herbert's *Dune.* Paul could spend his entire life in this room, just reading that which had been forbidden to him. He sat down again to read more of his history books.

Bryce came back a little while later and sat down at the table opposite Paul. "It's a very different story from the one we were taught, isn't it?" he said quietly.

"I can't believe it. I feel like I've been searching for this my entire life. Is there—is there any way I could take one of these books with me? I would pay you happily. How much does one cost?"

Bryce shook his head. "More than you can afford. One of our nicer volumes runs about five Sovereigns."

"Holy Jesus. That's more than my salary will be for an entire year."

"But I'm not going to give one to you or sell you one. We just can't risk it. I have a feeling if your travel companion found out, the monastery would be in trouble. We have to be very careful who we sell to."

"Does the Abbot know? He seems to be very friendly with Elder Eastman."

"They went to Seminary together. And yes, he knows. He's the one who initiated the printing and distribution of these volumes. The funds we earn from the sales—again, only for a carefully selected set of clients—help fund our operations here."

"Why does he do this? He must know that it could land him in prison, or worse."

"Of course, he does. Not all the members of the Church are opposed to knowledge and learning. There's an underground network of us who are working quietly on bringing about a more open and intellectual society. We believe that this doesn't have to undermine the Church but rather can work alongside it. We hope that by distributing these books, more and more people will become curious and want to learn more. We know it'll take time, but we're ready to play the long game. Meanwhile, we have to operate quietly."

"I promise you: I will keep this private."

"I had a hunch I could trust you. Here, why don't you take a couple of books with you to your room? You can at least read these while you're here."

"I would be most grateful." Paul picked out a couple of books, then Bryce led him to his quarters, a small room with a soft mattress on the fourth floor of the main building. Paul burned his candle to the base, reading late into the night.

The next morning at breakfast, Elder Eastman announced they would be staying one more night, and Paul couldn't have been happier. He spent most of the day in the Scriptorium, which is what they called the room where the books were made, and he read hungrily. In the afternoon, Bryce came in to check on him.

"Could I interrupt you for a few minutes? There's something else I think you might like to see."

Paul reluctantly put aside his book and followed Bryce outdoors. It was a cloudier day, with the threat of thunderstorms. Paul was happy to not be on the road. They walked some distance to the far side of the campus, to a long shed-like building, possibly the least attractive building on campus. As they approached, Paul heard a strange chugging sound coming from inside.

Bryce pulled back a big wooden door. Inside was another strange contraption, this one rattling and puffing out steam. The noise was tremendous.

Standing around it were three monks plus Turge and Archer. One of the monks grabbed a shovel standing nearby, scooped up some coal from a pile, and tossed it into a gaping hole down toward the bottom. Paul saw flames licking out. The monk closed a little door, wearing a thick mitt, enclosing the fire. The machine rattled and emitted more noise.

"What is this?" Paul shouted to Bryce. When Turge heard Paul's voice, he looked over at him and grinned like a little boy. Archer stood mesmerized by the machine.

Bryce gestured for him to follow him outdoors, where they could speak. "It's a steam engine. It's another artifact we've reconstructed from the past. It's even more complicated than the printing press. In fact, any second now, it'll probably stop working. It's something the brothers like to tinker with when they have the time."

Paul shook his head. "I am simply amazed. We've only just begun to figure out how to work with iron again in a serious way, and here you are, crafting intricate machinery! There's so much here that you've discovered. It really could make a difference in the world. We could restart our industries, start to build up this country again, maybe even rebuild the Empire…"

Bryce put up his hand. "Whoa. Stop right there. That would be a very bad idea."

"Why do you say that?"

Bryce started to lead Paul back to the Scriptorium. "Maybe you haven't read *The Fall of the American Empire* yet, but it's pretty clear that industrialization was a major factor in the country's downfall."

"How so?"

"I want to preface this by saying that nobody knows for sure. Nobody who's around today was actually alive back then to witness it, of course. From what I've read in our library, everyone was addicted to these machines, and the exhaust they released led to massive changes to the climate. Overall, the weather got a lot hotter, but also more extreme. Things spiraled out of control."

"But there were also a lot of things in that time that made life more comfortable and healthier for people, right? Don't you think we would learn from our mistakes, that we could do it right this time and not let things get out of control?"

Bryce sighed. "I'd like to think you're right. I am perhaps more cynical than you are about human nature. It seems to me that people are not very good at controlling their impulses. In any event, I know that for now, we here at the monastery have decided to be very careful about what we release into the world."

When they arrived at the Scriptorium, Bryce abruptly grabbed Paul's arm before they went in.

"You know, Paul, have you ever considered joining a monastery? I know it must seem like a retreat from action—and in some ways, it truly is—but in some ways, it's absolutely at the center of things. I think you're starting to see that. And sometimes it's okay to retreat from action, not be in the middle of the fray. A life of contemplation has many rewards and much less strife."

Paul blinked at him in confusion. "Are you suggesting I just abandon this journey and stay here?"

Bryce held his gaze steadily. "We could use a man like you, someone with an open mind. This is a place for free thinkers. I think you would like it here. And it doesn't sound like this journey is doing much for you. Why don't you stay with us? I can make the arrange-ments right now."

Paul's first reaction was, *Yes! Take me in!* But then he thought of his mother. He'd promised he would return to her. And don't monks take a vow of poverty? *All my money and belongings would belong to the monastery. How could I do that to her?*

But oh! All these books! The conversations we could have...

Bryce smiled at him. "I'm putting pressure on you. I apologize. I can see you're not ready for such a big decision. You're probably not ready to give up the hope of marriage yet, either! Still, sometimes, our lives do change. You might feel differently someday. If that time comes, our door will be open for you. Think about it."

The next morning, the entire monastery gathered in the courtyard to see them off. Their wagon looked different to Paul, and he was about to ask about it when Turge beat him to it.

"What's happened to our wagon?" he asked of no one in particular.

One of the monks stepped forward. "We saw that one of your wheels was cracked, so we replaced it. Then, we noticed that they were now uneven, so we decided to just outfit you with all new wheels. These have rubber on them, salvaged from the Olden Days, so your ride should be much smoother.

"And that's not all. We've also included another set of wheels that can be used on railroad tracks. They've got metal rims on them, spaced so that they fit just so. If you put these on and bridle all four horses to your wagon, you'll probably go twice as fast. There's a set of tracks just a little way away from here, going west. Do you want us to get you situated on them?"

"That would be lovely," said Eastman.

And so, the entire entourage moved over about a hundred feet to where the old railroad tracks from the Empire days ran through the village. The monk pulled out a wedge-like device made of wood that helped support the wagon while he and some others loosened the bolts on each wheel and swapped them out, quickly and neatly. The whole operation took less than a half hour.

Then, it was time to depart. Eastman and the Abbot embraced each other warmly. "Thou shalt abide, brother!" said Eastman in the middle of their hug.

"Thou shalt abide!" replied the Abbot. Paul waited until they pulled apart to give his thanks to the Abbot. He shook the hands of the other monks he had met, saving his last goodbye for Bryce.

"Safe journeys, Paul," said Bryce as he shook his hand. "Don't stop asking questions."

"I won't. I can promise you that."

9

The Inland Sea of California
Thursday, July 1

After a few weeks, the Clan's tour became something of a routine. In previous years, Alex had imagined the tour being non-stop fun and excitement, but now he knew that it involved a lot of waiting around. There were times when they would spend almost an entire week anchored somewhere in the middle of the Sea, waiting for the next Fairday to roll around. These tended to occur on the weekend, and so, they basically had nothing to do in the meantime, except for washing clothes, playing card games, practicing their instruments, repairing ropes and maintaining the boat. Uncle Evan tried to teach Alex about sailing, but he found it all kind of boring.

After Havenport, they had an interesting Fairday at New Accra, an African American city. This was on June 12, celebrating a holiday they called Juneteenth. African Americans came from all over the region for this. It was closed to most outsiders, but the Clan was let in since they're between a sixteenth and an eighth Black. The music and dancing were some of the best Alex had ever heard. They didn't make much money there, though.

The next weekend was the biggest one yet, the Solstice Celebration. This one was held at a hidden location farther north, not far from Agatha City on the eastern side of the Sea. Most of the people attending were a part of the Tribe. Alex felt a kinship with them that he hadn't in the other towns. People greeted each other warmly in the streets. There were open displays of the Sun and Moon symbols. The band performed at a Maypole celebration that went all through the night. Alex actually fell asleep on the stage; he awoke at dawn to find the dancing and celebrating still going on.

That was his fourth Fairday (although it was much more than a day; it lasted four days, three nights). The fifth one was kind of lame, Alex thought. First, it was held in Melbourne, which was several miles inland from the Sea. They had to hire oxen and wagons to carry their gear. Second, it was by far the smallest fair of all the ones he had been to. It seemed like it was mostly about selling produce. Alex did eat his first orange there, though, which was amazing. And he got to play for the dance. But he didn't think they made much money there, either, and the place was boring, a dusty village with adobe houses and a blazing hot Sun.

But now, they were about to go to one of the biggest Fairdays of the entire summer, or so he'd been told: the Fourth of July weekend at Modesto, one of the biggest cities on the Sea. Charles had called a Clan Meeting that evening. They sat on the boat in a big circle, waiting for Charles to begin. It was taking forever. All the shady spots were taken, and it was another hot day. Once again, Alex was bored.

"Can I jump in the water?" he asked his Aunt Mary, sitting next to him.

"Can't you wait? It won't be much longer."

"I'm dying of heat."

"I know. Remember, Delta, the goddess of the evening breeze, will bless us as soon as the Sun goes down."

A mosquito landed on Alex's arm. He tried to slap it, but it flew away.

"How come I can never get mosquitos? I'm slapping them super-fast."

"Well, remember that different beings live at different speeds from us. From the mosquito's perspective, your hand is moving like this—" she demonstrated a slow-motion swipe, making Alex laugh. "To a tree, we're probably buzzing around like mosquitos."

"Hopefully not as annoying, though."

"Oh, I'm sure we are. Especially the humans who chop them down."

"But the trees can't actually feel that, right? I mean, they're just wood."

"Alex! I'm surprised at you. Of course, they can. Just because we can't understand their sentience doesn't mean it doesn't exist."

Alex sighed. He didn't like being lectured at. Aunt Mary patted his knee and stood up. "I'll go find you a citronella candle. That'll discourage the mosquitos."

She got up and went down to the storeroom. As soon as she left, Alex felt a soft breeze from the west, almost as though Aunt Mary had called it into existence. The heat dissipated. She came back a little while later with a burning candle. She set it in the middle of the circle. Charles was now finally ready to break off the conversation he was having with Emma and Evan and start the Clan meeting.

"Sorry to keep you all waiting. As you know, Modesto is one of the biggest dates on the tour for us. In some years, we've made more money here than at any other stop. It's also a dangerous place for us. It's a KGL town, and I don't need to tell you what that means. We don't want any trouble here. That means not calling too much attention to ourselves. We're going to use the buddy system here; I don't want anybody to go anywhere alone, not even to the outhouse. Women: wear your head coverings at all times." There was a groan from the younger group of cousins.

"That's basically it. Just keep your head down, be smart, and we'll be okay. But if any of you are experiencing any kind of trouble, let me or Rosa or Evan know right away. Family before money. Blessings of the Sun and the Moon on you all."

"Blessings," said most of the group in response.

As the meeting broke up, Alex asked Jasmine, "What's the 'KGL?'"

Jasmine looked like she had just swallowed a bug. "Are you really telling me you don't know?"

Alex made a tiny shake of his head, embarrassed.

"It stands for the Kingdom of the Great Lakes. It's the most powerful country in America, the last remnant of the old Empire. A bunch of religious bigots. They're located way out east somewhere."

"I don't understand. Why would Modesto be a part of a country out east?"

Jasmine sighed impatiently. "The KGL used to be in charge of everybody. Some people wish we could go back to those old days, when we were all one country. You still see these little pockets of KGL enthusiasts everywhere, just waiting for the troops to march in so they can join back up." Jasmine rolled her eyes.

"Is that going to happen someday?"

"They'll have to get by me, first!" She mussed up Alex's hair and walked to the front of the boat to hang out with Ellie. Alex wished she hadn't left. He had a rumbling, uneasy feeling in his stomach.

The next morning, they sailed the short distance to the Port of Modesto. The harbor had a natural curve to it and at least a dozen piers for the boats to moor. As they pulled into the harbor, Alex could see beneath them old houses underwater again. The piers were built right on top of the houses. He thought it might be cool to go diving down and see what they looked like inside, but that also scared him a little. He imagined skeletons inside the houses.

The city was the largest he had ever seen, with some buildings as tall as ten stories or more. The streets ran in a grid pattern, diagonally rather than north-south/east-west, but with an extra-wide main street running straight from the harbor through the city. The Clan had to trudge at least two kilometers to the park where the fair was being held. There was a sign on a banner in red, white, and blue with words written in both Mojies and the Old Script. Alex asked Chi what it said, and he replied, "Welcome to Modesto's Fourth of July Celebration." Alex asked him what was so significant about the fourth day of July, and Chi just shrugged. "It's a KGL thing."

This time, they had plenty of space on the grounds. They were able to set up both tents and the stage in between. It took them all day to set up, though, because the harbor was so far away from the site. Alex was wet with sweat by the time they finished. Emma then poured lemonade for everybody. Alex thought he'd never tasted anything so good.

The park used for the fairgrounds was so large, Alex couldn't see the other side of it unless he was standing on the stage. There were mature trees running in long rows all through the park. A flagpole stood in the very center. At the top of the pole was a flag with red and white stripes with a blue square in the corner which contained an ornate golden cross. Underneath that was the California Bear flag that Alex was more familiar with. Alex thought it was strange that the California flag wasn't on top. At the far end of the park was a five-story building with a big clock at the top. Alex knew about clocks, of course, but had never seen a working one. He asked Aunt Mary about it; she said this was a "mercantile" city and therefore they needed to divvy up the day into small units. Alex had no idea what she meant by that.

After they got things set up, there was a long period of waiting for the gig that night. Once again, Charles stood up front all day, talking with people and handing out flyers for their evening concert. At one point, Alex saw him make the Sun symbol in the dirt again, but this time, the woman he was talking to surreptitiously put an "X" through it. Charles kicked dirt over the symbol after she left.

Alex was sitting in front of one of the tents with Aunt Mary, the one she did Tarot readings in, but she had no customers the whole day. One older man walked by, saw the sign they had over the flap to the tent, and got a disgusted look on his face. "Degenerates," he said under his breath, and hurried on. Alex had never heard that term before but could tell it wasn't nice. He turned to ask Aunt Mary about it but before he could, she said, "Don't ask." So, he didn't.

As the afternoon wore on, the fairgrounds became more and more crowded, the people louder and more raucous. Alex heard firecrackers being set off nearby. Some of them made him jump, they were so loud. One group of young men were so drunk, they kept falling down, laughing. Alex saw groups of women all dressed exactly alike, with heads covered in the exact same white fabric hat, whispering to each other and laughing.

Jordan and Chi came up to Alex. Chi said, "We're going to try to find an early dinner, if you'd like to join us. Charles says we should separate by gender." Alex jumped up, eager to do something. They walked toward the middle of the park and found a row of carts, all with food to sell. A lot of what was being cooked was meat, which made Alex's stomach turn, but they did find a place that made grilled cheese sandwiches on sourdough. *Delicious!* Alex could have eaten two more.

They took a long route back, checking out the other stalls. A lot of people were selling fireworks. Another popular stall was selling clothing all dyed red, white, and blue. One scary-looking bald man with a big moustache was selling swords and knives for fighting. They stopped briefly at a stall with a storyteller, like Charles, but he wasn't nearly as good. He was just holding a black book and telling everybody that they were sinners and that a day of reckoning was coming. "Jesus is coming back," he shouted. "It won't be long now; I can assure you!" They also came across another musical group, this one featuring a group of six women all dressed alike, singing a song about how much they adored their men and wanted to please them in any way. They sang in little-girl voices and giggled before they left the stage. *Weird!*

Back at their site, Alex could see that the Clan had started setting up to play already, so he helped move instruments and other equipment.

That evening, Alex knew he wouldn't be playing; he had to collect money with Alika, unfortunately. Charles announced the start of the show in his loudest voice, and the band kicked off with a lively tune, but nobody stopped.

Their show was poorly attended, and those who came generally didn't stick around for an entire song. Very few people gave Alex money when he circulated through the crowd. Even Charles couldn't keep the crowd's attention, even though he told one of his best stories, *Bilbo Baggins and the Ring of Invisibility*. Everyone seemed more interested in getting drunk than listening. There was constant talking through his entire story, and almost no applause at the end.

Alex didn't understand. Charles had said this was one of their most profitable cities. What was going wrong?

◦·————— ※ —————·◦

The next day was worse. When the Clan arrived at their site in the morning, they found drunk people sleeping in their tents, and somebody had thrown up right in front of their stage. They all pitched in to urge the drunks out of their space and to get things cleaned up. When people walked by in their groups, sometimes they would whisper and point at Alex's family, not in a nice way. Alex understood now what Grandma Meta meant when she said the "vibrations" were off. Alex wanted the Clan to leave. But he wasn't in charge.

At one point in the middle of the day, he overheard Charles and Emma having an intense conversation at the back of their little stage. Alex couldn't hear all of it, but he caught the general drift. Charles had run into members of The Reyes Clan (who had visited them once up north; they were distant cousins of some sort). This Clan was a little larger than Alex's and performed mostly juggling and magic tricks. They also included two midwives, who went around the Sea helping mothers give birth. Alex would have liked to have seen the magicians perform, but they were always performing at the same time. Alex knew that they were also members of the Children of the Sun. Charles was telling Emma that he'd been talking to their Clan Leader and learned they were leaving that day. They didn't want to take any risks.

"Maybe we should leave, too," said Emma. "We're not making much money this year."

Charles sighed. "I don't know. It seems like such a waste to have come all the way here and then miss out on the opportunities. Maybe this evening will be better."

"Maybe," said Emma doubtfully.

It wasn't. If anything, the crowd that evening was even louder and ruder than the night before. The drunk people in the audience tried to sing along with the band but did so in a disrespectful way, out of rhythm and off-key. The family was thrown off sometimes, distracted by the audience. During one song, some young men—who were really, really drunk—substituted naughty words for the real ones, making some people in the audience laugh. And when Alex and Alika circulated to collect money, very few people gave anything.

The one exception was Jasmine's dance. At least that got their attention. Alex didn't like the sexual things the drunk guys were yelling at her. But at least when it was over, they applauded loudly and whistled. Alex could see that Alika was extracting some coins from them, and that was good to see.

When Alex circled to the back of the crowd, he held out the hat to a man dressed in some of the fanciest clothes he had ever seen. He wore a long white tunic over white linen pants, all of which were spotless, and what looked to be a real gold chain around his neck. He had wavy blond hair and a chiseled jawline. His eyes were bright blue. He was one of the most handsome men Alex had ever seen, even more impressive than Charles, but in a very different way.

He dropped a coin in Alex's hat. "Tell me, young man, do you know the name of the dancer?"

Alex didn't want to tell him, but he also didn't want to be rude. "Yeah, she's my sister. Jasmine."

The blond man nodded. "There's another coin for you if you run along and fetch her for me." He held up what looked to be an actual gold coin. Those were worth a lot. Alex hesitated, then accepted it and ran back to find Jasmine.

She was in one of the tents, starting to change her clothes. She was startled by him. "Benson's Beard, Alex! Can't you give me some privacy?"

"Sorry, Jasmine. There's a man who wants to speak with you. He gave me this."

Jasmine's eyes widened when Alex showed her the coin. "That's a Sovereign," she whispered in awe. She grabbed it and looked at it hungrily, both sides, then put it in a hidden pocket. "Take me to him," she said.

She quickly put the rest of her clothes back on. Alex led the way to the back where the man was still sitting. The man smiled and stood up when they arrived, then bowed deeply. "You must be Jasmine. My name is Chad Benson."

Jasmine raised an eyebrow. "As in, *that* Benson family?"

Chad shrugged modestly. "One doesn't choose one's family. Please, do sit with me for a moment."

Jasmine sat down at the end of the wooden bench where he was sitting. Alex didn't know whether he was supposed to sit down, too. This whole situation made him uncomfortable.

"I wanted to have the opportunity to compliment you in person on your enchanting dancing. You truly have a remarkable talent."

"Thank you."

"I have been all across this country, including some of the biggest metropolises—Frisco, Benson, Dallas, Toronto—and I have never seen someone with quite your combination of artistry and beauty."

Was Jasmine blushing? She never blushes.

"I think you exaggerate, sir."

"Please, call me Chad. And I never exaggerate. I was truly transfixed. I am hoping I will have the opportunity to see you dance again. Tell me: will you be repeating your performance tomorrow evening? I certainly hope so."

"I don't know. We might be leaving."

"Before the fireworks? Oh, that truly is a pity." The man was staring intently into Jasmine's eyes. She seemed transfixed, then turned away and tried to divert his attention.

"Tell me, Mr. Benson, what's your relationship to the famous Emperor?"

"I am a direct descendent of Jack Benson, ten generations ago."

"I thought all the Bensons died out."

"Most of us did. After the Church took over the KGL, my ancestors went into exile in the west. As you can see, we managed to survive."

"And what do you do for a living?"

Benson put his hand over Jasmine's and spoke softly. "Mostly, I'm involved with importing goods. I'm also involved in politics, here and there," he said evasively. "But enough about me! I want to know everything possible about you." He reached forward, gently, and touched the scarf she wore around her hair. "Would you mind, terribly, if I removed this? I should like to see your hair." Jasmine leaned forward and let him undo her scarf. Her hair fell forward like a black sheet.

"Astonishing," he breathed. "You are a most stunning woman. Your skin is the most exquisite color. It reminds me of milk chocolate."

"I wouldn't know. I've never had chocolate."

"Never had chocolate! I find that hard to believe."

"It's true."

"Would you like some? I have quite a selection back at the hotel. I'm staying at the *Emperor,* just a few short blocks from here."

Alex would certainly like to try some chocolate, but he had a feeling he wasn't invited.

"Jasmine," Alex interrupted. "I really think we should get back. They're breaking down the stage. I think we're leaving tonight."

Chad Benson's eyes never strayed from Jasmine's. "By all means, do not let me detain you. If you must go, I will certainly understand."

Alex saw a strange expression cross Jasmine's face, like a cloud covering up the Sun. "Alex," she said. "You run along. I'll catch up in a little bit."

Alex didn't want to leave without her. "Come on, Jasmine," he pleaded softly. But she wasn't looking at him. She was staring at the blonde man. He stood up, held out a hand for her. She took it and stood up. It was like he was controlling her.

Alex was somehow surprised by this and not surprised. "Jasmine, please!" he whispered. "Don't go with him!"

Jasmine finally tore her eyes off Chad's. "Alex, you're being rude."

Alex started breathing heavily, and tears started forming in his eyes. He hated that he still cried like a baby. He didn't know what to do. He didn't want to leave Jasmine, but he also didn't want to start crying in front of this stranger.

Then, Alex heard Charles' conch shell in the distance.

"Jasmine!" he cried. "That's the signal! We've gotta go now!"

"No. I'm not going," she said fiercely. "Go back to the boat. *Now!*"

Alex turned and ran.

Alex ran all the way back to the boat. He passed some members of the family lugging equipment, but he didn't stop until he got there. He found Aunt Emma and Charles on the deck, deep in discussion. But he didn't care. He ran to Emma and started crying in her arms.

"Alex! What's the matter?"

He told them, trying to catch his breath between his tears. When he finished, Charles said, "Damn that girl!" and stormed off the boat.

"Should I go with him?" Alex asked.

"No, you'd better let Charles handle this. You stay here; I'll get you some tea."

R.J. and Ellie were just coming on board with a load of instruments. "What's the matter with Charles?" Ellie asked. "He looks furious."

Alex told them the story. Ellie's eyes grew wide.

"I want to go help," she told Emma when she returned with the tea.

"No, we've all got to stay here until Charles gets back. He wouldn't want anybody else to get lost in that city."

The same scene repeated itself with the next group that arrived on the boat, and the next. By that time, Alex was tired of telling the story, and Ellie picked it up for him. There were lots of worried looks when the family found out. Alex was glad that his instincts about this situation were shared by the others.

After a while, everybody was on board except for Charles and Jasmine. All the instruments and equipment had been stowed and a strange vigil came over the group. It was now quite late, way past Alex's bedtime, but there was no way he was going to go to sleep now. Everybody was quiet, waiting silently.

Finally, Charles came striding back. "She's gone," he said. "I looked all over the fairgrounds for her. I asked for her at the major hotels. Nothing."

"What should we do, Charles?" asked Emma.

"There's nothing we can do. We're not staying here another day. Jasmine knows we're leaving at dawn. If she's not here in the morning, we're leaving without her."

"Charles!" Emma exclaimed.

"No, that's it. Jasmine's a big girl. She should know better. The danger to the Clan is too great for us to stay. We'll circle around after the weekend is over and see if we can find her."

Alex buried his face on his Aunt Rosa's shoulder and started crying again.

10

Ariel Trunda's Story

Excerpts from Ariel W. Trunda, *The Decline and Fall of the American Empire* (Sydney: Oceana Publishing, 2313), p. 132–40:

…. As the twenty-second century neared its end, the American Empire was a shambling mess. The sea levels continued to rise, even after the end of the fossil fuel era, as the effects of human carbon emission reverberated through the ecosystem. This, combined with the increasing occurrence of hurricanes, tornados, fires, and other extreme weather events, pushed the emergency relief budget beyond sustainability. Recurring pandemics—especially the COVID-78 infection of 2179–80—taxed the emergency system of the nation's hospitals, exacerbated by decades of defunding the critical scientific research that would have enabled the nation to prepare.

Tellingly, talk of regional secession grew in frequency and vehemence. When Hawaii declared independence in 2159 (the 200th anniversary of her admission to the union, followed swiftly by Alaska's secession that same year), the government had neither the will nor the resources to offer anything more than petulant protestation. Puerto Rico followed, and by the end of the century several regional constitutional conventions had been held in preparation for a formal severing of ties (Cascadia, 2170; Deseret, 2186; and Texas, 2196). When California made a move to secede in 2192, a line was crossed. The U.S. economy could not sustain this loss. Embarrassingly, the rebellion almost succeeded; only the strongest form of military presence quelled the movement. Had any of these attempts in the "Lower 48" been successful, America would have been sheared apart a hundred years earlier than it did. As it was, the spectacle of California's defeat quelled the other secession movements for a time—and left the state stewing in seething resentment.

These succession movements were fueled by more than regional pride. The national inflation rate neared 500% in 2194, the same year that the U.S. defaulted on its debt, and the population—no longer sustained by the rejuvenating benefits of immigration and shrinking due to a century and a half of low birth-rates—fell to its lowest level since the Civil War of the 1860s. Citizens of these states knew they were giving more money to the federal government than they were receiving. It was imminently sensible to flee the sinking ship.

Escalating this situation was a pernicious instability in national leadership. Since primogeniture had been established in the previous century, Presidential succession had oscillated between orderly and chaotic. The Secret Service, with its privileged perspective on the First Family, often took matters into its own hands when an inbred moron was in line to be the next President. A well-timed skiing accident or yacht drowning might save them many a headache later. As the power of the Secret Service grew, the temptation to install one of their own at 1600 Pennsylvania Avenue became too hard to resist. Assassinations became more frequent and overt…

Jack Benson was born in 2172 in Washington, D. C., the grand nephew of the current President McConnell. Benson was a member of the Extended First Family, but fortunately for him, he entered the world only tenth in line to the throne. A palace coup when he was five years old ended in the execution of not only McConnell and his two sons, but also his grandson and nephew. Benson, spared perhaps because of his youth, escaped with his mother to the family compound in upstate New York, where he spent a relatively untroubled childhood, receiving an excellent education from a tutor whose name is un-fortunately lost to history. Benson displayed more affinity for literature, philosophy, and nature than he did for the arts of politics and war.

McConnell's successor, the head of the Secret Service, lasted in office two years before being assassinated by the next head of Secret Service, who in turn was thrown out in 2190 (but managed to escape into ignominious exile rather than martyrdom). This latest coup was engineered by former allies of McConnell, who now put a different family member on the throne (this would be the fourth President McConnell, for those of you keeping tally at home). He, too, would likely have been deposed in short order had not the California Crisis intervened and provided the cover of national emergency to distract the plotters. All McConnell family members were restored to their privileges, and Jack Benson returned to Washington, D.C., with his mother shortly thereafter.

As the political crisis in California deepened and military action became inevitable, all patriotic young men were exhorted to enlist. Benson was a reluctant soldier but found battlefield strategy fascinating. At this time, the weaponry from the old days—assault rifles, howitzers, and the like—was still in existence but faulty, unreliable. Benson took it upon himself to learn about their mechanics and make sure his troops were well armed and supplied. In several battles this technological edge proved decisive. For this, he drew the admiration of his troops and the attention of his superiors. He rose up in the ranks quickly, ending up a colonel by the end of the war, at only 24. His cousin, the President, seeing in Benson the face of a likely rival, appointed him to a government position out west in order to remove him from the center of power. This only served to prove his capabilities even more as he showed himself to be a just and able administrator.

When chaos erupted in Washington again in 2198, Benson found himself pressed into a leadership position he did not covet. McConnell's taxes to pay for the war had caused wide-spread rioting and looting, and his erratic personal behavior began to trouble his allies. Benson's friends wrote pleading letters insisting he bring his Army of the West to the capital to restore order. Benson claimed he acceded only to keep his cousin on the throne, but as he made his famous Long March and drew more and more numbers to his army, he was already being acclaimed as the next President. His cousin met him with the Federal Army in the fields just outside St. Louis in early 2199. By now, the die was cast, and the allies were now rivals.

On the morning of the battle, Benson awoke from a powerful dream, or so he told his aides: a vision of his troops marching to battle behind the banner of the Evangelical Church of America. The aides quickly procured several of these banners, and the consequent victory was seen as divine approbation. Word of Benson's victory—and of McConnell's death by one of Benson's sharpshooters—spread across the country, and his subsequent march to Washington became an inaugural parade.

The sincerity of Benson's sudden conversion has been the subject of scholarly debate ever since. While it is well known that his mother was a practicing member of the faith, Benson himself rarely attended church services. He treated the Elders of the Church as his political aides, summoning them to his office, presiding over their theological disputes, making use of their network to promulgate his messages. In all he did, he was a politician first and foremost, not a churchman. His alleged conversion most likely had more to do with the rapidly increasing popularity of the Church, which had grown from its obscure founding during the Fifth Great Awakening (2120–2145) to become the largest single denomination in the United States by this time….

One of Benson's first decisions as President was to move the capital to a new site. Over time, the dikes holding back the floodwaters in Washington, D.C., had grown less and less effective. Benson could see that Washington would soon have to be abandoned to the rising tides, just as Galveston, New Orleans, Miami, and several other cities had already been. The cost of maintaining the dikes was already straining the treasury, and the city's failing infrastructure made it vulnerable to sabotage and invasion. The next year (2200), he moved the capital to what was then called Chicago, which he now dubbed New Washington, but which quickly became known as Benson City, at first colloquially, then, after his death, officially.

Chicago had many advantages: it was far from the rising sea levels, and although the Great Lakes were not entirely insulated from climate change, the effects were notably less severe in the nation's interior; the temperatures were now relatively moderate due to the effects of climate change, no longer suffering the brutal winters of centuries past; it sat near one of the greatest sources of fresh water in the world; the transportation network that had first caused the city to be built in the 1800s—first waterways, then rail, then motorcars and air travel—still existed, in various levels of disrepair; and as the mass communication system collapsed in the wake of the population crash, its more central location in the continental United States could prove to be of strategic advantage. The symbolism of the fresh start, away from the intrigues and misbegotten history of the capital, was undoubtedly not lost on him.

Benson's leadership skills stabilized the country. He appointed able administrators to important posts, re-established meritocracy, and restored some moderate remnants of local democracy. He rebuilt the economy, almost from scratch, and he faced squarely the challenges of effecting an orderly transition to the new world of rising sea levels and more extreme weather. He opened a new University of the American Empire (or rather, took over the ailing University of Chicago), and for a while the city enjoyed a flowering of arts, sciences, learning, and erudition that would match any previous era. Unfortunately, this fine institution did not survive the purges of the ECA once they assumed control of the government three generations later. An exodus of scholars to safer havens overseas commenced, including your present author....

Benson spoke often about his dream to restore the democratic institutions of the days of the Republic, including elections for his successor. In the end, however, his familial pride got the better of him. In 2222, suffering from the viral infection that would soon take his life, he summoned his two beloved sons to his bedside and divided among them, with the folly of fondness, the administration of the nation that he had so effectively reunited. It was surely a difficult choice; he knew that the nation was not yet ready for a peaceful transition of power and the restoration of the long-atrophied democratic institutions. The decaying infrastructure and electrical grid—which he had only partially recovered—meant that communication and unification would be challenging at best. The hope was that a divided government, with its border running roughly along the Missouri River, and yet with ultimate authority resting unambiguously with the eldest, Jack Jr., would hold the country together.

This is precisely what did not happen. East and West remained divided, and soon the endless rounds of coups and countercoups in the capital would resume. The Western Empire fell first, upon the death of Benson's granddaughter Agatha, but the Eastern Empire only lingered a generation longer. By that time, the Eastern half had also been divided, into five Administrative Districts—New England, Greater New York, Mid-Atlantic, the Southeast (later renamed the New Confederacy), and the Great Lakes Region—but increasingly these behaved like independent nations as the dysfunction in the capital increased. Church and State were now so closely intertwined that it seemed only natural, during one of the vacuums of power in Benson City, that the Evangelical Church of America should step in to "save" the shattered government of the newly rechristened Kingdom of the Great Lakes, roughly contiguous with the five states of the original Ohio Territory that entered the union after the Revolutionary War.

This marks the effective end of the American nation, almost exactly 500 years after its founding, although some still claim that the Empire can and will rise again....

11

The Western Territories

Paul's Journal Entry: Iowa Monastery

Saturday, June 5, 2488

I am leaving the monastery with a heavy heart. In some ways, I've never felt so at home as I have these past few days. I could spend a lifetime reading these books. I can easily imagine myself living and working here, having lively conversations, and helping them recover the lost literature of the Empire and Republic. Even though this place is remote, it feels somehow like the work being done here is at the very center of things....

Even more curious to me was to see Eastman with his old friend. The man has a soul, after all! He seemed warm, engaged, full of good cheer. But as soon as he turns to me, his countenance changes, and a frown forms on his face. I can't seem to break through this icy wall he's put up, nor can I fathom why he seems to hold me in such contempt....

Paul and his companions headed away from the monastery in a new configuration: all four horses were harnessed to the wagon, and all five travelers rode inside. Archer took the seat up front next to Turge, so

Paul sat next to Elder Eastman on the bench inside. Opposite them sat Echleph and his dog. The group made rapid progress along the rails, moving at an exhilarating speed. Paul worried for a while that the horses would lose their footing on the tracks, with its frequent wooden beams, but they were sure-footed. Very soon they were out of the little hamlet and back into the countryside.

Paul decided to attempt a conversation with Eastman. "Did you get a chance to see the monastery's printing press?" he asked in Merican.

"Yes, I did," Eastman answered him in English.

Paul knew it was rude to speak in a language the others didn't understand but decided to continue in that tongue. "What did you think of it?"

"It is… interesting."

"I was surprised to see that they were translating the Gospels into Merican."

"I was, too. An utter waste of time."

"Why do you say that?"

"Trying to render the Lord's words in that barbaric tongue is like trying to put a dress on a pig."

Paul didn't know whether the Bible represented the dress or the pig in this metaphor but knew better than to ask. "Well, I think it's possible it can do some good, if the Word is spread more widely. This might encourage reading and literacy."

"And what good would that do? Do you really think your average farmer or builder would have time or interest in reading?"

"I suppose you're right. Still, isn't it true that literacy was widespread during the days of the Empire? If more people could read, it might help bind together the regions once again. Isn't that part of our purpose here, to restore some of the unity that we've lost?"

"I don't believe the printing of books in Mojies is going to magically reunite the old America. And besides, the risk of the printing press falling into the wrong hands is too great. I can see someone using that machine to spread lies or resurrect salacious material from the past. That would be a disaster."

Paul could think of several rejoinders but decided he'd better drop this argument. It was veering into territory too close to the truth of what Bryce and the others were doing.

Eastman continued. "And just to be perfectly clear, our mission is not to look for ways to reunite America. That would be a decision for the Supreme Elder and the High Council. We are merely investigating whether the faith is as strong as it should be as we travel west. Whether or not this means a political restoration of the old order is irrelevant."

"Doesn't the Book of Edgar talk about sewing up the torn fabric of America? I assumed that meant that we would be seeing a rebirth of the American nation."

"One could read it that way. Another interpretation is that it's meant in a purely spiritual way, not political. We live in dangerous times, very degenerate. Faith is rapidly losing ground among the young. You would be shocked how many nonbelievers there are among us."

Paul swallowed nervously. "Perhaps, if the fabric of faith is resewn, the political unity will follow," he said, somewhat disingenuously.

Eastman paused an uncomfortably long time. Just when Paul thought the conversation had ended, Eastman said, "Perhaps."

Not long after this, Turge pulled the wagon to a stop. "Whoa there!"

"What's the trouble?" Eastman called, reverting to Merican.

"Bridge out ahead. We'll have to ford the river."

Turge and Archer jumped down from their bench. Echleph hopped out the back with his dog. Paul followed. He walked down the little slope the tracks were on and saw some rusty concrete pilings emerging from the river up ahead, what clearly was once a railroad bridge. Fortunately, the river was only about fifty feet wide and shallow. The biggest challenge was getting the wagon off the tracks without upsetting the horses. When they walked down to the riverbank, Turge said, "You can get back inside the wagon. No need for you to get wet, too." Paul didn't know whether he should be insulted by the pampering, but he gratefully accepted the offer. Eastman hadn't bothered to get out of the wagon at all.

Paul could feel the wagon jostling from side to side as they maneuvered it off the tracks. After a minute or two, they rolled slowly down the slope and into the water. Paul could feel the wagon's buoyancy as they reached the river, but they stayed dry. Turge handled the horses expertly, with the help of Echleph and Archer, who rode the two lead horses across. Before long, they were back on the tracks and making good time again. After about an hour later, they had to ford the same river, not more than 15 miles away —The Skunk River, Echleph told him. Paul began to wonder if it would have been faster to take the roadway.

That night they camped in the forest. While Paul and Turge collected wood for the fire, Archer went out hunting. In a surprisingly short amount of time, he returned with two rabbits he had taken down with his bow and arrow. *It seems his nickname is well-earned,* thought Paul. Turge skinned them deftly and laughed at Paul's squeamishness. He was not used to eating game, but the meat was savory and delicious. That night, Turge and Archer put their food in sacks and hoisted them up a tree. When Paul asked why, he said, simply, "Bears." This did not make Paul sleep easily—nor the fact that he would be sharing the wagon with Elder Eastman (the three soldiers each had his own small tent). But sleep, Paul did.

The next day, the train tracks disappeared altogether into the tall grass after a few miles. The soldiers decided to remove the metal wheels and return to road travel. They also decided to unhitch the two extra horses here and return them to Archer and Echleph to ride separately. When Paul asked why, Echleph said cryptically, "We might need the flexibility up ahead."

After some time, they found the roadway again, but at this point it was rutted and broken up. Other travelers had clearly veered off the old road, creating a new path parallel to the first, sometimes running alongside it for several miles before rejoining the original roadway, and Paul's crew followed. They passed several ghost towns, some almost completely overtaken by forest. *In another hundred years,* Paul thought, *the land will have reclaimed most of this entire territory.*

In the afternoon, they crested a little ridge, and Paul saw a strange dark brown smudge on the land ahead, stretching across the horizon. "What's that?" he asked Turge, sitting next to him.

"Bison," he replied.

"You mean, animals? My lord! There must be hundreds of them."

"Thousands. And this is only one herd. They make good meat, if you can take one down. When the forest disappears, we'll use their turds for fuel for the fires."

"I hope you're kidding me."

"Nope!"

Paul shook his head in amazement.

That night, they camped out again, eating the remains of the rabbit. During dinner, Turge and Archer played little travel guitars and sang songs unfamiliar to Paul. After dinner, Paul found himself sitting alone with Echleph around the embers of the fire. The others had gone to bed. Echleph was smoking something, Paul presumed cannabis, an intoxicating drug strictly forbidden in the KGL. But they weren't in the KGL anymore.

Echleph rarely spoke to Paul, and Paul was happy enough with the quiet, listening to the crickets and frogs from a nearby pond. It was a new moon, so the stars of the Milky Way were especially vibrant, a wreath of light, almost bright enough to read by. Yet this time—maybe because of the stuff he was smoking—Echleph surprised him by starting a conversation.

"I understand you're a big fan of the old Empire."

Paul thought about this carefully. "I suppose I am. It seems to me that those times were more peaceful, people lived longer and healthier lives, and there was much greater interest in learning and being educated. And I will admit I'm fascinated by their technical wizardry. I keep learning more about the things they could do, and it seems like magic. It's hard not to wish we could have some of that."

Echleph grunted and took another puff on his pipe.

"I take it you're not a big fan?" asked Paul.

"No, I'm not."

"Why not?"

"Bread and circuses. That's all it was. People just wanted to be entertained. They bought more than they needed and then left their shit behind for us to clean up like we're their goddamn servants. They lived comfortable lives, to be sure, but they were so far removed from nature, they didn't even know what they were putting in their mouths when they ate. Their every move was monitored by devices they wore, for their so-called convenience. They gave up their freedom for frivolity and vanity. And peaceful? Hardly. They were constantly at war. Give me this world over your shitty, self-indulgent past, any day."

Paul was stunned, not least by Echleph's use of profanity. "I had no idea anybody felt that way," he replied. "I didn't even conceive of anybody considering this world to be better."

"For all your education, there sure is a lot you don't know."

Paul fell silent at this rebuke. And then Echleph surprised him again by reciting a poem from memory—in English, no less:

"The world is too much with us; late and soon,

Getting and spending we lay waste our powers;

Little we see in Nature that is ours;

We have given our hearts away, a sordid boon!

This Sea that bares her bosom to the moon,

The winds that will be howling at all hours,

And are up-gathered now like sleeping flowers,

For this, for everything, we are out of tune;

It moves us not. –Great God! I'd rather be

A Pagan suckled in a creed outworn;

So might I, standing on this pleasant lea,

Have glimpses that would make me less forlorn;

Have sight of Proteus rising from the sea;

Or hear old Triton blow his wreathéd horn."

Echleph took another drag on his pipe. "William Wordsworth, 1802," he said, staring into the coals.

"You know English?"

"In my line of work, it's strategic to know a lot of languages."

The next day, they at last encountered human habitation: the city Bryce had mentioned, Des Moines. This was another city that had once been much larger and now was huddled behind large walls. "The last out-post before the wilderness," Turge commented as they drove in. *Haven't we already been in the wilderness?* Paul thought.

They headed into the city. The ECA church here was much smaller than the previous churches they had visited. Paul would have been surprised if the sanctuary could hold more than a hundred parish-ioners. It was made from white stone and solidly built, but the insides had a neglected look about them. Paul noticed cobwebs on the wood-work. At the front of the sanctuary was a life-sized bronze statue of Jesus that looked like it dated from the olden times. Paul noticed that Jesus' big toes were worn down and shiny. He asked the elderly priest about this, and he told Paul that the congregation had a tradition of kissing the toes for good luck. When Eastman overheard this, he became enraged.

"This is idolatry!" he exclaimed. "It must be stopped immediately." The priest bowed in obedience. Paul sincerely doubted anything would change.

They stayed at an inn that night with a good evening meal and a hearty breakfast—the last such luxury they would enjoy for more than a month. Turge replenished their supplies at a local depot, then they exited the city. For the next three days, the travel was monotonous. The only other person they saw was an itinerant barber-surgeon, travelling in the opposite direction. Paul wondered how he found any customers to service in this desolated land.

On the fourth day out of Des Moines, the landscape began to change, the flat plains giving way to rolling hills. Later that morning they came to the famous Missouri River. They had to wait half the day for the ferryman to arrive to carry them across. It was a much shorter crossing than the Mississippi had been. They spent that night in the ruins of a town called Fremont on the Platte River. After this, the landscape became flat again. At night, they heard packs of wolves howling in the distance almost continuously.

Three days later, they were travelling through the numberless miles of open plains when Echleph called over to Turge to stop the wagon. When Paul climbed out of the back of the wagon, he saw Echleph kneeling, face to face with his dog, as though in conversation.

"Trouble's coming," he said, still staring at his dog.

"What is it?" asked Turge.

"Big storm. We gotta find some shelter."

Paul was perplexed. The sky was virtually cloudless.

He saw Echleph talking to Archer, then climb back on his horse and ride forward at a gallop. Archer went the opposite way, down the path they had just come.

Eastman emerged from the wagon. "What's this delay?" he demanded of Turge. "We're behind schedule."

"If the captain says we gotta find shelter, we need to listen to him."

Just then, Paul did see dark clouds forming in the west. They were small and distant but churning and crackling with electricity. The wind changed direction and became abruptly colder. A metallic scent filtered into the air. He felt the hair on his arms rise.

Archer returned, coming in at a gallop. "Any word from the captain?"

"Nope," said Turge.

The horses began to shift in place, whinnying uncomfortably. The black clouds were now filling a large section of the western sky. Archer rode briskly to the west, following Echleph's trail.

A thunderclap startled Paul. The clouds now blotted out the sun and had become a sickening greenish color in the middle. The wind picked up speed.

The soldiers returned. "I've found someplace," Echleph said in a raised voice. "Quickly."

He turned and rode at a fair clip up the road. Paul jumped back inside the wagon just as Turge clicked his tongue to get the horses started. After a quarter mile, Echleph turned left, leading them on what looked like a footpath through the tall prairie grass. Paul could hear the grass brushing against the canvas sides of the wagon, which rattled and tumbled on the uneven ground. Thick drops of rain now spattered the canvas top of the wagon. Another thunderclap struck, closer now. The light outside was now like nighttime but with an eerie greenish glow.

They approached an old, three-story yellow brick building surrounded by a black wrought iron fence. Paul noticed two chipped ECA crosses on either side of the gate. There was a lock on the gate, but Echleph made quick work of it with the mysterious tool he had used to pick the lock at the mall. He pulled open the gate and they hurried through.

The front door had a big brass knocker. Echleph ran up the short flight of concrete stairs and used the knocker loudly. By now, the rain was coming down heavily and the roof of the wagon was leaking. Since he was getting wet anyway, Paul climbed out of the wagon and joined the soldiers at the front door.

After some time, the door opened partway, and a woman's face peered out. She was middle-aged, her face long and care worn. "What do you want?" she asked in heavily accented English.

"We need shelter," Echleph shouted. "Tornado's coming."

Paul felt his throat constrict. There had been some tornadoes near Benson City as he grew up, but he had never seen one up close, thankfully. He glanced back at the sky over the wagon but couldn't see any funnel clouds.

"I'm sorry," she replied. "We are a solitary community. We do not accept travelers."

She moved to close the heavy door, but Echleph put his foot in it to stop it. Eastman had now climbed down to talk to the woman, too.

"Madam, you are speaking to an Elder of the Church! I must insist you provide us shelter."

Paul jumped in, "We can provide you with monetary compensation for your trouble."

Eastman shot Paul an annoyed look. But the woman only hesitated a moment longer before slowly opening the door.

"Are your stables around back?" shouted Turge. She nodded reluctantly. Turge and Archer took the horses and wagon around the side of the building, through the pounding rain.

In the short amount of time Paul had been out of the wagon, he had become thoroughly soaked. He desperately wanted to change his clothes, but all his dry clothes were in the trunk, in the wagon. He followed Eastman and Echleph into the building.

The space they were in was not large, only about ten feet square. There was a wide staircase leading up at the back of the room on the right, a sitting room on either side of this entry hall, and a room at the back on the other side of the staircase. As Paul looked around, he noticed that there were several girls and young women staring at them from the top of the stairs. *Was this an orphanage? Or a nunnery? And why was it out in the middle of nowhere?*

"Gentlemen," said the matron, "I hope you will forgive my rudeness. We have reason to be suspicious of strangers out here. We do have some extra rooms on the top floor—the former servants' quarters—where you can stay and wait out the storm. We will share our simple meal with you, such as it is. I will ask you to kindly respect the privacy of my girls."

"Of course," Eastman replied. "We are grateful for your hospitality. Do you have a tornado shelter in this building?"

"We have a cellar."

"Then we should get ourselves to it."

The woman led the way to a small door underneath the big staircase. It was nearly pitch-black down there, but she found a candle and lit it with some old matches most likely dating from the Olden Times, and Paul and the group followed. The cellar was shallow—none of the men could stand up to full height—and crowded with boxes and dusty furniture. The woman handed a second candle to Eastman and went back upstairs to fetch the girls. The travelers found an old sofa a few feet away and took a seat, a plume of dust billowing after they sat. A moment later, Turge and Archer came down, absolutely drenched. Turge wrung out his beard and a trickle of water fell. The woman returned with her girls, who huddled nervously at the bottom of the stairs. Some were crying, but a few snuck curious glances at the travelers. Echleph sat off to the side with his dog, who kept his head in Echleph's lap. The roar of the storm was tremendous. Paul worried about the old house standing up to torrential rain and intense winds.

After some time, Paul noticed light growing in the dusty, narrow windows. The thunder trailed off into the distance, although the rainfall continued, slowly subsiding. "I think it's safe to go upstairs now," said Echleph.

Eastman nodded, then turned to the woman. "We will need to take you up on your gracious offer. The roads will be impassable today."

She pursed her lips, as though she thought about raising some objection, then nodded curtly and walked upstairs. Her girls followed like ducklings. She led them all the way up to the third floor, but by the time they reached the first floor, the girls had all disappeared without a trace. The third floor had a musty odor to it, as though it hadn't been used in a century. Each of them was given his own room with a chair, a table, and a straw pallet for sleeping. This felt like luxury after the days of living in the wilderness. Paul sat in the chair and watched the storm move off to the east out his narrow window. After some time, Turge appeared in his doorway carrying his trunk.

"Your belongings, your Majesty," he said sarcastically, breathing heavily.

"Thank you, Turge." After he left, Paul changed clothes gratefully. He draped his wet robe over the back of his chair.

The evening meal was indeed meager, a thin soup and some hard, week-old bread. They sat at a long table with the woman; Paul caught fleeting glimpses of the girls peeking through the door to the kitchen, spying on the strangers. Paul asked the abbess about the convent—he confirmed that this is what it was—but she proved to be disinclined to conversation. They fell into a glum silence as spotty rain splattered the windowpanes.

As soon as they finished, Eastman stood up and thanked her for the meal. "We will leave at first light," he reassured her. She nodded somberly.

Paul found sleeping difficult that night. Maybe he was getting used to sleeping outdoors, but he found the third floor of this place hot and stuffy. He also found himself replaying the conversation with Echleph in his mind. He wasn't ready to concede that Echleph was right about the Empire—not yet at least—but he did find his attitude disconcerting. There was so much he didn't know about the past. And now, he was realizing, much of this had been deliberately hidden from him.

The books he had read at the monastery helped fill the gaps. He was starting to understand how the Empire fell. But this left open the question of why. He knew that the change in climate had something to do with the Fall, but he couldn't understand why the American people let this happen. Is it just human nature to ignore these kinds of things, and just look out for one's own material comfort and happiness? Surely, with all their knowledge and technology, they could have figured out that their own comfort and happiness depended on a livable world. Did they even try to find *something* to do to rectify the situation, without sacrificing too much comfort?

Also troubling him was the state of this convent. The difference between this and the monastery was staggering. The latter was well-appointed, the monks well-fed and happy. This place looked like it was going to fall to the ground in the next thunderstorm. The women and girls had an emaciated, malnourished look to them that bespoke food insecurity. Was this because they were that much farther away from civilization? Or was it the difference between the status of men and women? Paul had always taken this for granted, the natural order of things, but maybe—like the caste system he grew up in—it actually wasn't the way things had to be. Maybe this was cultural. He felt a wave of shame come over him, a deepening awareness of all the ways he had benefitted from his birth and sex without even being aware of it. He liked to think that this was all due to his hard work and intelligence, but he was starting to see the role blind luck had played. Lying in the dark, he shook his head at himself.

As he lay there, wishing he could sleep, he heard a faint pattering sound. Then his door opened quietly. His heart started pounding, suddenly on high alert. But it was only one of the nuns, wearing a white sleeping gown. He could barely see her in the dark. She closed the door quietly, then ran to his bed and abruptly lay down on top of him, knocking his breath out of him. He was confused by this at first, but then realization dawned on him as she started kissing him on the lips, hungrily. His first thought, strangely, was embarrassment. He had not shaven in weeks, nor bathed in nearly that long. But he soon forgot about himself and gave in to this perplexing situation. She pulled off her nightcap, letting her straight brown hair fall down, a sight Paul rarely saw. Then she pulled off her nightclothes in one deft move, revealing a young, thin body. She went back to kissing him urgently. And then she pulled down his pants, and before Paul could even register what was happening, his first sexual encounter was already over. He gasped for breath, and she put her hand over his mouth to keep him quiet. After a few moments, she began to rock and move on him, and he found them doing it for a second time.

Afterwards, she lay next to him on his bed, her body sweaty but warm against his, their breathing heavy and synchronized. Paul felt a kind of tingly afterglow. He was about to fall asleep when she spoke for the first time in a rough-hewn accent.

"Take me with you."

"What?" said Paul stupidly, half asleep.

"Take me with you. Marry me. I'll be your wife."

"But—but you don't know me! You don't know anything about me. How could you want to be married to me?"

"Whatever your life is like, it's gotta be better than this."

Paul swallowed. "I'm sorry. I like you, but there's no way the Elder would approve of this."

"Then stay here. Be my husband here. With a man of the Church in this place, you would automatically be given authority over the awful Mrs. Price. We all hate her."

Paul struggled to find the right words to say. "I don't think that would be right."

"Who cares? Don't you want more of this?" she started caressing his chest.

Paul did want more of this. He felt a weird temptation steal over him. It would be so easy. And he could escape his problems in an instant…

But no. He had made a promise. He shook his head sadly and sat up. The nun looked at him beseechingly for a moment, then abruptly slipped out of the bed, gathered her clothes, and ran out of his room.

He realized after she left that he had no idea what her name was.

The next morning, he was awakened by Turge, who noisily pushed open his door and said, "Get up! We're leaving!" Paul shook himself awake, then recalled the events of the previous night and felt a wave of shame come over him. And then, happiness. Then shame once again.

When he got downstairs, the group was already prepared to leave, standing just outside the doorway. Paul stepped out into the morning sun, the ground still wet from the thunderstorm. The head of the house—the abbess—was handing Elder Eastman some provisions. They looked like loaves of bread, by the shape of the bags. Turge and Archer were loading up the wagon, which had already been pulled around to the front. Paul looked around for the nuns, hoping to catch a glance at the one who met him in the night, to see her in full sunlight. No one was out. Paul imagined the abbess had ordered them to stay inside.

The abbess walked briskly to the gate, unlocked it, and held it open. The message was clear: *You'd better be on your way now.* Paul looked at the house one last time before climbing into the back of the wagon. It looked even more dilapidated than it had the night before, with gutters falling off the roof and paint chipping around the windows. Paul saw a curtain flip shut on the second floor.

Then they were off. Paul had wanted to thank the abbess but worried his guilt would be written on his face. He leaned out the back of the wagon to wave, but she was busy closing the gate behind them. She turned her back on them and strode briskly back to the house. Paul sighed and moved to the front, climbing up to sit next to Turge, now his usual position.

The path was sloshy from the rain the night before and it seemed to be a much longer distance to the main road than it was the night before. But find it, they did. The riding went smoother then.

After a mile or so, Turge leaned over and said quietly, "Sleep well last night?"

Oh God. He knows. "Yes, eventually," said Paul. *If he tells anyone, my career is over.*

Turge didn't respond, but Paul could feel the bench jiggling as he chuckled soundlessly.

12

Modesto

Sunday, July 4

Alex couldn't sleep that night. He kept listening for Jasmine. Sometimes at home, she would sneak out of the sleeping quarters and run off in the middle of the night. If he was awake, he would always ask her what she was doing as she was tiptoeing out of the sleeping room. And she would always say, "Nothing. Go back to sleep." And she would always be back before dawn. He was praying to the Sun and the Moon that she would just sneak back onto the boat, like always. Then, Alex started worrying about how angry she would be that he told everyone. *Well, she didn't tell me not to!* he said to himself defensively.

But she didn't return. The stars turned in the sky, the Moon set, and there was still no Jasmine. Just as the eastern sky was starting to lighten up before dawn, he heard some whispering down at the front of the boat. Hoping it was Jasmine, he crept toward the sound. There were several sleeping cousins sprawled out around the deck. Alex stepped carefully to keep from waking anybody.

It was Jordan, Chi, Ellie, and Junior having an intense discussion. When they saw Alex approach, they abruptly stopped talking.

"What? What is it?" he whispered to them. "Did you hear from Jasmine?"

The four of them looked at each other, trying to decide whether they should bring him into their conversation. Junior shrugged and then Jordan answered him.

"No, we haven't. And we're getting worried about her. We thought we might go in and try to find her."

"I wanna go too."

"I don't think that's a good idea, buddy. I think it might be better if we just took care of this. It's not a safe city."

"I'm not such a little kid anymore. I promise I'll be quiet. I'll listen to you."

The four of them looked at each other. Junior shook his head. This made Alex mad.

"She's my sister. I should be able to help find her. Besides, I know where she is."

"You do?" asked Ellie. "Where?"

Alex crossed his arms and shook his head. "Take me with you."

The older cousins looked at each other again. Junior, who was kind of the leader of their generation, said, "If you're lying about this, Alex…"

"I'm not. I swear," Alex said loudly, and the other cousins shushed him.

"Okay," said Junior. "But you have to keep up with us. And you have to listen."

"I will."

"Go and get your shoes on. Quickly."

Alex ran quietly back to his bag of clothing, found his walking shoes, and put them on. He didn't even bother tying the laces. When he got back to the front of the boat, Emma was there talking to them. She looked angry. *Uh-oh. Maybe she's going to put a stop to all this.*

But she wasn't. Or maybe, Jordan and Junior had already convinced her. She walked abruptly downstairs and returned with a backpack.

"All right, here's a little pack of provisions for you," she whispered to Junior. "I don't think you're going to find her anywhere in town; Charles looked pretty thoroughly last night. But if there's a possibility you can catch up to her on the road, you should try. Send word back to us. Charles is intent on leaving, but I'll make sure he's back here in three days' time. If you can't make that, our next stop will be Agatha City. After that, it's Vallejo, a long way away from here."

"We won't need that much time," said Jordan.

"And you take care of Alex," said Emma.

"Of course, we will."

"Then off you go, quickly now. I'll deal with Charles."

"Thank you, Emma," said Ellie.

"Just find our girl."

The five cousins climbed over the side of the boat and hurried down the pier and into the city.

The downtown area was crowded with groups of people roaming together, singing drunkenly. Alex wondered why they had gotten up so early, then realized that they had probably not gone to bed the night before. He didn't understand grownups. He had to jog a little to keep up with his cousins.

"All right, Alex, where are we going?" asked Chi.

"The Emperor Hotel," he panted, out of breath.

Chi whistled, as though to say, *impressive!* Alex hoped they wouldn't ask him which hotel it was, because that was the extent of his secret knowledge. But they all seemed to know—the very tallest building in Modesto. It was only a few blocks from the fairgrounds. It had a wide staircase leading up to the big front doors. Alex had never been inside such a tall building; he felt kind of dizzy looking up at it as they came nearer. He counted twelve floors. A man in a fancy uniform opened the door for them.

The inside was a big room with a red carpet covering the entire floor and luxurious stuffed velvet sofas and chairs. Alex wanted to sit in one, just to see how it felt—maybe take a nap. There was a long, tall desk off to the side. They headed over to it. Another man in the same uniform was behind the desk. He looked like someone had brought in a dead animal when he saw them.

"May I help you?" he asked reluctantly.

Jordan took charge. "We're looking for somebody, Jasmine Taiyo. We believe she's staying with a man named Chad Benson."

The man raised an eyebrow, then started flipping through a large book on his desk. "Mr. Benson checked out last night."

"Did you see my sister with him when he left?" asked Alex.

The man smirked. "Since I have no idea who your sister is, I wouldn't know if I had seen her."

"Well, she looks a little like me," said Alex sullenly.

"I was not on duty at that time. I do seem to recall my associates mentioning something about Mr. Benson departing with a dusky beauty."

Alex saw Jordan scowling at this remark.

"Do you have any idea where they might have gone?" asked Junior.

"I'm afraid that kind of information is held in the strictest confidence."

Junior pulled a coin out of his pocket and slid it across the desk. "Does this help jog your memory?"

The man raised a single eyebrow again. Alex wondered how he learned how to do that.

"My memory still seems to be somewhat foggy this morning."

Junior pulled out three more coins and impatiently slapped them on the counter. The man deftly slid them into his palm. "I do not know for sure where they went. However, I understand that they left by carriage, and they headed south. Everyone knows Mr. Benson's primary summer residence is in Los Altos Hills, on the Peninsula. The road south can take you there."

"Thank you," said Junior. They moved away from the desk to discuss the matter.

"What should we do?" asked Chi. Right then, the desk attendant cleared his throat loudly, indicating that he wanted them to leave the lobby. They retreated outside.

"We last saw her around sundown yesterday," said Junior. "He just said they left late last night. That means they couldn't be more than six or seven hours ahead of us. If Benson travels in a carriage, it would be slower than going by horseback. He's a rich guy, so he's probably got an entourage with him, also slowing him down. We can catch up with him."

"I think we have to try," said Ellie. "I saw some stables not far from here where we can hire some horses."

"All right," said Junior, "but we don't all have to go. One of us should take Alex back to the boat before they leave."

"No way!" said Alex. "I'm going with you!"

Then commenced a heated debate over who should and should not go. Junior argued he should go because—well, because he's Junior, Charles' son, and that made him important (he didn't actually say this, but that's what Alex sensed he meant). Chi argued he was the best with horses. Ellie argued that that she was Jasmine's best friend. Alex argued that he was her brother, and that he was the most useless member of the entire Clan on this journey. He noticed that nobody tried to contradict him on that point. But they also seemed to accept his argument that he might be valuable, as the only family member who met Chad Benson. Jordan didn't have to argue; everybody just assumed he would be going. In the end, the argument about importance to the Clan won out. They couldn't afford to have *both* Jordan and Chi gone, as the best fiddlers, and Junior was critical as Charles' right-hand man (or so he thought).

And so, it would be Alex, Jordan, and Ellie. Junior and Chi would go back to the boat and tell the rest of them the plan. The hope was that, with just three riders on horseback, they could catch up with the party before they got too far out of Modesto, then get Jasmine and bring her back. Junior said he would ask Charles to sail back to the pier at daybreak for the next three days, until they had to go on to their next stop. Alex was a little stunned that they were actually going to let him do something important, for once. They said a quick goodbye to Junior and Chi, who ran back to catch the boat before it left.

The stables were on the main roadway, not far from the downtown. They walked there quickly, anxious to catch up with Jasmine. Alex waited outside while Jordan and Ellie went in to hire the mounts. It took a long time. Alex was starting to get hungry.

Alex thought about Ellie while he waited. He didn't know her that well, even though they all lived together. He was suspicious of her for being the big sister of the repugnant Alika, but to be fair, she had never really been mean to him. She just didn't want him around when she was busy with Jasmine, which was, like, *all the time.* She was short, not much taller than Alex, really, and had curly black hair that she always wore in a ponytail. She was more athletic than Jasmine. She and Jordan seemed to be okay with each other. Alex would have preferred to have had Chi on this outing, but this would be all right. Besides, she really was Jasmine's best friend. If there was any possible way to help Jasmine out of a jam, Ellie would do it.

Finally, they came out from the side of the building leading three horses. One of them was smaller than the others, really just a pony. Alex was insulted at first, knowing this one was for him. After a moment, he conceded it was probably for the best. *But which horse will Jasmine ride, once we find her?* Alex wondered. They would just have to figure that out later, he supposed. All three horses came with saddles, which was a kind of a luxury. They only used blankets and ropes back at the farm. Ellie brought the little pony up to Alex and told him her name was Betsy, and Alex liked her right away. She was a creamy brown color with white spots on her face, with warm brown eyes. He patted her face and said hello.

"Do you need help getting up?" asked Jordan. Alex said he didn't, but he did use a little wooden box by the front of the building to help. He stroked Betsy's neck after he got on to make sure they were friends before they started riding.

They started out right away. To Alex's relief, Ellie suggested they stop at a food cart before they got too far and buy some treats. Alex had a piece of toast with some sort of creamy butter, topped with strawberries and blueberries in the shape of the KGL flag he had seen yesterday. It was delicious.

And then they were off, moving at a good trot. Alex felt a little worried for Betsy, struggling to keep up with the bigger horses, but he didn't say anything to Jordan and Ellie. He was as anxious to catch up with Jasmine as the rest of them. The road they took was wide, with solid, packed dirt, and they made good time. Before long, they were out of Modesto, traveling among the ruins outside the city walls. Yellow weeds grew through the broken concrete, mostly star thistle and field brome. It was already getting hot by mid-morning. Alex wished he had remembered to bring his sunhat. They passed by a tall sign from the Olden Times that had curly lettering in the old language. He asked Ellie what it said, but she didn't know, either.

After some time, they came to a little hill. Jordan told him this was a bridge over another road from the Olden Times. They paused up there to give their horses a rest. They could see for several miles in either direction. To their right was the Inland Sea. Alex knew it was narrower here. He thought he could see all the way across to the other side. Or maybe it was just some clouds on the western horizon. To their left, they could just barely make out the Sierras to the east. There was no sign of Jasmine or her group down the road.

"What should we do?" Ellie asked Jordan.

"I don't know. They must have gotten a bigger head start than we thought."

Ellie bit her lower lip, staring down the road. "I don't want to give up on her."

"I don't either. Let's keep going but not press the horses so hard."

"Okay."

Alex was even more worried now. *Where was Jasmine? How could they just disappear like that?*

They nudged their horses into motion. After a little while, Jordan pulled back so that he was riding next to Alex. He looked like he wanted to say something, then stopped himself. After a moment, he decided to just say it.

"Alex, I think we have to face the possibility we won't be able to find her."

"What do you mean?"

"I mean, the farther we go, the harder this is going to be. We know they went in this direction, but they could have turned off anywhere. Maybe this Benson guy has friends somewhere he's visiting. Maybe he wanted to go to the mountains…"

"Or maybe she's dead," Ellie interrupted, "and that's why Benson left in the middle of the night in such a hurry."

"She is *not* dead!" Alex shouted. He felt the heat rising to his face. "I know it. I can feel that she's still alive."

"You're not helping," Jordan said to Ellie.

"Sorry. I'm just worried about her, that's all."

"We all are," said Jordan.

"Look," said Ellie, pointing to a little wooden shack on the side of the road ahead. "Why don't we stop there and get something to eat and ask them if they saw Benson go by?"

"Good idea."

They steered their horses over to the roadside stand, tied them up to the hitching post, and stood in the welcome shade. The family behind the counter was Mexican, selling produce from the family farm, zucchini and cantaloupe. Jordan asked the woman selling the food if she had seen a fancy carriage go by earlier in the day.

"Si, si—big white carriage, six white horses. Moving fast. Early morning."

Jordan and Ellie looked at each other and nodded.

"Let's keep going," said Ellie.

They traveled through the rest of the day. The road was absolutely straight, as though drawn by a ruler. They passed more ruins of cities, then stands of eucalyptus and palm trees. For a long time, they couldn't see beyond either side of the road because the oleander had grown up so high, with alternating pink and white flowers. After several hours, they crossed the Merced River on a rickety old bridge. They didn't stop. But they never saw the carriage with six white horses—not even a plume of dust on the horizon.

When it came toward evening, they decided to stop for the night. Jordan led them off the road, over a small footpath that wound five miles or so to the Sea. They set up camp in a secluded location with a tent Emma had given them. Jordan got a fire going and grilled the vegetables they had bought at the roadside stand for dinner. Alex was so exhausted, he could barely eat his food before he stumbled to the tent and fell asleep.

The next morning, they got up early, hoping to catch up to them by curtailing their sleep. The road now started to veer to the west, following the curve of the Inland Sea. Late in the day they reached Los Baños, the southernmost city on the Sea. There was no sign of Chad Benson. They spent the night in an oak grove on the outskirts of town and pressed on the next day.

The third day, they began to climb up the golden hills of California. They passed a dry lakebed in the late morning— "an old reservoir," Jordan called it— and continued. There were dark green Valley Oaks dotting the hillside. At one point, Alex saw big metal towers on the top of a hillside. Jordan told him these were windmills from the Olden Times, but they didn't work anymore. The remnants of a rusted old guard rail ran alongside the road for a while, then disappeared. Alex saw a red-tailed hawk circling above them. There were several feral cats lounging drunkenly in the Sun by the road, including some as large as small dogs. When Alex asked about them, Jordan told him they were the descendants of genetically engineered pets from the Olden Times. Alex was confused by this but didn't ask.

They spent that night under an old viaduct off the road a considerable distance. Ellie explained that they had to keep a safe distance away from highwaymen. They had just crossed over the peak of the hills and were on their way down now. They left early the next day and now were heading mostly north. The landscape had changed, greener and lusher. They saw acres and acres of apricot orchards, spreading out as far as they could see. There were more villages along the road and more traffic. In the middle of the day, they felt certain that they saw the white carriage ahead of them and they set their horses to a gallop. But when they caught up, they discovered it was just a delivery cab, carrying produce. They slept in a remote place in the hills to the west of the roadway.

On the fifth day, after asking directions twice, they finally arrived in Los Altos. It was a wealthy town, full of big houses with gates in front of them. Most of them had guards and guard dogs. There was a little downtown area with tidy shops. They boarded their horses at the local stable and went from store to store, asking if anybody knew where Chad Benson lived. Nobody seemed to know. The people seemed a little afraid of Alex and his cousins, for some reason, and some wouldn't even say "hello" to them. They spent the night in an abandoned school from the Olden Times.

The next day was Fivesday. This meant that the Clan had probably just arrived in Agatha City. The three of them were all tired of traveling, and so, over breakfast at a little café in the downtown, Ellie and Jordan decided it was probably time to give up. If they left that morning and traveled quickly, they could reach Agatha City by Sun'sday and meet up with the Clan.

Alex started to cry. "We can't give up on her!"

Ellie reached across the table and covered his hand. "We don't want to, either. But we're losing their trail. And nobody here wants to tell us anything about Chad Benson. It's like we're invisible."

"Why? Why do they treat us like that?"

Ellie looked at Jordan, then back at Alex. "I don't know. It may be because our skin is darker."

At that moment, the waitress came by with more hot water for their tea. She was a kind-looking Mexican woman, but she spoke perfect

Californian. "I understand you're looking for Chad Benson?" she said quietly.

"Yes, we are," said Jordan quickly, matching her quiet voice. "Do you know him?"

"Yes, everybody knows the Bensons. Mr. Benson and his servants stopped in this café on their way out of town yesterday. I overheard them talking about going up to his second home in Frisco. You didn't hear this from me, by the way."

"Thank you, ma'am," said Ellie. "Did you happen to see whether he had a young woman with him who looks something like us?"

She looked up at them briefly, then lowered her eyes. "Yes, he did," she said softly. Then she left the table quietly.

Jordan and Ellie looked at each other across the table.

"She's alive," said Ellie, tears in her eyes.

"We're going to Frisco," said Jordan.

13

Traveling to California

Paul's Journal Entry: Ruins of North Platte, unclaimed territory

Thursday, June 17

We've made good time since we left the convent, probably covering nearly 200 miles in those three days. We arrived in this long-abandoned town from the Empire days in the mid-afternoon. We are now so far removed from civilization, the village is mostly untouched by raiders. Usually, these places have smashed windows, doors knocked in, the residue of generations of vagabonds scouting for treasure. Since we arrived early earlier than planned, Echleph had us set up camp in a place with an old, faded sign in English that reads, "Waggin' Tails Bark Park," whatever that means. We then went out on scouting expeditions to see if we could find anything useful in the old houses. Echleph went with Archer; I went out with Turge; and Eastman stayed behind, reading holy scripture.

Most of the houses we broke into were completely empty. Because this town hasn't been destroyed by the raiders, I must assume the original residents had time to move all their belongings with them when they left. Where did they move to? Did they know the country was dying? Or did they just concern themselves with their own situations?

In one house, though, we found the belongings still there. Clothes hung in the closets, with strange fabrics and styles, and furniture was still arrayed as the inhabitants had arranged it, although coated in a thick layer of dust. Every room had a rectangular black screen attached to the walls, which Turge says was part of their communication network with the outside world. I could almost imagine them walking around in this space. It gave me the chills. They must have left in a hurry, to leave everything behind.

After a while, I realized I had lost track of Turge. I found him in the kitchen area, opening jars from the cupboards and pantry. The old food was giving off an acrid smell. I was confused why he was doing thing, but then it became clear. "Bingo," he said, and he poured out a jarful of ancient coins and bills. He knew, somehow, that the people back then hid a stash of money in their kitchens. I walked over to look at the treasure. These things can bring a fortune on the black market. I had never held some of these particular coins before.

Turge looked up at me, almost as though he was nervous. "We's supposed to report this to Eastman, when we find something of value," he said cautiously.

I understood immediately. "I'm not seeing anything," I said. "It's all yours." He looked at me in surprise, then quickly scooped all the money up in one of his big paws and dumped it into a hidden pocket. I think I may have made an ally today.

Sunday, June 20

Yesterday, we crossed the border into the nation of Koolrada, according to Echleph. There were no signs announcing this, no guards at the border. He says this country is neutral in all disputes, referring to itself as the "Switzerland of America." But he warned that our church business will have very few takers; the ECA has all but disappeared in these parts. He refers to the politics as "Libertarian," meaning the people pretty much just want to be left alone. The land is utterly flat here; we had to go off the trail some way to find a secluded place to camp.

As usual, Eastman is insisting we hold a church service this morning. He usually reads from the Three Testaments, selections chosen according to the date on the liturgical calendar. The soldiers pretend to be listening, as do I. Within a day or two, we should be ascending into the fabled Rocky Mountains.

Wednesday, June 23

Yesterday, we passed by Denver, the capital of Koolrada. It's a large city, about the size of Benson, with a fifty-foot wall surrounding it (you can tell by the ruins surrounding it that it used to be much larger, though). We saw men on top of the wall holding rifles. I asked Turge if these were actual working firearms, and he said, "There's no need to find out." We gave the city a wide berth.

Traffic on this road has picked up again. We're now ascending into the mountains, which has slowed our travel. I am astonished by the size of this mountain range. I had no idea a landscape could be this dramatic! And there's snow on the mountaintops, visible from down here—snow, at the summer solstice! The whole vista takes my breath away.

Last night, I had another intense conversation with Echleph about the Olden Times. I think maybe he's opening up more, given the length of the journey we're on. We're also stuck with one another, since Eastman seems to prefer his own company, and Turge and Archer, each other's. I will try to record some of what he said here, although I wish I could capture his peculiar way of speaking, that faint accent, peppered with curse words.

I started it off by saying, again, that I think his viewpoint on the Republic and Empire is too negative. I said to him, "What about these roads we're riding on?

Wouldn't you appreciate having them in the condition they were back then? What about the access to education, the ability to move to different regions to find good work? What about the fact that I lost my loving father at the age of four from a disease that I know they had conquered back in those days?"

*He was having none of it. "Sure, they had fancy things, and better medicine. They needed it, because it was a sick society. Your heroes back in the Late Republic and Empire days didn't feel like they had to share the Earth with anybody. Certainly not with any other species. But not even other humans, outside their communities. It was all about them, them, them. They did whatever the f**k they wanted, whenever they wanted. They were spoiled children, suckling at the breast of underground oil, the ancient energy that wasn't theirs to spend. They diverted water out west to their homes in the deserts and showed off their wastefulness, just to prove they were richer than other people. They poisoned the ground with pesticides to kill weeds, then used more artificial chemicals to treat the illnesses these caused. They lived extravagant, unhealthy lives."*

I didn't understand how he could be so confident that he knew the ways of our ancestors. I mean, I'm pretty hazy about them, and I've done a lot more reading than he has. So, I pushed back, asking him how he knew all this. His answer was yet another surprise for me.

"To understand this, you have to understand something about the Sixth Caste. When the Caste system was being formed toward the end of the Empire, we were actually the first to form. We were a loose collection of laborers, farmers, mechanics, explorers, already forming into a kind of coalition as we watched the country starting to collapse. My caste was thus one of the only self-chosen ones, besides Castes One and Two. The upper castes weren't too interested in the composition of the lower castes, and we took advantage of their inattentiveness. We started by reviving the Freemason organizations from the early days of the Republic, secret mutual aid societies. We have lodges spread out across the country, right under your noses, but you're all too self-

absorbed to pay any attention. Thus, we have had our own private network in place for more than 300 years now, superseding any national loyalties our members might feel. I can call on any Caste 6 lodge across the continent and get any help I need. That's why rangers, like me, are all in this caste. We learn from each other the situation on the ground and pass this along from lodge to lodge."

I had no idea about this. It was interesting, but it still didn't explain how he could claim to know so much about the distant past. I pressed him on this, and he continued:

"We have our own system of education. It's just not connected to schools, like yours is. It's taught one-on-one, father to son, mother to daughter, master to apprentice. Each one of us is assigned an apprentice, separated by gender, and we teach them our lore. They follow us everywhere. The fact that you're seeing me without my apprentice is very unusual. I had to ask my best friend to take over my mentorship of a fine lad named Eaglefeather for me while I took this trip. It was hard to do it, but I know he'll be in good hands. We often share responsibilities like this. I promised Eaglefeather I would be back for his Rite of Adulthood ceremony in three years' time. This trip was just too long for him to be away from his home and his friends. I doubt your Church would have agreed to this, anyway. And the less you all know about our ways, the better. Anyway, my master passed along this information to me twenty years ago from his master, who learned it from his, and so on back to the Empire itself."

I asked him why, then, he was willing to share this with me.

"Because I like you. Because you asked. Nobody in the upper Castes has any real curiosity about us. But also, because I don't have to worry about you. No offense, but you don't have the fire in the belly to do anything with this information. You're too embedded in the system. Someday, maybe you will. If you find that fire, if you do decide to step forward into the arena, I want you to remember me. I can be of use to you. I've only scratched the surface here."

I wanted to ask him more, but I sensed he was done talking. I intend to press him for more information as we go.

Disputed territory between Koolrada and Deseret

Tuesday, June 29

I haven't had time to write lately. Eastman keeps insisting that we're behind schedule—a schedule I've never seen, I might add—and has been pressing us cover more territory each day. We had to change our horses in a small town in the Rockies—a fascinating village that seemed to have working solar panels from the Olden Days, powering some of those electrical devices that I heard about earlier. I could see artificial illumination in one of the houses. I wanted to investigate, but Eastman didn't let me interact with the locals. They did seem wary of us, so maybe it was for the best.

The mountains were just staggering to me. Words cannot describe their beauty. It took days to get from the plains up to the pass, where it was cold enough that I had to scrounge in my trunk for warmer clothing. It still wasn't enough. Then, on the west side, the pine forests gave way to scrub land, more desolate, and we entered another long passage with no human inhabitants. Out here, scavenger birds are common; we passed by a group of them arguing over a dead mountain lion.

I finally had a chance to probe Echleph again around the campfire last night. I figured that, with this Sixth Caste network he described the other day, he probably had a pretty good idea of what we were going to face in California. It turns out, he does. We could probably have saved the Church a lot of money and cancelled this trip if we had just bothered to ask him. Specifically, I asked him if it was true what they said about a new religion cropping up out there, and he said it was.

"Oh yeah, there's definitely a new religion brewing out West, full of zealous environmentalists. Several religions, actually. There are probably at least two dozen

*factions, not quite aware of one another. They're disorganized, but they're passionate, and they're growing. All it'll take is one charismatic messiah figure to spring up out of this soup, unify and organize them, and then the KGL will be in real trouble. The Church has good reasons to be scared. If your Church was smart, you would send an army out there and f**king slaughter them wholesale, smother that baby in the crib, or else you're probably done for. But I don't think you have the stomach for this. My money is on the Californians."*

I was shocked by all this. I asked him if he knew of any such messiah. He said he didn't. But he was pretty sure one was coming. "I don't know if this messiah figure is going to be religious or political. The gods help you if it's both."

Somewhere in California

Friday, July 9

We are camping tonight in a forested area in what Echleph calls the Coast Range. We are close enough to the Pacific that I sometimes see seagulls circling overhead and catch a whiff of saltwater, or I think I do. But we haven't made it to the ocean yet, let alone Frisco. It's beautiful country but hot and dry. I found it hard to sleep last night, partly because we seem to be utterly lost.

Yes—lost. I never thought I would write these words. My confidence in Echleph's guidance has never been shaken until now. Tensions between Echleph and Eastman are running high. We are so close to our destination, yet so far…

Paul looked up from his journal at Echleph, sitting on a log on the other side of their campfire. The ranger was studying a map closely with a grim look on his face. Paul still couldn't quite believe that Echleph had let them down. His instincts had been unerring until now. A couple of days after leaving the convent, for example, he directed them to take a sharp left turn and leave the comfortable east-west roadway. When Eastman asked him indignantly why they were making this detour, Echleph said, "The Dakota Federation lands are up ahead. Not too friendly to Americans. Best to avoid them." Paul could see no signs or other indications that they had passed into a new territory, but he had come to trust Echleph's knowledge.

Because of Echleph's guidance, their journey had been relatively untroubled. But that was partly because of how *empty* the landscape was. They travelled for days, even weeks at a time without encountering another human being. Animals—yes, animals in abundance. The farther they went, the more emboldened the creatures became. Deer would routinely visit their campsites, curious about them, as well as raccoons, possums, prairie dogs, even a huge elk. One night, Paul couldn't sleep because the noise of the frogs and the insects was too deafening. The roads became thin and irregular, with tall prairie grasses, twice the height of a man, encroaching and sometimes covering their path.

Occasionally, Paul would see remnants of the old world along the way—crumbled piles of concrete and metal that once formed a building, a rusted truck now barely recognizable, piles of white plastic bags, still holding ancient garbage. They passed one small city that had walls built entirely out of old automobile tires, thirty feet tall, but the city was abandoned, long ago. For the most part the land was eerily empty.

They fell into a general routine as they travelled. They would camp at about the same time in the late afternoon, near a river or a creek if they could. Archer would go off hunting if their supplies were low, and almost always returned with some game. After they ate, Turge and Archer would play a board game that used dice that entertained them endlessly. Paul tried to follow along occasionally but never could quite figure out the rules, even though he was quite good at the popular strategy board game *Xerxon* back in Benson. Echleph would sit with his dog, smoking his pipe, staring into the flames. Paul would sometimes engage him in conversation, but other times, Echleph refused to talk. Eastman would read from the Bible or other religious texts. In the morning, he had a very particular routine he had to follow, shaving his face and trimming his hair, gargling with water noisily, brushing down his clothes meticulously, and praying silently for exactly the same length of time. Paul imagined it was the same exact prayer, running through his mind ritually. The Elder still showed little interest in having any sort of conversation with Paul, despite Paul's occasional efforts.

After leaving Koolrada, Echleph told them to hide their Church paraphernalia as they entered Deseret, the nation between Koolrada and the Nevada Wasteland, governed by Mormons. "They're not too keen on the KGL here," he said cryptically. Eastman reluctantly obeyed. The roadways in Deseret were wide and smooth, better kept than any roads they had been on, even in the KGL. They made it across quickly, stopping on the outskirts of Salt Lake City. Echleph and Turge went into town alone to purchase supplies for the next leg of their journey.

After this, the landscape turned desolate, a huge expanse of salt flats followed by an endless desert. It smelled of sage and dust. In terms of human habitation, they saw only ghost towns, some almost completely reclaimed by the wind and sand. Still, they made good time, and soon were coming up to another huge mountain range—the Sierras, Turge called them—nearly as large as the Rockies. They passed a big alpine lake, Lake Tahoe, and then they were in California, at last. After several more hours of winding down a long slope, the view opened up and they could see a massive panorama before them, golden hills dotted with dark green trees and the huge Inland Sea at the bottom of the valley.

When they approached the Inland Sea, Echleph again had them take a detour to the north. There was a ferry across the Sea to Frisco, he told them, but it was run by the local pirates of Sacramento. He knew of another ferry several miles up the coast that was safer. But when they got there, they discovered a blackened landscape. The town he was looking for was gone. The charred landscape looked like a war zone, but Turge assured Paul it wasn't.

"They have fires in California every year. The people are used to it. They pack up and leave and then they rebuild the town a few years later."

Soon, they were out of the burned area and came to a nice seaside village named Lincoln. Paul was shocked to see women wearing pants, just like men, and walking around without their hair covered. *No wonder the Church is worried about California!* They passed through a nondescript village called Northpoint at the northern end of the lake, but it was too small to offer a ferry service. They spent the night in a larger city inland a few miles, called Chico. Elder Eastman was disturbed when he discovered the one ECA church in the city had been closed and boarded up.

The next day, as they were travelling down the west side of the Inland Sea, was when they got off track. The road they were on circumnavigated the Sea, leading from one walled village to the next, but at one gate they were refused entrance. No explanation was given by the guards. Their language was hard for Paul to understand—although Echleph spoke it fluently—but it was clear from the body language that visitors were not welcome.

So, they took a small road west from the city. This led them into some forested hills, and after some time, they struggled to find their way out. Echleph and Turge pored over an old map—possibly the one they had picked up at the Trash Mountain—and used a compass to guide them, but a path that might have led them back to the Sea was too narrow for the wagon to pass through, and the road ahead led them south and west. Echleph suggested abandoning the wagon here and carting their essential supplies via horseback, but Eastman rejected this plan. Eventually, they gave up and set up camp for the night.

And now, here they were, lost in the coastal range of California. After Paul finished writing in his journal and after a heated discussion between Echleph and Eastman, it was decided that they would give up on finding the Sea and just continue on the next road that was wide enough for their wagon. Eventually, they would have to hit water again. Hopefully, they could find a ferry from there to Frisco. The mood of their party was dark, compounded by a drizzly rain that set in and seeped into their clothes. They were so close to Frisco, their ultimate destination, and yet so far away. They rode until dark but remained lost. They camped out again in the wilderness. Paul didn't dare try to get Echleph talking that night.

The next morning, they found a road wide enough to travel on, but it did not seem to be leading them toward Frisco. Instead, it wound its way up and through yet another mountain range—this one smaller, but still hard to navigate—winding east, then west, even north for a while. There were some ruins of old towns and villages occasionally, but no other signs of human habitation. At one point they came to a small valley filled with overgrown grape vines and were able to eat their fill of sweet green fruit. Echleph said this was once a vineyard for making wine. The forest dissipated as they climbed over a ridge, then got thicker than ever as the road led them southwest, thinned out again—and then closed in on them completely. They spent another night in the wilderness, feeling no closer to Frisco than the day before.

The next morning brought them into a forest with remarkable trees, incredibly tall. The barks had a reddish-brown color to them and a distinct scent, warm and spicy. The ground, covered in soft needles and ferns, smothered the sound of the horses. The trees mostly blocked out the sun. It felt moist and cool. It was one of the most amazing places Paul had seen, on a journey full of amazing sights. Paul felt a strange tingling sensation, a kind of religious awe—something he had never felt in any church service—and began to understand for the first time what the devout must experience. The others in his group seemed to be feeling something similar, because they all slowed down, as if thinking with one mind. Paul climbed out of the wagon to get a better view of the forest. He looked up at the forest canopy, hundreds of feet above him, struggling to believe that trees could grow to be this tall. The only point of reference he could think of was the Black Pyramid back in Benson City.

Paul noticed that Echleph had stopped and was now holding up a finger while looking at his dog. Rex's nose was working overtime, his ears rotating rapidly. Archer slipped off his horse and pulled an arrow out of the quiver strapped to his back. He notched an arrow, pointing down, and quietly rotated 360 degrees.

Suddenly, about two dozen people seemed to appear out of nowhere, dropping out of the trees and landing in a circle about thirty feet away from them. Most of them had bows and arrows, aimed at the group, but three or four had actual rifles from the Empire days. Turge leapt from the wagon and drew his broadsword, but they were far outnumbered. Echleph gave a hand signal, and Turge reluctantly placed his sword on the soft ground and held up his hands. Archer followed suit.

It was possibly the strangest group of humans Paul had yet seen. They were all dressed alike, loose-woven tunics and pants out of the same material, shades of white and brown and yellow. Their hair was long and pulled back. Paul couldn't tell if they were men or women, except for a few with patchy facial hair. Even there, he wasn't certain. They had a wide range of skin tones and hair colors, with a number of them graying. It looked like it had been even longer since they had bathed than it had for Paul.

When he looked closer, he got a further shock: some of the smaller people had ears that went up to a point, like the ears of elves or fairies from the children's books he once read. They had fine bones and almond-shaped eyes. Paul blinked, wondering if his eyes were deceiving him.

One of them spoke to the group, in yet another new language. This one, though, sounded a lot like English, strangely enough. Paul could almost make out what they were saying. Echleph responded and the two of them exchanged a brief conversation.

Echleph turned around to address the travelers. "We are to follow them."

"Why is that?" said Eastman, now out of the wagon and standing next to Paul. "What's their intention? Are we their captives?"

"I'm honestly not sure," Echleph replied. "I don't speak their dialect very well. I tried to communicate to them that we're lost, just passing through. I don't think they mean us any harm. But I suggest we not make any sudden moves toward our weapons."

After a few hundred feet, the road ended. The same person spoke to Echleph, who translated, "This is the end of the road. She says our horses and wagon stay here, and we continue on foot."

"Absolutely not!" said Eastman.

Echleph conveyed this to their captor, listened to the reply, and translated back. "We are promised that the wagon and the horses will be looked after. I don't think we have much of a choice, Elder."

Eastman pursed his lips. "Very well."

Three of the elvish humans who had descended from the trees took the reins of the horses and led them away. Paul and his group followed the strange people through a winding footpath deeper into the forest. Paul lost all sense of direction and time. The stillness of the forest, the dappled light, the strange smells, all gave him a surprising sense of peacefulness, despite the situation.

After some length of time—was it ten minutes? Or was it two hours? — they came into a wide clearing with a dozen small huts in a circle beneath the trees. The reddish trees surrounding them had staircases circling around the trunks, going up and up, to circular platforms and treehouses in the trees at varying heights. There were rope bridges connecting the treehouses and platforms. These dwellings went up to a dizzying height. Paul saw somebody up high take a rope swing across from one tree to another, landing gracefully and tying up the rope on a nearby hook. These people seemed to live completely in a three-dimensional space.

A woman with long gray hair, held back in a braid down her back, came forward to greet them with a smile. "Welcome, gentlemen," she said, in heavily accented English. "I hope our greeting didn't alarm you." Paul noticed that she had normal ears.

She went to Echleph first, holding his hand in both of hers, then moved on to Turge, then Paul. She was unaware, it seemed, of their relative rankings.

"We have to be very cautious with outsiders," she continued. "Some are quite hostile to us."

Eastman replied to her in his best Church English. "We apologize for any intrusion. We are simply lost in your forest. If you could direct us toward Frisco, we would gladly be on our way."

"Oh, I'm sorry to say that won't be possible, not at the moment," she said, still smiling. "We must escort you from our village, and no one is available to do that right now."

"We do not need to be escorted."

Her smile faltered, then returned. "We must insist. And you will be blindfolded. You see, we are very private people here, and do not want our whereabouts known." Eastman opened his mouth to object, but she continued. "But I am being rude. You must be tired and disoriented. Please, come to our hearth and share a meal with us."

Paul was hungry. He was also curious about this place. Was it really being run by a woman? He started to follow the others toward the center of the clearing, when Eastman stopped him, holding onto his arm.

"We cannot stay here," he whispered in English.

"Why not?"

"These people are not of the Faith. Some of them look like devils. It will be… dangerous to spend too much time in their presence."

"I don't understand. We've stayed with others on this journey who aren't of the Faith. I can think of several inns that were hardly godly…"

"No, those were all good Christians. These people—I think they might be devil worshippers."

Paul was surprised to see real distress in Eastman's face. For the first time, he began to feel a touch of pity for the man. Just a touch.

"Elder, I don't think we have much of a choice. But we can always be assured of God's absolution, right?"

Eastman stood still for several moments, his brow furrowed, then at last made a gesture with his head, not quite a nod, but indicating assent. They moved to the circle surrounding the fire and partook of their nuts and dried apricots.

The meal was a casual affair, with people coming and going at will. They spoke to each other in a strange dialect, related to English but pronounced differently, hard for Paul to follow. He and his companions were served a strange honey-flavored liquor the natives called mead, sweet and sharp-tasting, unlike anything he had ever drunk before. It seemed to be coming upon evening, but it was hard to tell with the trees blocking out the sun. Lanterns were lit in the treehouses, reminding Paul of the fireflies back home. At some point, Paul began to hear music being played. He wasn't sure what the instruments were. It sounded like someone was playing some sort of keyboard instrument made of wood planks with a mallet, soft and warm, but it was out of Paul's visual range. The instrument was tuned in a strange scale he had never heard before. Then some drummers joined in, then singers high up in the trees, singing what sounded to him like nonsense words in a weird kind of yodel. They exchanged vocal lines back and forth across the forest. It surrounded him, like the music in the church, but it was more organic, more unstructured. It had a kind of hypnotic effect.

After some time, the music picked up in speed and intensity, and some of the members of this tribe started dancing. It was a highly irregular dance, not choreographed like the dances Paul attended back home. To Paul's surprise, Turge joined in, moving his large body with surprising grace, then Archer. Paul suspected they had been drinking a lot of the mead. At this display, Eastman stood up abruptly, brushed off his robe indignantly, and asked their host if he could be shown to his sleeping quarters. She took him up a winding staircase to a treehouse. Paul followed Eastman with his eyes. By the time Paul looked down, Turge and Archer had left the circle, too, walking off holding hands with their dancing partners. Paul had to assume these were women, but he still didn't know. Echleph, meanwhile, was engaged in a rapt conversation with a man who looked a lot like him, tall and scruffy, with long hair in a ponytail and a faint beard. He also sat with a dog. Rex generally disliked other dogs and strange people, but he seemed to have acclimated himself to this stranger and his dog. Paul wondered if Echleph had found another member of his caste.

The gray-haired woman returned and sat down next to Paul and resumed speaking in English. "My name is Celestian, by the way."

"Mine is Paul." He reached out to shake her hand, but she bowed deeply instead. He was still trying to digest the possibility that a woman might be the leader of this group of people, or whatever it was. How was that possible?

"What do you think of our little community?" Celestian asked.

"I have never seen anything quite like it. Your place is beautiful. It seems like you've found a way to live in real harmony with each other and with nature."

"Oh, we have our share of squabbles, I can assure you! We had a splinter group break off from us and form their own village a couple of miles from here. But that was long before I was born. We're on good terms with them now."

"Before you were born? How long has this village been here?"

"A very long time. Hundreds of years."

"Really? How have you managed to survive all that time?"

"What do you mean?"

"It seems like you're living in isolation. Don't you need to have contact with the outside world, for medicine and other supplies?"

"We do venture out when we need to. But we find ourselves to be pretty self-sufficient. We have a clearing not far from here where we raise sheep for wool and cheese, and where we can grow our crops. We find that there's very little from the outside world that we need. Still, we do go out occasionally, if only to find out what's going on in the world."

Paul shook his head in wonderment. "Hundreds of years. This means your people have managed to avoid the chaos of the fall of the Empire and its aftermath."

"Well, not entirely. Sometimes the world has a way of intruding. As you saw when you entered our territory, we do our best to keep the troublesome elements at bay."

They were quiet for a while. The woman seemed comfortable with the silence, and Paul appreciated that.

"I'd like to hear more about your perspective on that time," he eventually said.

"Do you mean the Fall?"

"Yes. It's kind of an obsession of mine. I've been trying to figure this out my whole life. I feel like I've gotten closer to the answer on this journey, but I don't have all the pieces to the puzzle yet. It's just so hard for me to understand how this could have happened, how such a great Empire could collapse."

"Ah. You'll want to talk to the Seer, then."

"The Seer?"

"Yes, they're the leader of this village."

They? Is this one person or several? "I had assumed you were the leader."

"Not really. I run the day-to-day business of the village, but the Seer is really the one in charge."

"Well, yes. If you wouldn't mind, I'd like to meet this—this person."

"I will take you to them right now."

Paul followed the woman to a nearby tree, then up the winding staircase that circled a trunk at least ten feet in diameter. The stairs were supported by diagonal trusses. The way the trusses and the stairs were partly swallowed by the tree made Paul suspect it was all decades old, if not over a hundred years old. Paul didn't know trees could live that long. The stairs had only a thin rope handrail on the outside, making him nervous. He stayed close to the trunk as they climbed. Fortunately, they stopped at the first level, about fifty feet off the ground. There were at least two levels of treehouses above them on this tree.

The treehouse encircled the tree, and surrounding the treehouse was a platform about ten feet wide. Connected to this platform were six or seven rope bridges leading to other trees, as well as one of those rope swings Paul had seen earlier. The treehouse itself had a second floor above the first, cradled in a branch that was easily as thick as Paul's body. The doorway had a rounded top. Celestian knocked gently. Paul heard a voice inside say, "Come in!"

As they entered the space, it took Paul's eyes a moment to adjust to the dim light. It was a cozy room, with pillows and over-stuffed chairs strewn haphazardly. There was a small staircase at the back, leading up to the second floor. In the middle of the room, in front of the massive tree trunk that dominated the space, there was a table with pieces of fabric and earthenware jug and cups. Sitting behind it was an old person with short-cropped white hair. Paul struggled to determine the person's gender and ultimately decided it must be a "she," given her small stature. Paul could probably lift her up with one arm. Her face was wrinkled and scarred, and it seemed like she had only one working eye. She was wearing glasses, presumably to do whatever work she was doing, the weaving of some sort of tapestry. Celestian introduced Paul and exited quietly.

The Seer took off her glasses, put them down on the table next to a guttering candle, and looked at Paul with a hint of a smile on her face. She unnerved him a little. After a moment or two, she gestured to an overstuffed sofa, an invitation, he supposed. He sat down. She followed nimbly.

"Would you like some tea?" she asked him. Her English was perfect but strange. Paul couldn't place what it was about it that struck him so.

"That would be lovely," he responded. She moved to the side of the room where she had a little fire burning under an iron teapot. She poured some water in a cup, sprinkled some herbs, and brought it back to him.

"You're a part of that religious group that's come to us," she said after she placed the cup and a candle on a little table next to the sofa. Paul was surprised she knew what was going on down on the forest floor fifty feet below.

"Yes, although only two of us are actually officials in the Church," he replied.

She stared at him steadily with her one clear eye. "Yes, but you're not terribly religious, are you?"

Paul felt a chill come over him. *How can she possibly know this?*

"Why do you say that?"

"When you've lived as long as I have, you learn to see through the façades people put up pretty quickly. Don't worry: your secret is safe with me."

There was something about this woman that made Paul feel comfortable letting his guard down. "You're right. I admit it. I've been involved with the Church my entire life, but I've never been very religious. It just seems like magical thinking to me, all of it."

"Being skeptical is not a bad thing. Don't dismiss magic, though. It does exist. Just not in the ways you might think."

"Well, I'm hardly going to reject one superstition for another. I've always been pretty certain that what you see is what you get in this world."

"Ah! So, you're a rational materialist. Interesting!"

"I don't know what that is."

"You believe that the world is a concrete entity, that it can be perceived but only through careful observation and rigorous adherence to the rationality of the scientific method, so that we don't delude ourselves. The dominant paradigm in the late Republic and early Empire."

"Yes, I suppose that's right…"

"That's fine. Just remember that the best scientific method is only poking pinpricks of light into a vast black velvet curtain. And this also requires faith, just as does Christianity, Judaism, Islam, and all the other creeds."

"I take it you don't consider yourself a rational materialist?"

"I am an evangelical agnostic."

"I've never heard of such a thing."

"I believe the state of *not-knowing* is divine and should be promulgated as widely as possible."

Paul was starting to lose the thread of her reasoning, and she seemed to sense it. "I am sure you're not here to discuss metaphysics with me, are you? I sense you have a question to ask me. Go ahead and ask it."

Paul swallowed. He suddenly felt foolish, but he pressed ahead anyway. "I'm wondering if you know why America fell, all those years ago."

She nodded, accepting his question. "I cannot tell you *the* answer. I can only tell you *my* answer. Because I lived through it."

"I don't understand."

"I was alive during that time."

"What? How could that be? You would have to be…"

"I am over four hundred and fifty years old."

Paul waited for the punch line. Surely this was a joke.

The Seer laughed at his expression. "It's true!"

"I don't get it."

"Back when I was born, in the 2030s, some new technology had been developed which enabled scientists to modify the genes of fetuses using a bacterium called CRISPR. It was illegal to use this on humans, but if you had enough money, those rules could be circumvented. My parents paid an exorbitant amount of money to have my genes altered so that the telomeres in my DNA would never degrade. My body is constantly repairing itself. I essentially stopped aging at about sixty."

"I don't understand half of what you just said."

"That's okay. You don't have to understand. But do you believe me?"

"In all honesty, I don't know what to believe."

The Seer laughed again. "Now you're starting to get it!"

Paul put his palms on his temples, trying to focus. "You're saying that you've been alive for over four hundred years, and that you witnessed all this history?"

"It could be. Or maybe I'm just a batty old coot who is making stuff up. I can tell you this much: this is the reality I know. Of course, our minds construct our realities, based on pre-existing assumptions. Most of what we experience is constructed by our minds. Our expectations drive our perception of what's happening. We can never tell for sure how accurate our memories are."

"So, you're saying nothing is real? That our memories are just made up? That seems pretty nihilistic to me. I refuse to believe that there isn't a Truth out there, somewhere."

"That's fine. Just be skeptical when you think you've found it. Keeping a truly open mind takes effort. Do you have an open mind?"

"I like to think so."

"Good. Would you like to hear my story?"

"Very much."

"Then I will tell you it. But first, you must try not to interrupt me. There will be things you don't understand, because the world back then was very different than it is now. I can't be stopping every other minute to explain some piece of technology to you."

"I understand."

"People always interrupt me because they cannot grasp the strings of my thought. My language is archaic, and I know my mode of thinking has become strange to others because of my long time-horizon. But this doesn't mean I don't like to talk. Listening to me without interruption will be your gift to me, in return for my hospitality."

Paul nodded. As the Seer began her story, Paul finally figured out what was strange about her English: she used it in a less formal way, with different pronunciation of the vowels and different word formulations, somewhat slangy. It was like it was a living, breathing language for her, not the precise but dead language Paul had learned in school. It was probably more like the English as it was actually spoken back in the days of the American Empire.

My God. She could be telling me the truth.

14

Frisco

Monday, July 12

Alex dreamt that night of a young man with curly brown hair, handsome and confident, staring out at the ocean. He is wearing fancy church clothes. When he sees Alex, he turns and says, "Don't worry. I can save you."

Alex woke with a start. It was another one of those strange dreams, leaving him feeling tingly. This one didn't make any sense to him at all. He didn't recognize the man in the dream, although he seemed vaguely familiar, like someone he may have met a long time ago. Why did he say he was going to save Alex? From what? It was *Jasmine* who needed saving, not Alex. It didn't make any sense. He decided to keep this dream to himself. He got up out of his sleeping sack in the room they had occupied in downtown Frisco.

Alex had been hearing about Frisco his entire life, how big and impressive it was, but being in the city was an entirely different experience. He had no idea any city could be this big. The streets seemed to go on forever, some straight, some winding. And the buildings! They were already closely packed and very tall as they entered the city, with big cisterns on top to collect water, but as they got closer to the downtown, the number of super-tall buildings increased. They dwarfed the Emperor

Hotel in Modesto. Jordan told him that the city was even more impressive back in the Olden Times; most of the tall buildings had fallen in the Great Earthquake of the last century. In one part of the city, the streets were mostly underwater. You could pay a gondolier to take you from place to place. Other parts of the city were on hills, though, and the old roads were still intact.

The size of the city presented a problem, though. They didn't know where to begin looking for Jasmine. The people were friendly, if a little strange. One of the most talkative people they met was a weird-looking man with bug eyes and a brown beard that went down to his belly, riding something Ellie called a "unicycle." He told them he had seen Jasmine just the other day, that she was wearing a crown like a queen, but after a while they realized he was just making stuff up. Or he was crazy, which is what Ellie thought.

They learned that quite a few of the tall buildings were unoccupied, and by the end of the first day, they found one they could sneak into. They camped out on the fifteenth floor, above the other squatters, some of whom looked like they had lived there for years. Every day they would get up, walk through a different part of the city, asking about Chad Benson. Nobody had any answers. Jordan, Ellie, and Alex didn't feel like the people were lying to them about his whereabouts; they just honestly didn't know. They were starting to run out of money and time, if they wanted to meet up with the Clan in Vallejo. Alex had begun to lose hope.

This morning, Ellie suggested they try farther north. After breakfast, they went straight up one of the main thoroughfares and then hired a gondola to take them into a new district. They passed by a strange building from the Olden Times that was tall and pointy, shaped like a white, thin triangle with broad shoulders jutting out. Then the canal turned diagonally to head northwest. The water ended after a block or two, they got out, and Jordan asked the first person they met on the streets if they had ever heard of Chad Benson. They hadn't, but then Alex had a different idea.

"Can you tell us where the fanciest residential area is around here?"

The pedestrian mentioned someplace called Nob Hill, not too far from there, and pointed them in the right direction. It was only six or seven blocks due west, climbing up steep, steep hills, passing old houses painted in vibrant colors. When they reached the top of the hill, Alex led them to one of the tall buildings. They pushed their way through a fancy rotating glass door. At the front desk, they asked if Chad Benson lived there. The attendant—much more kind and helpful than the one back in Modesto—told them he thought Benson lived at the Marquis, up near Grace Cathedral. They followed his directions up another hill to where the big gray church stood, blackened with soot from fires from the last century. There were three ancient apartment buildings still standing in the vicinity.

"I have a hunch she's in this one," said Alex, and led them to a spectacular beige brick building that looked to be sixteen stories tall. It stood on a street corner and had three archways for the entrance. Again, they pushed their way through those heavy, rotating glass doors and into an elegant lobby with white marble on the floor and three chandeliers hanging down from the ceiling, each one flickering with dozens of white candles. There was a wide staircase in front of them at the back of the lobby. To their left was a long, curving wooden desk. A man in a green uniform was sitting behind it, reading a book. They approached him quietly.

"We're looking for a Mr. Chad Benson," said Jordan.

"May I tell him who's calling?" asked the man.

Jordan and Ellie looked at each other excitedly. "Actually, we're looking for Jasmine Taiyo, who's staying with him. Tell her it's her cousins and her brother."

The man nodded and rang and little bell. A boy about Alex's age came out of a back room, dressed in a similar green uniform. The man gave him the message, then the boy nodded and ran to a staircase nearby.

"You may wait in the lobby area," said the man. They politely moved to the overstuffed beige sofas in the middle of the space.

They waited for a long time. Alex began to get fidgety. Then, they heard footsteps on the stairway, and they all stood up. The boy in the uniform ran down the stairs first, darting back behind the desk and into the back room.

And then, there she was.

Jasmine was wearing a dark green dress with sparkling things running down her sleeves. She was also wearing a necklace with some sort of precious jewel, white and glittering. Her hair was combed and pulled back into something silvery to hold it in place. She looked concerned as she entered the lobby, then her face lit up when she saw her family.

Alex ran to her and gave her a hug, and she hugged him back, then she hugged Ellie and Jordan. They all began speaking at once, then laughed, then Alex started again.

"Where have you been? Why didn't you rejoin us?"

"Here, let's sit down," she said, and they did.

"It's been quite a journey," she said, looking mostly at Ellie. "Chad's pretty amazing. I can't believe how much money he has. We have running water up there! And servants! Every day, this woman takes care of me and makes me feel beautiful. There's always enough food to eat. And he buys me things."

"Wait a minute," said Ellie. "Are you telling me you *like* it here?"

"Of course! What's not to like?"

"Um, how about the fact that we've been worried sick about you?"

"I'm sorry. I just didn't know how to get word to you."

Alex could tell that Ellie was getting angry. She said icily, "Well, we've been following your trail for the past two weeks. You haven't been easy to find."

"I'm sorry. You didn't have to do that. I distinctly remember telling Alex to let me go."

"Well, I didn't think you really wanted that," said Alex defiantly.

"I don't either," said Ellie.

"Come on, Ellie! Wouldn't you like to live comfortably for a change?"

"Not if it meant giving up my family. Not if it meant being away from my best friend."

"I think you would change your mind if I could show you our apartment."

"Our apartment? It sounds like you've moved in permanently."

Jasmine blushed and shrugged her shoulders coyly.

"Come on, Jasmine! You should know better! This is a man we're talking about, here! A rich man, to boot. He's found a sexy little plaything to entertain him for a while, then he's going to dump you out on the street when he finds another."

Jasmine stood up, her mouth set. Alex knew that look.

"You don't understand him at all. He's not like that. He's loving, and kind, and he says he's never going to leave me."

"Yeah, right." Ellie was now standing, too, but Jasmine stood several inches taller.

"You know about my abilities, Ellie. I can *read* people. I know what's in their hearts. I also can perceive their past and their future. I can see my future with Chad, and it's amazing."

"Your powers are not foolproof. Have you ever considered that someone else might have powers, too, that you're being manipulated?"

Jasmine's eyes flashed. Alex wondered if they were about to get into a physical fight. Jordan stood up and held out his hands. "I don't want us to fight. Jasmine, why don't you show us your apartment? I think we're all curious about it."

Jasmine looked away. "I can't do that."

"Why not?"

"Chad says he doesn't want me to have any visitors."

"See what I mean?!" shouted Ellie. "He's already controlling you! I can't believe you can't see this."

"Shh!" whispered Jordan. "Let's try to remain calm. Sit down, the both of you."

Jasmine was glaring at Ellie. After a moment or two, she sat down. Ellie followed suit.

Jordan tried a different tack. "Look, Jasmine, everybody's worried about you. Can't you at least just come with us to Vallejo and meet the Clan? I know they all would want to see you and make sure you're okay."

"Yeah," said Ellie under her breath. "Maybe my mom can talk some sense into you."

Jasmine's eyes flashed. "No. I'm not going. My place is here."

Alex's eyes started filling up with tears again, which he hated. "Jasmine, please. Don't stay here. I miss you. I need you."

Jasmine's face softened. She reached over and mussed up his hair, just like she always did. "I actually don't think you do. I mean, look at you, travelling all over the countryside with these lunatics we call our cousins. Pretty impressive, little man."

Ellie was not about to be diverted. "I can't believe you, Jasmine. I can't believe you'd abandon us so easily. Abandon *me.*"

"Don't be so overdramatic. I mean, maybe you're right. Maybe he'll get tired of me. I don't know. Nobody knows. But think about this: I have a hold on him, and I can influence him. He's on his way up. He doesn't quite see it yet, but I can. He's going to be a powerful person in this region. Once he rises to power, I will be in a position to help our people—far more than by doing those sexy dances that you detest, Alex!"

"How can you trust him?" asked Ellie, plaintively.

"I just can. I know it. Anyway, this isn't goodbye forever, I promise."

She stood up, reached into a little purse she had tucked into her sleeve, and pulled out the golden coin like the one that Chad Benson had given her on that first night. "Here, take this, give it to Charles. Tell him there's one less mouth to feed. Tell everyone I love them, and that I'm okay."

She handed the coin to Jordan, then turned and ran up the stairs just as she started to cry. The three of them stared after her, stunned. Ellie put her hands to her mouth and started to cry herself. Jordan put his arm around her.

"Let's go. We're done here." He led them out of the lobby, slowly.

Alex felt a weird sort of numbness come over him. He couldn't quite comprehend what had just happened. He couldn't believe Jasmine would *choose* to stay with this man, whom she barely knew, instead of coming home with them. When he started to think about it, his mind went blank, like it was too much to handle. He let Jordan lead them back to their place, where they silently packed up their things, carried them downstairs, mounted their horses, and headed north. By unspoken agreement, they were heading up to Vallejo where they knew the Clan was currently docked.

Alex hardly registered what was happening. He was vaguely aware of Ellie crying softly as they rode through the old part of the city, but then his mind would go blank again. He felt like the world had been drained of color and life.

Nobody said anything. After about an hour, they reached the northern edge of the city. There were some tall reddish metal towers jutting out of the water here, the remnants of an old bridge long since fallen into the bay. The towers had X-like shapes going all the way up. A newer bridge made use of these towers plus some newer wooden pilings, running along the top of one of the cross shapes in the old bridge. Unless they wanted to wait for a ferry, they would have to cross this bridge to get to Vallejo. To the left, Alex could see the bay opening to the Pacific Ocean, so vast, it seemed to go on forever, all the way to the horizon. The Inland Sea seemed puny by comparison.

The bridge took them a long time to cross. There were some places where the wooden planks had rotted through, leaving a gap. In the middle of the bridge, the wind seemed to pick up energy from the ocean, making the roadway sway. It was already slick with spray from the ocean. Alex's little pony made nervous whinnying sounds.

They were nearly across the bridge. Alex could see a group of men on horses and a wagon on the other side, waiting politely for them to finish crossing before they began. Two of the men were wearing fancy red robes. The wind caused the waves to crest, salt-water spray stinging Alex's eyes. And then, a huge gust of wind swung them away from the ocean. Betsy lost her footing, stumbling and staggering to the right. Alex gripped the bridle and tried to bring her under control, but she kept sliding. To his horror, she banged into the side rail and knocked him off the saddle and over the side of the bridge. He was falling, his arms flailing helplessly. Then he hit the water with an impact that knocked the wind out of him. He sunk down into the bitterly cold water.

Then everything went black.

15

The Seer's Tale

I was born in 2032 in Palo Alto. My father was a tech billionaire, which probably means nothing to you. It hardly means anything to me, honestly. I will give you the short explanation, though. In those days, money wasn't a tangible thing like it is today, in the form of coins. It was all electronic, which means, essentially, that we all had to have faith that our invisible transactions were real. Rich people would buy and sell various kinds of virtual properties, vaguely representing something in the "real" world, but mostly just vehicles for them to make more money. If the prices went up, you got richer; if they went down, you felt poorer, even though none of this made much of a difference in the physical world. My father, using some very complicated mathematics and very sophisticated computers (don't ask), created a new way to predict these rises and falls very accurately. People who subscribed to his service got very rich. Therefore, he got very rich, very quickly. After several years, the government decided, belatedly, that what he was doing wasn't entirely kosher, so they made new laws that forbade it. It wasn't illegal while he was doing it, so he never got into trouble. He retired at the age of thirty and lived extravagantly for the rest of his life.

He and my mom had three kids, me and my twin sisters. He decided we would be named after his favorite elements, so I was called Carbon and my sisters were Hydrogen and Nitrogen, a typical move for him. We all hated the names. Nitrogen asked everyone to just call her "Jenny." Hydrogen eventually changed her name to Heidi Jones, trying to be as anonymous as possible. As for me, I appreciated the fact that "Carbon" was gender-neutral, but it did cause all sorts of logistical problems down the road.

We were born into this very particular culture, south of San Francisco, a place called Silicon Valley at that time. All my parents' friends were tech billionaires, too. I told you already about the gene editing that I underwent when I was in utero. When I was an angry teenager and asked my dad about this, he said that he was only trying to keep up with the other tech billionaires. He knew that their kids were all getting this treatment, too. At first, this treatment was just about switching off certain genes so that your kid wouldn't get breast cancer down the road, or Alzheimer's, or Parkinson's, or Sickle-Cell Anemia. Yet, it quickly started to become what you might call boutique gene editing. Kids who are ugly are shown to be at a disadvantage and live less healthy lives. Wouldn't you want your child to be healthy? And how about brains? Again, this isn't about vanity, they argued; it's about insuring the best possible future for your child. My parents felt like they couldn't not agree to this, if all their friends were doing it. They said, aren't you glad you've got a body that regenerates, and that you were given especially good looks and good brains? And honestly, at that time, I thought I was the ugliest and the stupidest person in the world, so I didn't believe it had worked on me.

Regarding our childhood, here's where things start to get ironic, if they hadn't already. We grew up in the technological capital of the world, but our parents didn't allow us to use any of it. They knew that the technology they had designed was actually not good for children. You set them up with a device that they fall in love with and that seems to adore them right back. You make it fine-tuned to their particular wants and desires, so that they become inseparable. Then, you've got an addict for life, begging you for an upgrade, another add-on, another hit. Yes, these guys were playing the long game.

Instead of doing some soul-searching and finding some other line of work, possibly earning them only millions instead of billions, they thought that the best solution for their designer children was to cart us off to a boarding school up in the redwoods and absolutely forbid us from using any technology. And so, that's how we came to be here: as a refuge from the very world our parents were helping to create. Later, though, we would make it into something very different, as you've already seen.

There were about twenty-five of us living here. Our parents founded the school, hired the best instructors in the world, who taught us not only the traditional subjects but also gave us special training in the natural world, which would later prove invaluable. We loved it. We thrived. I used to think that all children should have that kind of experience. It was only later that I came to realize how sheltered I had been. At the time, I was blissfully unaware of the chaos going on in the world outside.

So, I was living in this boarding school in these beautiful redwoods with my fellow gifted children. We had all be given the same gene treatment, so we were all bright, had generally agreeable personalities, and all had the potential to escape the scourge of old age and death. We talked about it, of course, but found it hard to believe. The correct term for us was amortal, not immortal—we could still be killed by accident or a virus or by some other means, as we would eventually learn, sadly. Still, we lived charmed lives, happily oblivious to the world around us. Being the children of the elite, with ample wealth, and genetically programmed to excel in this world, we could go to any college we chose. I went to a small liberal arts college in the Midwest, probably not too far from where you're from. I majored in English, then followed this by graduate school in library science.

After school, I returned home to the Bay Area. My parents had gotten divorced by this time, and I sensed that my mother needed me. I got a job in one of the branches of the public library in San Francisco—the city they call Frisco now—and lived with her in the city. I never would have been able to afford this had I been reliant on the income for my livelihood. They couldn't pay me anything close to a living wage. I wouldn't have been able to live if it weren't for the trust fund my father had set up for me.

It was now the 2050s, and the world around us was beginning to fall apart. As income inequality and the climate crisis grew, more and more people took to the streets and to a life of crime. My mom and I had to move several times to safer neighborhoods, but each time we moved, the criminals eventually caught up with us. Nowhere in the city was safe.

During this period, some of my former boarding school class-mates had bought up hundreds of acres of forest land near where we had spent our happy childhoods. One of my best friends from our boarding school days invited me to join the commune they had created there. It frankly sounded too weird to me, and I turned them down. I didn't think it was right for us privileged types to just turn our backs on the world. We needed to fight to make the country better.

Then things got even worse. It was the election of 2056 that really started it, at least for me. There were three authoritarian Presidents in the twenty-first century, each one worse than the last. Each one took more power, took away the power of anybody to oppose them, committed more crimes, and got away with more. The first one occurred before I was born. He was considered an aberration, an embarrassment, so obscene and vulgar. He was utterly incompetent, so the country eventually sort of laughed him off after we got rid of him. After this, we were able to get back on track for many years. Nobody believed we would ever let ourselves do this again. But we did. People like to fall in love with charismatic charlatans. The truly thoughtful leaders tend to not be that charismatic. People even know that the charismatic figure is a fake, but they don't care. It's built into our DNA to follow them. Part of the reason is also that these characters are a godsend for the media. They make news, every day, cause outrage and consternation. They love attention, and the media love to amplify it, a kind of demented feedback loop.

The second authoritarian President was elected in 2056, right when I was a young person trying to make my way in the world. This one was a lot smarter than the first, cannier and more brutal. I joined the protests against him, fought hard, and to my utter devastation and disbelief, he was re-elected in 2060. He tried to serve a third term, but fortunately, we still had those guard-rails in place. He was replaced, and everyone heaved a sigh of relief. But not me. I knew it could happen a third time, and I didn't want to be around when it did. And sure enough, there would eventually be a third, and this one pushed us over the line into permanent dictatorship. People thought it could never happen in America, but it did.

I told my friends in the Redwoods I had changed my mind.

When I told my parents that I had decided to join the Redwood commune, my father was adamantly opposed. He thought it sounded like a cult. "It's not a cult, Daddy," I told him. "I can leave and visit you any time. It's just that I find the outside world abrasive. Why don't you visit me? Other parents do." He said maybe he would, but I knew he wouldn't. A few years later, he died on a skiing vacation with his fourth wife. His remains are in a cryotube underground, waiting to be regenerated when the time is right, counting on a future that never came about.

As for my mom, I distinctly remember her saying to me, "You can be whatever you want to be. As for me, I'm going to be a drunk."

So, I quit my job and moved north. I used my trust fund to help the commune purchase a lot more land. This gave me a kind of high status in the group, which made me uncomfortable. Still, I immediately felt at home. It's beautiful here, surprisingly isolated, and we could live "off the grid," as we said in those days—almost completely self-reliant. We could also live in a way that harmonized with nature, rather than always exploiting it. We thought, we can wait out this crazy time and come back when America finds its footing again. We've got time.

Of course, it never did.

Part of the problem was purely demographic, although we didn't actually see this at the time. For some time now, young people had been turning away from parenting. The replacement rate for any population is just over two kids per woman. It had already fallen below this line well before I was born. For a while, the country filled up the gaps with immigration. But as the economy faltered, immigrants were less welcome. Sometime here, the country's population slowly started to shrink. Then the fall picked up speed. Pretty soon, the population was in rapid free-fall. And this had huge economic consequences. Fewer babies meant fewer workers and consumers, which meant lower profits, which meant fewer jobs, and then fewer people willing or able to have children, and so on. The economy spiraled down.

When the government finally woke up to what was happening, they tried to reverse the trend. The bullied and cajoled women to have babies again. They outlawed abortions, made birth control harder to obtain. They tried to make it more attractive with financial incentives. But they couldn't do enough to make it worthwhile. It was too little, too late.

And now, I see it very differently—a conscious decision by the human species to control its own reproduction that was so visibly harming the planet. I'll come back to that later.

With all this, you may be surprised to learn that I actually did have a child. But I did, not long after moving to the Redwoods. A daughter. She was my best friend. I was forty when I had her, very much in love with a man in the commune, someone who did not have the gene editing I had had. At this point, I didn't really believe I was going to live this long. Obviously, I did. I outlived my husband, of course, then I outlived my daughter, even though she herself lived longer than normal, perhaps due to my genes. I outlived my grandchildren, too. My great-grandchildren both opted to leave the commune and I lost track of them. Occasionally some stranger comes by, claiming to be my great-great-great-whatever, and I let her stare at me for a day. Very awkward for both of us.

You're probably wondering why I let myself fall in love, given this awful world and the possibility that I might live so long past my partner. As I said before, at that time, I didn't really believe I was amortal. A better way of phrasing it was, I just couldn't comprehend it. But love! You can feel when love is true. It may falter, it may fade, but it can still be true while the flame is alit. It can happen at any time of life. My first real love came in my thirties as I said, and I fell head over heels. I thought we would grow old together. I knew that I would probably outlive him, because he was a man, and people who were born with two X chromosomes somehow almost always outlived those with an X and a Y. But then, I saw him start to fade, while I didn't, and the reality sunk in. After he passed, I promised myself I would never let myself fall in love again. It was too much sorrow to bear. And I thought there could never be another soulmate. Yet I did fall in love again, when I was in my hundreds. I knew I would outlive her, of course, but it somehow didn't matter, to either of us. Then it happened to me again, twice in my two-hundreds, and once again in my three-hundreds. And I cannot honestly tell you which I've loved the best. This has been one of the biggest surprises of living so long.

This small group of us, now about fifty, was living in isolation in the redwoods. At first, we felt pretty smug. Let the world go to hell, we said. We have each other. And that sort of worked. But as things got worse out there, we started seeing more refugees coming through. Some were fleeing the violence, some were running from the latest pandemic, others were afraid of the police, who had new powers in the latest regime. We helped those we could, but it strained our capacity. We had to start turning people away. And some of them surely died because of this, which made us feel terribly guilty. Slowly, the numbers of refugees started to fall, and after fifty years or so, there were no more. It was kind of haunting.

By the end of the twenty-first century, the era of fossil fuels was essentially over. It was too expensive to extract them from the ground, and the damage to the ecosystem was undeniable. As the population began to fall, with less money flowing through the system, all kinds of infrastructure began to break down, which inhibited travel. When the electricity grid collapsed around 2150, there was very little communication between the far-flung communities. We could feel the outside world slipping away. And that's the way it's been ever since then.

What is it like, living as long as I do? You go through several phases. At first, it's not that different. You don't believe it's really going to happen. Or you believe that something will come along and do you in, as does, in fact, happen. There are a lot of opportunities for accidents and stupidity. A human life is a fragile thing. Thus, you just kind of ignore it. The second phase is a growing acceptance of this reality and a kind of excitement. It comes about when you approach and then pass your hundredth birthday. You think, I may have cheated death! I can do anything I want with these years! I can learn any language, any musical instrument, literally travel the world on foot…

The third phase is depression. It usually happens when your youngest child dies, but it happens to those who don't have kids, too, sometime after you pass the far end of the human lifespan, in your early to mid-100s. This is very real and very debilitating. Half of my cohort took their own lives at this time. The problem is that there's no human story that can help us to understand this kind of life—and we rely on stories to explain ourselves to ourselves. Of course, there are myths and legends, people like Methuselah, but nothing truly believable. What are you supposed to do with this incredible privilege? How do you make a meaningful life? After you've done a few of the items on your bucket list, you realize that you don't really have that big of a bucket after all.

Then, the fourth phase slowly dawns, where you realize that there actually are new things to learn, new ways to observe, new knowledge to unlock. You grow and change. You gain a whole new perspective on the human experience, as though you are floating above it. You become grateful for this opportunity, curious to find out what you can do with it, what the boundaries really are of human potential. You have time to slow down, attempt to learn the language of the squirrels and the trees, the rhythms of the seasons, what the earth is trying to say to us.

The fifth phase will be when I die. I used to be scared of death, but not anymore. I've learned enough to realize that death isn't exactly what we think it is.

As far as I know, I'm the last of the amortals now, but there are a few I've lost track of over the years, people who have just drifted away, including both of my sisters. I miss them. I assume they've all died, one way or another, but I don't know for sure.

What have I learned in this fourth phase I'm currently in? I will try to explain it to you, but it may be hard for you to understand. It started when I began to think less about myself and more about the world around me. When I was in my two-hundreds, I noticed that I was more in synch with these beautiful, ancient trees, than with your average human. My lifespan was more like theirs. I noticed that the young people spoke differently and found my ways to be strange and archaic. I began to think about the way trees communicate, reading what I could find about them, which wasn't much. I learned that trees are not really individuals, as we think of them, but are more a part of a larger entity that you would call *forest*. I mean, they are individuals, too, of course, but there's this other level of existence that's just as real. We just have trouble seeing it. And they do communicate with each other, just in ways we can't understand, through the release of bio aerosols, the underground mycorrhizal network, probably through other mechanisms, too.

I could tell that the birds and chipmunks and squirrels were talking to each other, too, but I couldn't understand them. Oh, my weak, weak senses! The longer I lived, the more I realized how limited they are in scope! We take such pride in our vision, but we can only perceive a fraction of the electromagnetic spectrum. If only I could see infrared, like some rodent cousins! If only I could hear with the range of a cat or pick up information in odors like a dog. We are given a narrow bandwidth for our window of perception. How much are we really able to grasp? How much is it just our brains filling in information, based on what we expect? It's the height of arrogance to think we really understand anything, given our limitations.

I started to meditate and learned how to heighten my senses and disrupt my normal mode of perceiving the world. It's not easy, but when you have time on your hands, you can get better, albeit slowly. I began to see more clearly that we are much more like trees than we think. We have a fundamental bias in our species, that the individual is paramount. Some other species are like that, but most are not. When you take on a species perspective, you begin to see through the veneer of individual expression, as powerful as that may be in a particular person. If you step on an ant, that individual dies, and perhaps feels some pain, but it's mostly just a cog in an ant colony. The colony has an agency of its own, its own goals. And the entire species of ant has its own agenda as well. The same is true of humans.

In that way, there is really no life, no death, for an individual—or it matters less than we think. We are all embedded in the river of life, roaring across the landscape like an angry god. We are Sapiens, an entity wholly apart from what we think of as being a human. We are ants in a colony, bees in a hive, a flock of birds, turning at once in the sky. We are so much more influenced by other humans than we recognize. We are a part of that Sapiens River, a little molecule, and without the molecules, there would be no river, but we are an incredibly small part of it. All this is brutally simple but impossible to fully comprehend if you only have one lifetime. For me, I feel like I'm a canoeist in the rapids of our species, exhilarated by the meta-human ride.

But there's more. I now see humans in five dimensions. There are the three you think about, amounting to the physical space you occupy. This is where most people think being human begins and ends, but of course it doesn't. The fourth dimension is time. While you are aware of time as a component of your existence, you tend to not actually see it, like a fish cannot perceive water. In a way, I've been freed from the constraints of time, and so I can see it more clearly. You are in a life-stream, flowing through your physical dimensions plus time. This is important. It took me until I was in my mid-one-hundreds to really be able to understand this.

The fifth dimension took me another hundred years to grasp. And that is this: we are also in a web of life, cascading out. We are members of a family, a tribe, a region, a race, and so forth. We are also all members of the human species, of primates, of all life on Earth, of all matter and energy on Earth, and then, ultimately a part of the life-stream of the entire Universe. These different layers exert various kinds of influence on you as an individual, most of which you cannot perceive. I now look at my fellow humans as hopelessly blinkered, living their lives thinking they understand so much more than they do, even about themselves and their own motivations.

That's why to answer your question, "Why did America fall?" it helps to look at the situation from the species' perspective. As a species, we had been very successful. Too successful. We were burning up the resources of the planet, and our very survival was at stake. Sapiens made the brutal but rational decision to prune itself. Is it an accident that women all over the world stopped having babies at almost exactly the same time? This is an example of the collective unconscious at work. It's taken all this time, but I think we're finally getting through most of the damage we've done to the planet. I've noticed the weather is less extreme, and I hear that the glaciers are growing again, finally. The air smells cleaner. Sapiens was right to rein it its reproduction; by doing so, we've managed to survive as a species. It really is a miracle—or else you could say that it was a broader intelligence at work.

Meanwhile, I'm seeing signs that the human genome is changing. You've probably met some of our elves. Back when I was young, some rich people used to use genetic engineering to transform themselves into fantasy species—humans with extra-keen hearing, super-fast running abilities, special gifts of intuition, even some with tails. But that was over by the end of the twenty-first century. The elves you've seen have all come about the natural way—there was some sort of genetic modification that was passed down, all those generations later. And I've encountered some people with uncanny mental abilities, abilities that would have been considered witchcraft in an earlier age. It's like Sapiens said, "Hey! I like that trait! Let's keep this around, try mixing it with some others, see if we can amplify it, then see if it conveys any evolutionary advantage." Never mind that we had already won the genetic lottery; Sapiens is always looking out for more.

In the 2200s, some of these "mutant" humans started trickling into our little community. I had thought that we were the only people who received these genetic modifications at birth. But of course, we weren't. There were rich people in New York, Los Angeles, Chicago, London, Paris, Stockholm, Berlin, Buenos Aires, Rio de Janeiro, Jakarta, Sydney, Tokyo, Shanghai, who were all doing the same thing. And these are just the ones we found out about. We learned later that many of these experiments backfired, or the genetically modified people were killed in the mayhem of the late 21st century. But enough lived, and enough bred with other modified humans, that the modified genes started drifting through the gene pool. Strange new children were born, some of them grotesquely transfigured, some of them with incomprehensible new powers. I think our genetic engineering experiments have only begun to manifest themselves in our species.

These young people found living around those without these enhancements very difficult—they referred to them as 'Normies,'—and found themselves isolated. Word seemed to get out that we were a community particularly friendly to the genetically diverse, and as they arrived, we found we couldn't say no to them. And as you saw, in order to protect ourselves, we became very cautious with letting Normies just waltz in and get word out about us. Everyone you see here is somehow touched by genetic modifications—either the descendants of our first group, or of the other genetically modified people who flocked to us from around the country.

Anyway, I'm getting sidetracked. Back to your question: Why did America fall? Because "America" was no longer serving the needs of the species and life itself. It had become toxic. When you live as long as I have, you start to realize that this sentimental attachment to this thing called a "country" is really just an arbitrary idea, concocted by humans to organize themselves. We have, in essence, decided that a new mode of organization is needed…

16

The Redwood Forest
Monday, July 12

Paul awoke inside the Seer's treehouse. He didn't remember falling asleep. He was still in a seated position on the sofa where they had been talking the night before. He looked around and found the Seer in the far corner, working at a spinning wheel and humming quietly to herself. Without taking her one eye off her work, she seemed to know that he was stirring.

"Sleep well?"

Paul blinked a few times, then sat up. "I hope I wasn't rude to you by falling asleep on your story."

The Seer smiled to herself. "Not at all. I never take offense at sleeping. I just don't do as much of it as I used to."

Paul rubbed his eyes with both hands, then used his fingers to comb his hair. "I wanted to thank you for your story last night. I learned a lot."

"Thank you for listening."

Paul hesitated, wanting to ask more of her, but not wanting to push it too far. "Can I ask you one more thing?"

"Sure."

"What happens next? To America, I mean."

The Seer was feeding some flax into her wheel, which whirred smoothly and made a soft *click-CLICK, click-CLICK* sound. She took a few moments to consider his question. "Well, America is no more. It's never coming back, not like it was. But something new can be reborn. Something better. Maybe you can play a part in this."

Paul didn't know how to respond to that. He listened to the hypnotic sound of the spinning wheel for a while.

"How so?"

"Oh, I wouldn't want to tell you what to do. That's not my place. But I can see that you have a strong life force within you."

"What do you mean by that?"

"Do you remember what I talked about last night? How we're all like molecules in the river of humanity? A better way of thinking of it is that the river is massive, made up of millions of little rivulets. Each one represents a person. Some of these rivulets are soft and yielding and dissipate into the Earth without leaving much of a trace. Others are stronger, and can move boulders, especially when they gather other rivulets to help them. Neither way is better, by the way, just different."

"And you see this in me?"

"I do. It's just not fully developed yet. You remind me a little of Jack Benson in that way."

"Wait a minute! You actually *met* Jack Benson?"

"Oh, sure. He was traveling here, not long after he came to power—it must have been around 2201 or 2202—and he had heard about me and wanted to meet me. He sat right there where you are, and we had a nice little chat."

"My god. What was he like?"

"In some ways, just a normal man, but in some ways, absolutely not. He radiated confidence and control. He had a magnetic pull on other people. When he walked into a place, everybody could feel that lifeforce, and would automatically turn their attention to him. It didn't matter if they agreed with him or liked him: they paid attention to him. They couldn't help it.

"That kind of charisma—it's a powerful thing. And it's utterly neutral. You can decide what you're going to do with it. You can use it to stroke your ego and get attention, or you can use it to serve your people and the human species as a whole—ideally, the entire planet. In other words, it's as much a curse as it is a blessing. Do you understand?"

"I think I do."

"Good. Now, you'd better get ready to go. I don't think your Elder wants to linger with us pagans."

Paul nodded and stood up, stretched. He didn't know what to say to the Seer, so he just said "thank you" again. She nodded, still not looking at him.

He stepped out onto her deck. The morning light from the east was filtering in, to his left, making the dew on the redwood needles glisten magically. The air smelled earthy and fresh. He could see people down below, coming and going, including Elder Eastman. He was already wearing his official red robes of the order, which Paul found a little pathetic, honestly. Yes, they would arrive in Frisco today, but would anybody really be noticing?

He walked down the winding staircase, somehow less frightening in the morning light, and walked up to his group. Eastman looked aggrieved at Paul as he approached. *He probably thinks I slept with one of the natives last night. If only he knew what I was really doing!*

"Change your clothes," said Eastman brusquely. "We need to be presentable today."

"My robes are in my trunk, in the wagon," said Paul. "I'll change later." *And how is it that you have your clothes with you?*

Eastman stared at him for a moment blankly, perhaps surprised at Paul's defiant tone, then turned around without a word to discuss their departure with Echleph. After a few words with him, Eastman approached Celestian. "We are ready to leave," he said to her abruptly.

"Very well," she replied in her heavily accented English. "Our guides are ready to lead you out."

"I'm not going," said Archer.

The group turned at once to stare at him. He was standing off to the side, holding hands with a young elvish woman from the group.

"What?!" cried Eastman.

"Me and Thorne, we're in love. I'm staying with her."

"You're in love?" shouted Turge. "You don't even speak the same language! How can you be in love?"

"Sometimes, you just don't need words to know," said Archer piously.

"This is absolutely out of the question," said Eastman. "You signed a contract to get us to Frisco. We're not there yet. If you bow out now, you will forfeit your pay."

Archer shrugged blithely. "Money don't matter here."

"Have you checked with anybody besides Thorne about this?" asked Echleph. He turned to the mayor and spoke to her in their language. She then addressed Thorne, who smiled when she answered.

"Yes, it seems that your colleague is reading the situation correctly," said the mayor.

"And is it all right with you, that he stays?" Echleph asked Celestian. "You don't seem all that keen on outsiders here."

"We can make an exception when love is involved."

Turge was starting to get red in the face. "Don't be ridiculous, man! You can't stay here. You got a life back home. You got friends, you got family, you got a career…"

"Doing what? Leading around a bunch of spoiled church men across the wilderness? Or are you talking about being a soldier in their stupid wars, and getting shot up for no good reason?"

Eastman put up a hand. "We don't have time for this. If this soldier intends to throw his life away, so be it. I wash my hands of him. Let's get out of here."

Turge clenched and unclenched his fists several times. Paul thought he might be able to punch a hole right through one of the giant trees. Eventually, he calmed himself down, with effort. As for Paul, he never actually liked Archer much, but he found himself sad at the breakup of their squad. He walked over to him and held out his hand. Archer hesitated, surprised, then shook it.

"Thank you for your guidance on this trip, and all the excellent game you brought down for us," said Paul sincerely.

"You're welcome," Archer mumbled, then quickly dropped the handshake so he could resume holding hands with Thorne.

The four remaining members walked to the edge of the clearing where a path led into the woods (Paul thought it was south, but he still wasn't entirely sure). Four young members of the commune, all dressed alike, stepped forward with eye-masks in their hands. Before they put them on, the villagers gathered around them and started to sing.

It was some of the strangest music Paul had ever heard. It was in a weird scale or mode, and he couldn't understand the words. It seemed to be a hymn of farewell, with a touch of melancholy in it. Frankly, Paul found it a little embarrassing. They had only been there less than twenty-four hours. It seemed like overkill to him.

At the end of it, the Seer stepped out of the group. Paul hadn't noticed her coming down from her treehouse. "May your journey take you where you need to go," she said to all of them, but Paul felt like it was especially addressed to him.

Then, the blindfolds were put on. Paul saw Eastman argue about taking off his glasses, then concede and slip them into one of the many hidden pockets in the robe. Then Paul's mask was slipped on, and he truly couldn't see anything. He felt a soft touch on his arm, and a young woman's voice said, "This way, please." He moved forward.

It was a strange experience. He had to completely trust this person, someone he hadn't met and hadn't even seen, really. Yet she guided him deftly. "Step over a little log here," she said. "Get ready to duck your head." They turned left, then right, then left again. Paul began to wonder if they were deliberately taking them in circles to disorient them, so that they couldn't find their way back. He felt a tinge of regret about not being able to return, even though he knew it was implausible that he could ever find the time to do so.

As they went on, Paul began to become more acutely aware of his other senses. He heard strange bird calls, high up in the trees, and the sound of big water drops hitting the earth. There was a quick rustling sound in the ferns at some point. He began to be aware of the position of his travel companions, Turge breathing heavily behind him, Eastman up front, Echleph probably walking noiselessly in between. The smells shifted, at one point becoming like perfume, at another, distinctly smelling of saltwater. He could even hear, faintly, the sounds of the breakers of the Pacific Ocean some distance away.

And then he felt, rather than heard, when they exited the forest, the sun beating down on his head. His guide squeezed his arm and said, "We're here."

Paul pulled off his mask gratefully and saw his guide for the first time—nothing more than a teenager, really, small and elfin. "Thank you," he said.

There, waiting for them, was the wagon and all their horses—even Archer's, though the rider was left behind. "Check to see that nothing is stolen," Eastman whispered to Turge, but not so softly that Paul and their guides couldn't hear.

"We will leave you here," said one of the guides. "It's not far to the bridge—less than ten miles. Just follow this road. Safe journeys to you all." And without a backward glance, they all melted into the forest.

Paul reluctantly changed into his formal robe before they started the final leg of their long journey. Turge and Echleph tied Archer's horse to the back of the wagon, not wanting to misbalance the team with three horses. Paul almost volunteered to ride it, but that was hard to do in these robes, so he sat in the wagon with Eastman. He would have sat up front with Turge, but the big man was in a dark mood, brooding over the loss of his friend.

Paul found himself brooding as well. He was finding it hard to process the story the Seer told him. He didn't understand everything she was telling him. One thing was for sure: her cosmology was unlike anything he'd heard of before. If it's true that she was over four hundred years old—he was still reluctant to believe this, for some reason—she sure didn't arrive at the Church's way of thinking about the world in all that time. Quite the contrary. And yet she had also challenged him on his hidden atheism in a way that made him think that his range of understanding of religion was very narrow indeed.

And what of her hint that he might have some nascent greatness in him? He had to admit that this appealed to his vanity. He also took her warning very seriously, however. As much as he liked the idea of playing a role on the world's stage, a part of him understood Archer's desire to retreat from it—although Bryce's monastery held more appeal than living in a remote forest, as beautiful as it was.

They rode down a hill, a winding road, nice and wide. It was sunny and warm. They passed through a tunnel of some length, perfectly round, probably one of the artifacts of the Empire that had survived the great earthquake, somehow. This made him think about what the Seer said about the past. It was so much less glamorous than Paul had thought. All through his childhood, the history of the Empire had called to him, a glorious time of wealth and glory. He felt like this journey had begun to disillusion him about America. He didn't like it.

Then, they came around a hill and could see the vast bay in front of them, and Frisco, off in the distance. Far, far away, just a little pin prick, Paul could see the White Pyramid rising above the rest of the buildings in the city. Even from this distance, Frisco looked enormous, at least as big as Benson City. Paul felt a little flutter of excitement.

They came to the edge of the land. There were enormous concrete pilings towering over them, once supporting a massive bridge that spanned the bay. Now, there was nothing but a rather cheaply made wooden bridge, just wide enough for two carriages to pass each other, built on wooden pilings and the metal and concrete remnants of the old bridge. Just as they moved closer to the start of the bridge, Paul could feel the wind pick up, as though it was being funneled through the straights that led into the bay. He felt uneasy about crossing the choppy waters on this little bridge.

"Hold up," said Echleph. "Let's wait for this other party to cross."

Paul could see three riders on horseback coming toward them, maybe a man and a woman and their son. They looked like peasants, with dark skin and homespun clothing. They seemed to be having trouble with the movement of the bridge. Paul thought, *Maybe I'd better walk across rather than ride. It looks unstable out there.* He hopped out of the wagon. A gust of wind blew into his face.

Then, just as they were nearly across, it looked like the wind just picked the boy up and dumped him over the side of the wooden railing, right into the water.

Time seemed to slow down to a crawl. He could see the boy's parents, or whoever they were, notice the boy's fall, but they couldn't control their horses. Paul turned to look at his companions, but they all seemed to be staring at this horrible scene, dumbfounded. Paul turned back to look for the boy but didn't see him. The waves were choppy here, so maybe he just couldn't see him swimming. After a moment, the waves subsided, and it was clear that the boy had definitely not come up to the surface.

Paul realized it was up to him, if it wasn't already too late. He ran the twenty feet or so remaining, dove headfirst into the water and was shocked by the cold. Here it was, mid-summer, and this felt like Lake Michigan in the winter! Paul's second thought was, *Why didn't I take off this stupid robe?* It was like trying to swim with lead weights on his legs.

He had a pretty good sense of where the boy had fallen in, near one of the wooden pilings not far from the shore. He did the crawl stroke over to that spot, took a huge breath, then dove down. It was deeper than he expected it to be. The water pressure began to make his ears ache. The cold was quickly seeping in. He had to go deeper, though. Finally, he could see the bottom of the bay, although the water was murky. It was probably ten or twelve feet to the bottom.

After looking for a moment, he spotted the boy, lying on the seabed near some rocks. Paul's first thought was, *He looks dead.* Still, he had to try. He put his hands under the boy's arms, then used the rock to propel himself upward. His lungs were now bursting, desperate to take a breath, while his robe wanted to pull him down to the bottom of the bay. He fought as hard as he could against it, then at last broke the surface. He took a huge breath.

The boy was dead weight in his arms. It was hard to swim with him to the shore, with the waves jostling them. As they got nearer to the shore, Paul cut his leg on some sharp object underneath, maybe a piece of metal. It went right through his thick, water-logged robe. The saltwater of the ocean stung it. *That's going to hurt,* he thought lamely, even as he struggled to get the boy up and out of the water. He stumbled as he tried to find his footing.

Turge and Echleph were waiting for him, halfway into the water, and they got the boy out of his arms as soon as they could. Together, they got up to a grassy area. Paul fell to his knees on the sand, gasping for breath. After a moment or two, he had recovered enough to clamber up the sandy hill to where Echleph was trying to revive the boy. He was holding the boy's nose, breathing into his mouth, then pumping his chest rather roughly. Paul had never seen somebody do that before. Just as Paul arrived and knelt next to him, the boy seemed to vomit up a gallon of water. He coughed, spluttered, and then more water came out. The three men all laughed with relief. Turge thumped Echleph on the back.

The boy looked up at Paul. He had vivid blue eyes, very strange against his brown skin. Staring at Paul, he said, in crystal-clear English, "Are you the Supreme Elder?"

This made the three of them laugh even harder. "No, I'm just a regular churchman," said Paul, then realized how untrue those words sounded to him.

The boy started to tremble, and Turge ran to the wagon to bring him a blanket. He brought one for Paul as well. Now that the adrenaline was wearing off, Paul was starting to feel the chill. He stood up shakily and peeled off his water-logged robe angrily. *This thing almost killed me!* he thought. He pulled the blanket around his shoulders and tried to stop trembling.

Just then, the boy's family members arrived, both weeping. They hugged the boy, each in turn, and expressed their gratitude to all of them, shaking hands one by one. Paul couldn't understand what they were saying, exactly, even though Californian was probably closer to English than

Merican was. Paul didn't need a translation, though; he could tell how grateful they were. They had seen everything. The young woman helped the boy to his feet, then gave Paul a long hug.

Finally, the moment was over. With a final expression of thanks and a deep bow, they led the boy toward the place where they had left their horses. They had gone only a few feet when the boy stopped, turned around, and held out his hand to Paul.

"My name is Alex," he said.

Paul walked up and took his hand. There was a kind of electric charge between them that Paul couldn't quite explain. He didn't want to let go of his hand. There was something about this kid, something uncanny.

"Nice to meet you, Alex. My name is Paul."

17

Here, There, and Everywhere

Everything was black.

And then, Alex could see a flickering white light in the middle of the blackness, growing slowly but steadily. He thought it might hurt his eyes. He tried to look away, but everywhere he looked, the light was there. It gradually filled the space in front of him. Even though it grew, he found it actually didn't hurt his eyes. It felt warm, like sunlight.

Where am I?

He looked down and saw his own body curled up at the bottom of the bay, as though he were floating in the water above himself. It should have been scary, but for some reason, it wasn't. He found he could move around just by thinking of it. He floated out of the water. He saw Jordan and Ellie on the bridge, looking surprised and horrified at Alex's fall. Then he looked over at the group of men on the other side of the bridge. Two of the men wore fancy red robes. One of them was already running toward the water, but was frozen in place, like a figure in a drawing. Alex was somehow within time and floating outside of it.

That man is going to try to save me, he thought.

He could float higher if he wanted to, up into the sky, and look at Frisco like he was a bird. He wanted to explore this new ability, but something told him he had to come down to Earth. He came down on a grassy hill not too far from the bridge. And there, sitting on a park bench, was Grandma Meta. He ran to her, or flew, rather, and she gave him a hug.

Grandma! I can't believe you're here. How can that be?

—Don't you understand, Alex?

I don't know...

—Come, sit down. We need to have a little chat.

She patted the bench next to her and he snuggled up until their hips were touching, just like they always did. He felt her body at first, and then he felt nothing, like she was a wisp of smoke.

—You've been having quite an adventure, haven't you?

I sure have. I don't understand what's happening to me right now.

—Well, you're in an altered state of being.

What does that mean?

—It means you're not entirely here, or there. Your spirit has become disconnected to your body.

Don't I need to get back? Jordan and Ellie are going to start worrying about me soon.

—They already are. But don't concern yourself with that right now. We can sit here and be outside the flow of time for a bit. Oof! It's such a blessing to be out of that cage! I can't tell you. I'm sorry you have to go back to it. But go back to it, you must.

I don't understand.

—I know. There's a lot you don't understand. That's okay.

Okay.

—There are a few things that I need to tell you, while we're in this moment. First of all, do you know who I am?

You're Grandma Meta, of course.

—That's right. But you understand that you're not talking to the physical version of me, right?

I kinda figured.

—Right. Are you curious about that?

I guess so.

—Well, our souls are communicating.

How is that possible when we're so far apart?

—Our souls are not just contained within our bodies, silly! Your soul is so much bigger than little old you. It stretches out, like a lotus of countless petals.

It does? How come I can't see that?

—When we assume physical form in this world, we are limited by the senses our bodies come with. If we could sense more, we might be able to see it. Here's another way of thinking about it. You know how we use the Sun symbol in our religion?

Sure. The Sun is the giver of life energy.

—It signifies our allegiance to the Sun, of course, but we have equal allegiance to the Earth, whom for us is of equal power. So, it's not just the Sun. The reason we use the Sun symbol is because it also represents the soul, a perfect circle with lines emanating representing different ways of reaching out to the world, as well as that which we allow to come in and touch our core. Our souls are constantly reaching out and touching other souls, and being touched, in turn, by others. You collect little pieces of other people's souls, like a bee collects pollen. And those you touch also get a little residue of you, whether either of you want this or not. You are literally a part of me, and I of you. That's why I can talk to you even when I've left my physical body behind.

I don't understand. If you've left your physical body behind, how are you still YOU?

—My body was never me, not entirely. It was the cloak I wore for a time to help me get out and do the work that can only be done on the Material Plane.

I don't understand.

—Okay, let me try this another way. You know how you feel good around some people, but others you don't?

Yeah, like Alika. Bleah.

—That's because you receive energy from others. Some of this resonates with your field, like strings tuned a fifth apart. They can't help but vibrate together. Some just naturally create dissonance with you. They can be operating at a higher or a lower frequency, but it doesn't matter. In truth, there are multiple kinds of frequencies, all simultaneously in vibration, some faster and some slower. The real question is how many of these parameters are in synch? How many are not? The more dissonant, the more you naturally resist taking in the other soul's energy. A little bit of negative energy is okay, but not a lot.

—Positive or negative, when we're around each other for any length of time, we will pick up energy and absorb it into our system. You and I had a lot of each other in our systems. When you would come to see me in the mornings, you were seeing the material me, but also the image you had in your mind of me, your expectations, your concerns. All those things are real. It's just that it's not all one thing or the other. Some would say we're only our physical manifestation, that no soul exists. Some would say we're only soul. But neither is true. We are both physical and spiritual. We do tend to forget our souls, though, because they are not visible to the normal way of seeing.

I still don't understand.

—You will understand more later. But right now, you have a mission to fulfill. The first part of your mission will be to learn how to see this. You have to pierce the veil of illusion that's between our physical selves and the other plane of existence. When you gain access to this plane, you will be able to see these truths more clearly. The second part of your job will be to remind people of these truths, so that they don't make so many foolish choices. There's a third part of the mission, but I think we can leave that for later.

I don't understand why I have to have a mission.

—We all do. That's why we choose to come into the physical plane and exist in these limitations for a while. I think part of my mission was to get you ready to take on yours. Since I've now departed from the physical world, I think my work must be done now.

No! I don't want you to go!

—Well, you can't always get what you want! And anyway, you don't get to decide. That's a contract between me and my material self. But really, there is no "me." I am just a manifestation of a broader soul. When you leave the material plane, you start to understand how interconnected we all are, how we're really all a part of the same thing. I've just removed the garment of this material world. You will still see me in your dreams and in your thoughts, because that's just as real as the other way of experiencing somebody, only different. Do you get that?

I guess so. But I don't like it.

—I know. I'm sorry. I wish I could be with you longer physically. But I don't think my time would have ended if you weren't ready to take the next step without me.

But I'm not ready! I don't know anything. I'm just a kid.

—Don't even try to lie to me, young man! We know all about your visions. You've already been visiting this plane, haven't you?

No, I don't think so.

—What about our dream conversation?

That was real?

—Nothing is real. And everything. But dreams should not be dismissed. We have them, in part, so that we can escape the bounds of the material world for a time. You need to dream, because that which you think you know through your material senses is just the smallest fragment of the total.

Can you see the total?

—No, I can't. Not yet. But I can see a hundred times more, now. You will get close to this level, without having to take off the cloak of the material world.

How will I do that? I don't know anything.

—You cannot do it alone. You need guides to help you. Fortunately, they're waiting for you. They don't know this, but they are. And they aren't going to be hard to find. It's going to happen soon.

What about Jasmine? I don't understand why she left us.

—She is on her own' soul's journey. And the sooner you learn this, the better: you cannot dictate another's soul journey. It's like trying to tell a rabbit which way to jump.

I could scare the rabbit and make it jump…

—You could, but that would be mean. And could you really know which way he would go? Yes, you can try to scare people into obeying you, but that's not the Way. Down that path is darkness. Don't forget this.

Okay. I won't.

—I know you won't. You're a good person, Alex. I know you're going to be able to do these important things.

What if I don't want to? What if I just want to be a normal kid?

—Oh, you will be a normal kid, too. But the thing is, you actually do want to be doing these things. Otherwise, you wouldn't have chosen this life-stream. The choices you make in life can divert your stream. But it's still your stream. Some people allow another person to harness their energy, letting their stream follow another's path. You can lose your connectedness to your own life-stream. And that can make you miserable.

—This will be part of your work, too—to help people find their truest path. Remember: you're not telling them. You're not scaring the rabbit into jumping a certain way. You're helping them remember what they actually want.

—It doesn't have to all be done at once. It's a process. It is time for you to begin. It's time for you to go back and rejoin your life-stream. Just remember that I love you, and that it's all going to be okay.

I love you too, Grandma.

18

Frisco

Monday, July 12

Paul's teeth were chattering as he rode in the wagon across the flimsy bridge into the city. It didn't help that the wind was howling across the water. Occasionally the wagon would slip sideways, buffeted by the gale, but Turge had a steady hand. Paul trusted him. He wondered if he would ever get warm again, though.

Still, it was worth it. Pulling that kid out of the water—that was something. He had never actually saved someone's life before (well, he and Echleph saved him together, to be fair). If he accomplished nothing else in his life, he could feel good about this.

And there was something about this boy—*did he say his name was Alex?* He had an intense look about him. Even though they interacted very briefly—less than an hour—Paul felt like he had met him before. Or that he was somehow destined for greatness, and Paul was lucky enough to have encountered him early in his life.

Okay, now you're starting to lose it!

Then he thought about his long conversation with The Seer. "Do you have an open mind?" she had asked him. He had promised her he did. He had seen so many strange things on this journey, he felt like only a fool wouldn't have an open mind.

Let's just imagine the Elders are right. Jesus is due to come back at the turn of the century. How old would he be right now? If this kid was about twelve, he would be 24 in 2500—a little young for Jesus, but certainly old enough, older than I am now. And Jesus appeared in a small village in an ethnic minority out on the edges of the Roman Empire. Wouldn't this be about the equivalent thing for today?

Did I just meet the new Messiah? Is this the figure Echleph was warning me about?

Paul laughed out loud. Elder Eastman shot him an annoyed glance, but didn't ask what he found so funny, thankfully. Paul shook his head and brushed aside his fantasies. He wasn't ready to believe in such nonsense. Not yet at least.

Looking up, the city was starting to come into view. It really was impressive, sitting on the tip of a large peninsula, at least five miles wide. Paul could see the white sails of tall sailing ships to the right, running into the port just to the side of the bridge. *If they could just build a taller bridge, these boats could sail under it and have access to a lot more ports inland,* he thought. *Maybe Frisco likes being the bottleneck to all this commerce.* There were a few tall buildings like in Benson City, but the White Pyramid towered over all of them. It probably wasn't as tall as the Black Pyramid back home, but in a way, it was more impressive. It seemed to be made of gleaming white marble, with two wings off to the side, like shoulders. Unlike the Black Pyramid, this building was more of a genuine pyramid, rising to a perfect point at the top. Paul wondered if this pyramid shape had enabled the building to be one of the few survivors of the Great Earthquake.

They exited the bridge in one piece and rode into the city. At first, they were in forested land, undeveloped, but then the road they were on slowly veered to the east. They passed through a tunnel and out into the waterfront area. The buildings here were close-packed, all about three stories tall, painted in vibrant colors. Paul was amazed at the street life— vendors pushing carts selling fish, musicians on street corners, what looked like cowboys with broad hats on horses, raggedy-looking people with long hair and beards riding bicycles—people of all different races and positions, mingling comfortably with one another. Trying to determine the caste of these people was impossible. *Are there different standards for dress here? Or is the caste system just less defined?* In fact, Paul had trouble even distinguishing the races here. Very few people seemed to be fully white or black or Asian or Latino—most people being some sort of blending. The women went around with their hair uncovered, wearing pants like there was no difference between the sexes. It was all very disorienting. Paul noticed that the women were much more willing to look him directly in the eyes. The women back home were more demure.

After a few miles, they took a diagonal street to the southeast, and now the White Pyramid was in full view; this street led directly to it. Before they reached their destination, however, the road they were on dipped down below the water level. Paul could see that this was not in the original design of the city; the waters had infiltrated this part of the city as the sea levels rose over the last half millennium. Up ahead, he could see that the White Pyramid had a concrete wall built around it to keep the floodwaters out, about five feet tall.

There were several packet boats lined up here to take passengers through to various destinations in the city from here, for a fee. Turge leaned over his shoulder from the driving bench and said, "All right! Everybody out! That's the end of the line for us."

Paul wasn't sure what he meant by that, but he climbed out of the back of the wagon, dragging his trunk with him. Eastman and Echleph walked over to one of the boat operators, presumably to negotiate passage to the Pyramid. While he waited, he helped Turge unload Eastman's things from the wagon.

"Do you know what's going on?" he asked Turge.

"We're done. We got you to the White Pyramid. This is where we depart."

"Really? I don't understand. I thought you would be coming back with us."

"You and the bossman are taking a clipper ship back to Benson. You don't need us to help you anymore."

"But how will you get back home?"

"The captain says he's got another gig for us, out here. And besides, I've gotta try to knock some sense into Archer and get him out of those trees."

"How will you find your way back to him? We were lost when we went in and blindfolded when they led us out."

"Yeah, but they never told me I couldn't peek!"

Paul laughed. Then, he felt a wave of sadness at the prospect of losing his companion. Turge was rough and vulgar, but Paul knew he had his back. He also didn't relish being alone with Eastman for the remainder of their journey.

He held out his hand to Turge. "I want to thank you for everything. You've been an excellent guide and travel companion."

Turge looked skeptical at the hand, then took it, practically enveloping Paul's hand in his big paw. "You're okay, kid," he said quietly.

Eastman and Echleph approached. Eastman said to Turge, "Right. As I've indicated to your captain, the funds promised you are available at the First Bank of the ECA down on Market Street. You two may dispense with the horses and the wagon as you see fit. On behalf of the Supreme Elder and the High Council, I want to thank you for your excellent service."

Turge looked uncomfortable. "Okay," he said, finally. Then, to break the moment, he carried the trunks to the boat. Paul shook hands with Echleph, who looked at him with that peculiar half-smile of his and said, simply, "Good luck." Paul sensed he implied more than one meaning.

Paul and Eastman got into the boat. Paul waved to Echleph and Turge as they led the horses and wagon away on foot. Soon, they were out of sight. He was alone with the Elder.

The boat was long and thin, with a prominent prow. The boatman stood in the back and used a long pole to move them through the shallow water. There were several other water taxis in this canal, and Paul could see still more as they passed through an intersection. They reached the Pyramid quickly. Eastman asked the boatman to carry his trunks up the ramp that brought them over the little dam that protected the Pyramid, which he did. Eastman paid him some coins.

And then they were there. They stepped down from the concrete wall into a plaza. The Pyramid had square concrete pillars surrounding the base of the structure to help support it. This created a broad overhang all around the building. Underneath this, the entrance to the building was all glass, guarded by Church military personnel in uniform. When they saw Paul and Elder Eastman, two of them raised their bows and arrows while another one approached them, hand on the hilt of his sword.

Eastman, at least, was dressed in his church robes; Paul was still wearing his linen undergarments and the old blanket he had put on after he had rescued the boy. He now saw the wisdom in Eastman's orders to wear his formal wear. The guard noticed Eastman's robes but was clearly not going to take any chances. When he got to about six feet away, he spoke to them in Californian. Paul couldn't quite understand him but suspected he could pick up the dialect if he were to stay there for a few weeks.

Eastman responded in English. "We are Elders Eastman and Girard from the Central Church in Benson City. We are expected."

The guard removed his hand from his sword and visibly relaxed. "Yes, we have been expecting you," he replied in English. "Please, follow me. And allow my soldiers to carry your things."

The guard led the way to the entrance, first giving an order in Californian to the two archers. They marched over to the retaining wall to gather the trunks. Paul and Eastman walked through a revolving door into a lobby area, the walls of which were mostly made of glass. Most of the panes had a wavy quality to them which indicated they had been in place for years, if not centuries. Paul noticed some panes were missing, boarded up and not replaced. Still, the space was impressive, almost as impressive as the lobby of the Black Pyramid.

At the front desk, the guard spoke to another uniformed officer, also speaking in Californian. This one nodded and said to Eastman in English, "Welcome, Elders. We have been awaiting your visit. I have been told to show you your rooms. We will prepare an evening meal for you shortly; please be ready at six o'clock. Now, if you will follow me."

He led them to a staircase with carpeted steps, a real luxury, then led them up and up. They paused at the tenth floor to catch their breath, then finally exited the stairwell on the twentieth. The square footage of the building was noticeably smaller here, but still sizable. And they weren't even halfway up. Down a short hallway, the guard led them to two rooms, one across the hallway from the other, opened the doors for them, and handed them each a brass key.

"If there is anything we can do for you while you are here, please let me know," he said. Then he bowed and left.

Paul was stunned. He would have his own room, for the first time in weeks. And it was huge, as large as the entire house he shared with his mother and their servants back home. As he entered, to the right he found a bathroom with *running water!* And in the middle of the room was a huge bed, large enough to sleep three or four people. Paul decided to lie down on it to test it out. It was like lying on a cloud. He quickly fell asleep.

When he awoke, he found his trunk in his room. The guards must have brought it in without waking him. He found his robe draped over the top, still a little damp from his swim in the bay. He hung it in the bathroom to dry further and examined the tear near the bottom. He would ask later if there was a sewing kit available. He got himself cleaned up, put on his second-best robe, and walked downstairs for dinner.

Eastman was already there, speaking with two elderly men in red robes. One of them was an Associate Elder, with two stripes on his sleeve, rather portly, but the other was a High Elder, three stripes, out-ranking Eastman. Paul approached them, and Eastman introduced them, in his elegant Church English: Elders Hageman and Richter, the latter being the High Elder. Paul noticed that, unlike out in the streets of Frisco, all the church officials were clearly white, just as they were back in Benson. *The White Pyramid must have a double meaning for the locals,* thought Paul.

"And this is Assistant Elder Paul Girard, although one wouldn't know it from his clothing."

Paul ignored the gibe and bowed to the Elders. A servant in fine livery appeared with a glass of wine on a tray. Paul gratefully accepted it.

Richter politely brought Paul into the conversation. "We were just providing Elder Eastman with a quick summary of the situation here. We are most grateful for your arrival. I'm afraid the situation is not good."

Paul took a sip of wine. "How so?"

"Church attendance has been falling every year for the past several years—five percent, six, sometimes ten percent. Tithes have fallen even faster. We have had to close churches in several cities, due to shrinking attendance. We cannot afford to keep some of them open any longer. Our congregations are aging, too. We have been trying to boost attendance through greater outreach and evangelizing, but nothing seems to be working. We are hoping you are bringing us some fresh ideas."

Eastman evaded the implied question. "We read in your letter that the Church is facing competition from a new cult in the area?"

"That's right. There have been several new religions as well as just a general drifting away from the Church. But there is one new religion that seems to be growing rapidly. The adherents call themselves the Children of the Sun."

"Who is the leader of this cult? Sometimes, if you cut off the head of the snake, the rest of the animal dies with it."

"That's the thing. I am not sure there is a leader. Or if there is one, he is very well hidden. But I suspect there isn't one. I don't think they're that organized."

"Well then, this should be an easy thing to root out."

"One would think. But they're elusive. When you shine a lantern, they scatter like cockroaches."

"Is there anything you can tell us about this new religion?" asked Paul. "Perhaps if we understood the appeal, we might be able to address some of the needs our Church is not fulfilling."

Eastman frowned at this question. *I feel like I can't say anything right!* Still, something about his visit with the Seer made him feel emboldened.

"We do have spies in their congregations, of course," said the other church official, Hageman. Paul was trying to guess their ages, and which one was older. They were both in their early seventies at least. "It is hard for us to understand the appeal, frankly. It is very pagan, tied to the changes of the season, fertility rites and so forth, with lots of vulgar music and dancing. They act like children. I suppose that makes sense, given their name."

"Do you know who it appeals to?" Paul pressed on. "If we had some sense of the demographic, maybe we could understand why they find this religion more congenial."

"It does seem to have an especial appeal to the lower orders, not surprisingly," answered Elder Hageman.

"And now, gentlemen, shall we repair to the dinner table?" Elder Richter gestured toward a big table being set with fine silverware and ample servings of meat and bread. "We are most anxious to hear about your journey here. Surely, you must have some tales to tell!"

Paul certainly did, but he let Eastman take the lead. His version of the story was very pallid compared with the journey Paul remembered. Eastman's description of the Redwood Commune made his two elderly colleagues gasp with shock.

"You are fortunate indeed to have made it out alive," said Richter.

"The Lord was undoubtedly looking after us," replied Eastman. Nothing was said about the rescuing of the boy, or their visit to the Trash Mountain, or any of the more interesting stops they made. In Eastman's telling, they were walking through a wilderness of evil, saved only by the grace of God and the steadfastness of his prayers.

They stayed two nights with the aged church leaders. On the second day, there were several meetings, and this time, Paul was allowed to attend. In a way, he wished he hadn't. From his perspective, the situation was clear: The Church was dying out here, probably because it was out of step with the population it was meant to serve. If it was more dynamic and responsive, there would be no need for the parishioners to seek their spiritual guidance elsewhere. He tried to nudge the leaders toward realizing this themselves by the nature of his questions, but they seemed unable or unwilling to entertain his ideas.

As they waited for a mid-day meal in the meeting room on the second day, Eastman said to Paul, "I will be preparing a letter to be sent to the Supreme Council today, in advance of our return, in case you have any letters you would like to post."

Paul did have some letters to his mother, but this news concerned him. "Why are you sending a letter? I had assumed we would just report our findings in person."

"Mail routes over land are faster than sea. A letter will be the fastest form of communication. And it provides insurance, in case anything should happen to us at sea."

"May I ask what you intend to say in this letter?"

"The truth. That the situation is exactly as we had feared. If the Church takes no action, the entire region might be lost."

"I don't know that we actually *know* that."

"What do you mean?"

"I mean, we haven't actually seen this for ourselves. We're just taking their word for it."

"Their word is unimpeachable. And I think we saw enough, as we crossed the country."

"I disagree, respectfully. Why don't we stay here longer and see for ourselves? We can talk to local churches, maybe find some members of this cult. I mean, why did we come all the way out here if we were just going to affirm what they sent in their letter to us? That seems like a waste of time."

"We cannot stay longer. The sea voyage takes several weeks. We need to depart soon before the weather turns."

"Then we can stay over the winter."

"How free you are with the Church's money," Eastman said sarcastically.

"I'm just urging you to think about this before you send out your letter. You know the probable outcome as well as I do. The High Council will authorize a holy crusade to this region."

"And so?"

Paul was starting to feel his blood pressure rising. He knew he was getting into dangerous territory, but he felt that he had to press on. Maybe this was his moment to affect the course of history, as the Seer had foretold. Somehow, he felt like he had been changed over the past few days, maybe by his talk with the Seer—maybe even by his baptism in the Bay, to borrow an idea from the Church.

"And so? That means an occupying army, coming in here to try to force people to believe something against their will. It will essentially be a war, and wars have unintended consequences. There will be bloodshed. There will be lives lost on both sides."

"That's not a decision for you or for I to make. We are merely observers. Our job is to report, not to make policy."

"But don't you see? We have the opportunity to affect that policy. We can frame this in such a way that the High Council turns its attention to other matters."

"I frankly am appalled at you, Elder Girard. Why do you have such a soft spot for these people? Is there something here you're not telling me?"

"I'm just saying, you don't win converts to the Faith at the sharp end of a sword."

"Well, you're wrong about that. Of course, we prefer that people find their way to redemption through the power of Christ's love, but we would not have had the success we have had for nearly 2500 years if we hadn't been willing to use the sword as well."

"The Evangelical Church of America has only been around for some 350 years…"

"I am not talking about the ECA!" Eastman shouted. "I am talking about the long tradition that brings us back to Jesus Himself. The ECA is merely the current manifestation of that tradition. It wasn't the first, and it won't be the last."

"Maybe it will be, if we ram it down these peoples' throats…"

"You are so ignorant; it really astounds me. This Church—I mean the long history of the Church, not the ECA—is one of the greatest monuments of human history. For over twenty-four centuries—each one of which was burdened with seemingly insurmountable crises—she has held together her people, following them as they moved around the globe, tending to them when they were sick or broken by this cruel world, forming their minds, fixing their moral compasses, drying their eyes when they were facing the loss of a beloved family member, lifting their eyes up to see how their transitory lives fit into the eternal battle between Good and Evil. The Church has survived every kind of heresy and revolt, outlasted nations and empires, rebuilding every broken support of her power. Yes, sometimes she has had to exert her power through the instrument of war. Yes, sometimes people resent the Church's power. But they also respect it. They may succumb resentfully, but they eventually discover the beauty in the order the Church brings. And if they don't, their children do, and if not their children, then their grandchildren. For millions of souls around the world, the Church provides a beacon of hope in this shattered world, the knowledge of Christ's love and the possibility of canceling death.

"You think you are being kind to these people by giving them a choice. In fact, you are being cruel. People don't need a choice. People need the Church, whether they realize it or not. I cannot believe I have to spell this out to a fellow Elder."

With that, Eastman turned around and walked away.

Paul and Elder Eastman did not speak to each other for the rest of that day. Their hosts gave them a farewell dinner with a half-dozen other Church officials, all equally elderly, and Paul let Eastman do most of the talking. The next day, they gathered at the retaining wall to leave, said goodbye to their hosts, and took a water taxi to the edge of the water, to a two-seat cab, and then to the waterfront where their ship awaited. They went through these phases in a chilly silence.

The Port of Frisco was huge, even larger than the one in Benson, and Paul admired the tall ships moored there. He learned they would be taking a three-mast clipper called *The Merciful,* one of the fastest ships in the KGL fleet. It would still take them nearly three months to sail south through the Panama Canal, the Caribbean, up the eastern seaboard, then through the St. Lawrence seaway and into the Great Lakes to Benson City. There would be several stops along the way as well.

As they sat in the waiting area, Paul decided he would try to break the impasse between them. "Elder, I hope I did not cause offense yesterday. If I did, I hope you will accept my apology."

Eastman pursed his lips and did not meet Paul's eyes. After several heartbeats, he replied, "Your apology is accepted." Paul did not believe him.

This is still going to be a long journey.

19

Alex awoke on a sunny beach, water gushing out of his mouth. He coughed violently, then coughed again. His chest hurt badly. Three men were looking down at him, concerned. One of them was dripping wet, wearing the robes of a Church official. He was handsome and confident-looking, and Alex immediately recognized him from his dream that morning. He asked him if he was the Supreme Elder of their Church. They all laughed at that. Normally, Alex would have felt embarrassed or defensive, but not now. He'd been through so much, it just didn't seem worth it. And anyway, he didn't know. Something about the man seemed like he was an important leader or was going to be.

Grandma Meta! He remembered his encounter with her with a start. He felt a pang of sadness, but then something else—an emotion beyond words. It was all okay. She was okay, even if she wasn't here physically. We all were okay. In fact, if death isn't the final event he'd always feared it was, there really wasn't anything to worry about, ever. It was hard to wrap his head around that.

He now found himself shaking. He wasn't at first, but now it was like his body was waking up and deciding it was cold. Which he was. One of the three men ran over to a wagon and brought back a thick woolen blanket, very nicely made. It helped a little, but he was still cold.

And then Jordan and Ellie came running up, tears running down their faces. "Alex! Are you okay?" They didn't even wait for an answer before they hugged him. He didn't think Ellie had ever hugged him before, but she did now, and it felt like she meant it. She didn't even care that he was getting her wet.

"I'm okay," he said quietly.

Jordan held out his hand to the churchman and shook it. "Sir, I cannot tell you how grateful we are for rescuing our cousin. There's no way we could have done it ourselves. Is there any way we can repay you?" He then shook the hands of the other two men.

Alex could tell they weren't understanding him, but they seemed nice about it. He wondered briefly how they were able to understand him a moment before, but he felt like he couldn't think straight. Ellie helped Alex to his feet. He found he was shaky, too wobbly to walk very well. She helped him walk slowly toward their horses. He was glad to see that Betsy was there, doing okay. Before they got there, though, he decided he wanted to know the name of that churchman who had rescued him. Even though he felt funny about doing this sort of thing with grown-ups, he turned around and held out his hand.

"My name is Alex," he said.

The man looked him straight in the eyes, like he was an equal. It was unusual for a grown-up to treat any kid that way, let alone someone who seemed to be in a high position, like this one. It felt like they were cousins, or long-lost brothers. Alex had never felt this kind of connection with a stranger before.

"Nice to meet you, Alex. My name is Paul."

They shook hands. Alex felt a strange sensation when their hands touched, almost like a charge of static electricity on a dry day. He had a feeling that he and Paul would someday meet again.

Jordan and Ellie decided that Alex needed to rest for a while before they continued. "Don't worry about reaching Vallejo today," said Jordan. "We'll just take it easy for now. They'll still be there tomorrow."

Alex wasn't worried about reaching Vallejo, but he appreciated Jordan saying this. They decided to eat some bread from their packs even though it was in between mealtimes. At first, Alex was worried he might throw up the bread, but it went down okay. And then he felt like he was starving, so he ate more.

They were sitting on a bench overlooking the bay. It was nice to just watch the people coming and going on the bridge. Alex could see that it was still windy out there, and how the bridge swayed with the gusts. Nobody else fell in, though.

After a while, Ellie stood up and brushed the crumbs off her shirt. "Do you feel ready to travel?"

"I saw Grandma," said Alex abruptly.

Ellie sat down again. "What?"

"I saw her, when I was underwater."

They were quiet for a while, then Jordan said softly, "Buddy, I don't understand."

"She's crossed over. I crossed over, too, but I came back."

"Oh, God!" said Ellie, putting her hand to her mouth, and she started crying.

"It's okay," Alex found himself saying. "She wants us to know that she's all right. She said she's just removed the cloak of this material existence, or something like that."

Jordan said, "Alex, I want you to tell us everything you experienced down there. Don't leave anything out."

Alex swallowed and told them the story. It was all very clear in his head. When he was done, Ellie gave him a hug again.

"We're glad you made it back to us," she said.

"We'd better get going," said Jordan. "Everyone needs to hear about this."

The road they took was an Olden Times road, nice and wide, with concrete paving. There were times when it got broken up and they had to move carefully through the wreckage. As they came up to a city called Sausalito, they saw a sign advertising boats for hire, written in Mojies. "Do you think we could afford that?" Ellie asked Jordan.

"I think it might be worth trying."

They headed off the road and into the town. It was a hilly village, with a mixture of houses, ramshackle huts, a few buildings still standing from the old days, but mostly ruins.

Down at the harbor, they found a marina with several small boats. They went into the main building and Jordan asked about boats to Vallejo. The man behind the counter named a price. Apparently, it was a lot, because Jordan and Ellie had to discuss it at length off to the side, quietly. Jordan then negotiated with the man. They went back and forth several times and finally settled on a fee about half as much as the original amount. Alex didn't really understand currency and money that well, so it was all meaningless to him. Alex was a little sad to say goodbye to Betsy, but they obviously couldn't take the horses with them. They found a stable not far from the marina and received some money for the horses. Alex assumed it was less than they had paid to rent them back in Modesto, but it gave them enough to pay the boatman.

A little while later, they were in a little keelboat with a spinnaker sail, captained by the man in the boathouse himself. He handled the craft expertly, moving through the water much faster than the Clan's boat ever did. Alex felt a combination of excitement and fear, sailing so fast, so near to the water. They passed between a little peninsula and an island, heading northeast. They generally hugged the southern shoreline as they sailed, and Alex could see the ruins of several old cities on the hills that they passed.

It was getting near sunset when they pulled into Vallejo harbor. It was a big city, with a little inlet river that led north to the harbor. Alex didn't see the Clan's barge there at first, which worried him. They got off the boat, Jordan paid the captain, then said to Alex and Ellie, "Wait here. I'll go ask for them." Alex and Ellie sat down with their legs over the side of the pier and watched the captain maneuver the boat out of the harbor. He used a paddle at first, but soon found the wind and sailed quickly out of the channel.

Jordan returned with Uncle Evan, Aunt Rosa, Aunt Mary, and Emma. Alex was a little worried they would be angry with them for running off to look for Jasmine, but there were hugs all around. Mary was one of Ellie's moms; Alex could tell she was just relieved Ellie had made it back okay.

"I take it you couldn't find Jasmine?" asked Emma.

"Oh, we did," said Ellie. "But it's a long story."

"Let's get you three back to the boat," said Rosa.

The barge was docked at a different pier, five down from the one they were on. Alex could see people coming and going, probably to a Fairday in the city. Strangely, he felt no interest in going to this himself. He felt now like all that was behind him, somehow. It was like he was a different person than the one he was back in Modesto. It made him a little sad, like he was saying goodbye to the old Alex, but there wasn't a new Alex to take his place yet.

Everybody was there on the boat, and the three cousins were greeted warmly. Even Charles didn't seem angry. Ellie and Jordan told them the story of Jasmine, which caused several family members to shake their heads and make "tsk" sounds. "She may come to regret that decision," said Emma.

"That's what we told her," said Ellie.

"But she did give us this," said Jordan, presenting the gold Sovereign to Charles. Everybody gathered close to look at it. Alex wasn't the only one who had never seen a coin that valuable before. Charles nodded solemnly and handed it to Evan, who took care of the finances.

After this, Jordan said, "There's something else. Alex, do you want to tell your story?"

He felt self-conscious. He was also getting very tired, so he just shook his head no. Jordan seemed to understand. He told the story for him. Aunt Rosa was the most upset at the news. She was Meta's little sister. She started crying. Emma, Rosa's daughter, comforted her.

"Well, that settles it," said Charles. "We're going home in the morning."

Everybody just nodded, like it was the only viable solution. Alex felt a little uncomfortable that this big decision was being made because of him. He honestly didn't know, still, if what he experienced was real or not. He hoped it wasn't, because he wanted Grandma Meta to still be alive. He was also suddenly ready to be done with the tour.

Charles ordered Junior, Emma, and Evan to collect their things from the fairgrounds. Alex felt so tired, he just curled up on the side of the boat and fell asleep, wrapped up in the blanket the churchmen had given him.

It took them three full days to sail home. They made good time the first day, but the second day was hot and still, the Delta breezes reluctant to pick up. Alex didn't mind, though. He found some comfort in just sitting on the deck, watching the seagulls circling overhead.

At one point, Alika passed by Alex and said, "You'd better be right about Grandma. Otherwise, you're costing us a lot of money for the remaining Fairdays."

Alex fixed his eyes on her steadily and said, "I should think you would hope I'm wrong. I sure do." Alika blanched and hurried away.

They arrived late the next day, on a Monday. The little dock at Northpoint looked different to Alex now, so much smaller and shabbier. The family started unloading their supplies while Charles and Rosa walked on ahead to the family homestead. Alex helped unload some of the items, but they didn't want to take everything out. If Grandma Meta was okay, they would just spend a night or two and return to the fair circuit.

Alex waited. He hoped he would see Grandma coming down the hill on her little donkey, waving to them like she did every year, followed by the children of the Clan. In his heart, he knew he wouldn't. As soon as Charles appeared on the road alone, Alex sensed everybody else knew as well.

"Is it true?" asked Emma.

Charles nodded solemnly. Without anybody saying anything, they got to work unpacking the rest of the boat. There would be no more Fairdays this year.

Grandma Meta had died on July 1. The family had tried to get word to the tour group, sending letters to three different places, but it was always hard to track down people on the fair circuit. They had thought about sending someone out to find them, but it seemed too risky. Besides, the clan needed the money. They had had to go through the cremation ceremony without the family that was on the tour, but they held off having the full memorial service until the group got back.

The remainder of the week was spent getting ready for the service. It would be on Sun'sday, of course. The family baked bread and sweets for three days. Grandma Meta was well known in the community, and two days before, people started arriving and pitching tents on the property. The ceremony itself must have had over a hundred people in attendance.

Alex had never been to a memorial service, not that he could remember. His mother had died giving birth to him, and his father only a few months later ("of a broken heart," Grandma Meta used to say). If he went to those, he was only a baby. He wished Jasmine were there, then he realized what he *really* wished was for Grandma Meta to be there, just like always. But she wasn't, not even in his dreams. Charles read little scraps of paper from Grandma's Memory Jar, including some funny items from Meta herself that she had dropped into the jar over the years. The family sang some of her favorite songs from their repertoire, then invited everyone to the square in the middle of their compound for the big feast. People told their favorite stories of her, and that made Alex feel a little better. But not really.

The next day, things started to return to normal. There was always work to do on the farm, and Alex slipped easily back into his usual chores. They had come back just in time for the corn harvest, always a labor-intensive activity. Uncle Thomas, Rosa's spouse, said they were pulling in the harvest twice as fast as normal, with so many hands.

It was the routine, but things felt different to Alex. He tried playing some of his old games after his chores were done—working on the tree fort he'd started years ago or racing the go-cart he'd built with Uncle Evan down the long hill—but they didn't hold any appeal. After the work was done for the day, he found what he liked best was taking long walks by the creek that ran down to the Sea.

Alex thought about Grandma Meta a lot, trying to hold on to her memories. But these made him miss her so much, he had to turn away from them. The same was true of Jasmine. Instead, he found himself thinking about that churchman he met, Paul. Maybe because he had just had that conversation with Grandma Meta, he wondered about that feeling he had when he shook Paul's hand. It felt like the two of them had exchanged little pieces of their souls, even though they interacted so briefly. It was like he became just a little bit like Paul and vice versa. He still didn't trust himself to know whether this was real or not.

July rolled into August, and August rolled into September. Alex felt weird during this time, almost as though his soul had become detached from his body. He knew he was still there. But he had to prove it to himself, deliberately burning his hand one evening around the campfire (which caused worried looks to be quickly exchanged among the grown-ups). Alex knew they were worrying about him. He could see them whispering and looking at him. He overheard the word "depression" more than once. But he wasn't sure that was the right word. Transformed seemed more like it. He felt like he had been jolted forward into adulthood, rather violently. And he knew he would never be able to go back to the way he was.

September was when they usually started school. It had been run by Grandma Meta and Uncle Thomas. Alex didn't want to start up again without her as the main teacher. On the first day of school, Alex just didn't go, sitting instead on the little bridge over the creek, dropping seedpods into the water. He wasn't really thinking about anything. After some time, Uncle Evan walked over to him and sat down next to him, their legs dangling over the edge. Neither of them said anything for a while.

Finally, Evan broke the silence. "Not feeling much like school, are you?"

Alex stared out to the creek for a while, then shook his head.

Evan nodded. "We've been talking about you, some of the grown-ups, and are starting to think that maybe being here isn't so good for you."

Alex looked up at him quizzically. "If I'm not here, where else could I be?"

"We've been talking about your visions. We don't really understand them, but we think they might be important. There's a boarding school, up in the mountains, run by some members of the Tribe, meant to help people in their spiritual practice. They might be able to help you learn how to make use of your gifts."

Alex nodded slowly, taking this in. "I've never heard about this school."

"We don't talk about it much. It's a secret place. I'm sure you know there are people out there who don't like our kind of people. They might try to shut it down, or worse. If you went there, you should know that there's some risk involved."

"I think I should go," said Alex decisively.

"Really? Just like that? I didn't tell you that you would have to live up there. It's much too far away from us for you to still live here."

"That's okay. I think maybe this is what Grandma was trying to tell me, from the other side." *And besides, I miss Grandma Meta and Jasmine too much, staying here.*

"All right, then. I'll go tell Charles and the others."

Evan stood up, ruffled Alex's hair, and headed back in.

The next day, Evan and Alex packed up a few belongings and took the family cart to head up to the Sierras. The clan gathered to see him go, but the mood was very different from when they left for the tour. Ellie and Jordan gave him extra-long hugs, and Ellie said, "Take good care of yourself, Alex." He could almost feel Grandma Meta's presence there with him. It gave him a heavy feeling inside. He climbed up to sit next to Uncle Evan on the old oxcart and nodded at him, ready to leave. Evan nodded back and released the brake on the cart. Alex looked back once, gave a little wave, and then turned to face the road ahead.

20

En route to Benson City

Paul had never been on a tall ship before, and in that regard, he was excited about the voyage, even though it meant more time alone with Eastman. He and Eastman were each given their own cabin, first class, on the top deck. The ship held about forty passengers, most of them in steerage, plus some cargo in the hold (Paul never found out what this was). He admired the way the sailors climbed up the masts and onto the bowsprit so deftly and nimbly, all the while singing sea chanteys to coordinate their work. There was even a kind of music to the creaking of the floorboards, the whoosh of the water, and the thrumming of the ropes as they moved through the water so quickly.

Unfortunately, on the third day out of Frisco, a sickness swept through the lower decks. Paul tried to keep his distance. It seemed possible that he would escape it for a while. Then it struck him. And it hit him hard. He couldn't hold down any food, was feverish and delirious, and spent almost the entire voyage in his cabin, miserable. At one point, he thought he heard the ship's doctor come into his cabin and say, "Yeah, he's got it. He might not make it, this one." He wasn't sure whether this was a dream. He also dreamed—or possibly really experienced—Eastman giving him Last Rites.

He had been looking forward to seeing the sights on the trip—the cities of Ellaya and Cabo San Lucas down at the tip of Baja, then through the famous locks of the Panama Canal, into the Caribbean, past the ruins of Florida, now mostly underwater—but he missed all of it. He only felt well enough to come up to the deck when they were already in the Great Lakes, wending their way toward Benson City, more than a month later. He was only drinking the thinnest broth, still, and had probably lost twenty pounds. His mother would hardly recognize him. He arrived on deck just in time for a ceremonial burial of a shrouded body, done quickly and without much sentiment. He wondered how many lives had been lost.

Not Eastman, though. Paul saw him standing at the railing, looking ahead into the distance. Paul reluctantly walked over to join him. He found he needed to hold onto the railing for support as he walked. Eastman noticed his arrival and nodded.

"I see you are recovering," he observed.

"Slowly but surely," replied Paul.

"That is good," said Eastman, after a pause.

They stood there in silence for a few moments. Paul enjoyed the feeling of the wind in his hair and beard after weeks of stuffy air in the cabin.

"What happens next?" he eventually asked the Elder.

"I am sure that some members of the High Council will want to meet with us to discuss what we've seen. They will have had time to read our letter but will undoubtedly have questions."

Our letter?

Paul wondered if he might have an opportunity to speak his mind, but Eastman seemed to be a step ahead of him. "Of course, you will only speak if you are asked direct questions."

"Of course."

"After this, you and I will await our next assignments. And of course, how you comport yourself in this last phase will affect my willingness to offer my most sincere recommendation for you."

Paul sighed. "Of course."

Eastman nodded, satisfied, then turned and left Paul on the deck.

For a while, Paul just stood there, holding onto the deck railing, looking out at the forest lining the lake, now changing colors to autumn. It was a beautiful day, and he was going home. He had survived whatever plague this ship had given him, survived this perilous journey through the untamed wilderness of the West, and would be seeing his mother again at long last. He should have felt something akin to joy, or at least relief and gratitude, but these were not the emotions he felt. Instead, he felt a kind of constriction inside his chest. He didn't quite know why.

Was it just Eastman, and the feeling of utter powerlessness? That was certainly part of it, but there was more. He could see now that his whole life plan was untenable. He had thought he could fake his way through, keep up the façade of faith, work his way up on the government side of the KGL, and create a good life for himself—respectable, if not dramatic. He didn't realize how much compromise this would require. And this plan for some sort of holy crusade to California struck him as not only wasteful and pointless, but potentially a kind of crime against humanity. That boy he met in the Bay kept coming back to him. *I don't want any part in the persecution of those people,* he thought.

His visits to the monastery and the Redwood Commune also kept running through his mind. What he had learned from Bryce, Echleph, and the Seer really upended his entire worldview. He didn't know quite what to believe anymore. And he was growing more comfortable with that. Maybe the Seer's Radical Agnosticism, or whatever she called it, was starting to take a hold of him. The offer from Brother Bryce to move to the monastery was looking more and more attractive, too. A life of contemplation, removed from this sordid political business, seemed very appealing now.

Increasingly, he was thinking perhaps he should renounce his position entirely and pursue some sort of career outside the Church. One idea was to become an attorney. He knew that journeymen lawyers had to travel a circuit through the KGL at the start of their careers, but he no longer feared traveling like he used to. That would be one benefit from this adventure. Assuming he could afford the extra schooling, this career would enable him to extricate himself from the Church and perhaps earn enough to support his mother, get married, and start a family. And maybe he could venture outside Benson and the KGL again. He hadn't realized how small his world was until he left it. There was an unimaginably vast world out there. He was just starting to comprehend how little he comprehended.

Paul heard the bells indicating the start of the noon meal down in the mess hall. He noticed he now had an appetite. This was good. He held the railing as he moved slowly toward the stairs.

Two days later, they passed through the straits that connected Lake Huron to Lake Michigan, past Mackinac Island, once inhabited but now abandoned, then south along the shore of Wisconsin. Paul's strength was returning, but he still enjoyed just sitting on deck, watching the scenery roll by. Wisconsin was sparsely populated; some of the cities along the coast had only the faintest hint of the ruins of the Empire, swallowed up by forest now. Milwaukee was their last stop before Benson City, another hamlet built on reclaimed Empire lands. Paul could tell this had once been a thriving metropolis. Several passengers disembarked, some on stretchers, and there was an exchange of goods, carried by an efficient group of stevedores.

And then, the next day, the Black Pyramid came into view. His heart skipped a beat. He had wildly mixed feelings. He was eager to see his mother and his friends. He was not eager to endure having to fake it through the upcoming hearings about their journey. And he had a huge task ahead, to begin the process of changing his career path. Yet the prospect of removing the shackles of the Church and the likes of Elder Eastman lifted his spirits.

As they pulled into their berth at Navy Pier, Paul could see a small crowd gathered. He scanned it eagerly to see if he could find his mother. He thought he spotted her, but he wasn't sure, then the ship pulled into its position and Paul could no longer see the crowd. He went down to his cabin to haul up his trunk, difficult to do in his weakened state, and add it to the pile of luggage to be taken ashore. He then joined Eastman in the line to disembark, organized by caste. He stayed with Eastman in the Fifth Caste section, even though he could have moved forward to be with his kind.

Before anybody was allowed to leave the ship, however, three Church Guards came aboard. *What's this about?* Paul wondered. To his horror, they came right up to him.

"Elders Eastman and Girard? Please follow us."

Paul looked at Eastman, wondering if he knew anything. He looked just as surprised as Paul felt.

"What's the meaning of this?" Eastman asked them.

"That will be explained at the Black Pyramid."

"What about our belongings?"

"They will be taken care of."

Paul's heart was thumping in his chest. He was racking his brain, wondering what he had done wrong. His first thought was that Eastman had betrayed him in his letter, revealed something of his doubts about their mission. Then, with a sickening feeling, he wondered if it was Brother Bryce who had betrayed him, or someone else at the monastery. He didn't want to believe this, but it was possible. Could it be that their conversations were overheard by another monk? Whatever it was, this was not good.

They were taken down the ramp and into a black carriage waiting for them. Paul felt unsteady on his feet, unused to being on solid land after so long at sea and from his illness. He looked desperately for his mother as they entered the carriage but couldn't see her. The blinds were drawn, so they could not be seen as they travelled, but nor could they see out. It was dark inside, but Paul still scanned the faces of the guards and of Eastman, sitting across from him in the dark carriage, to try to glean what was happening, to no avail.

It was not far to the Pyramid—a few blocks east, a few blocks north, then just a couple of blocks east again. Paul could hear the driver call the horses to a stop. One of the guards got out of the cabin, held open the door, and said, "This way, please." Paul saw that they were at the back of the Pyramid. The guard led them through a thick wooden door into an unadorned room. Paul and Eastman then followed the guard up two flights of stairs. Behind them on the stairs were two more guards. Paul felt a fleeting urge to push past them and run away, but he knew he was still too weak to pull this off. And where would he run to? The KGL's power in Benson was absolute.

They came into a large room with a tall ceiling. Seated at a table were three Elders, including one High Elder, in purple. Seated off to the side was the Abbess of the convent they had visited in Iowa. Next to her was one of the nuns. The one who had visited him in the middle of the night, Paul guessed.

Now he knew what this was all about.

Paul felt a constriction in his throat. He tried to swallow, failed, and succeeded on the second try. Eastman shot a curious glance at the women, then back at Paul, then his eyes narrowed.

"Gentlemen," said the High Elder, "I hope you will forgive our rude welcome, after your long journey on behalf of the Church. A little matter has come up that requires our attention before we can give you a more appropriate greeting."

"What's this all about, sir?" asked Eastman.

"Well, it seems our Sister Aurelia here has a very serious accusation to be made against one member of your party. She claims that you stopped by her convent—unannounced, against her express wishes— demanded shelter for the night. And then one of her novices had her maidenhood violated by one of your men. I am afraid to inform you she is with child."

Paul swallowed again. The nun—whatever her name was—studiously avoided catching Paul's eye. He could now see how young she was. She was pretty, he thought, although it was hard to tell with her hair covered. He didn't see any physical evidence of a pregnancy, but of course that didn't mean anything. *Still,* he thought desperately, *how can they be sure?* His knowledge of women's reproductive systems was woefully impoverished.

"We are here to determine if you can tell us which member of your party violated this poor woman."

She hasn't identified me yet, Paul realized. He began to formulate a plan. Archer was still in California and not likely to be coming back. *Maybe we could pin this on him...*

Then Paul thought twice. *I'm tired of lies,* he thought. *I've been lying my whole life.* He had never liked Archer, honestly, but it wasn't right to pin this on him. And who knew whether the nun would go along with this? It was cowardly. He was responsible.

The Abbess was now speaking with asperity. "I cannot believe you would let this happen. My girls are kept away from you men for a reason. They are exemplars of womanhood and devoid of any kind of carnal desires. Your group has brought the corruption of sex into our peaceful enclave..."

The High Elder interrupted the Abbess. "I would like to ask your acolyte if one of these two men was your assailant," he asked her.

The nun looked like a hunted animal. She looked at Paul with a panicked expression, hesitating, then looked back at the High Elder.

"It was I," said Eastman.

❋

The next set of events happened in a blur for Paul. There was an angry denunciation from the Abbess, a wearied scolding from the High Elder, then Eastman was led away to await his punishment. He steadfastly refused to meet Paul's eyes as the guards led him off. As the Abbess and the nun walked out of the room, the young woman looked at Paul pleadingly, but he felt immobilized. The Elders talked among themselves briefly, then told Paul he was free to go, that he would be summoned before the High Council in a few days to give a full accounting of the journey, and then they left him alone in the room, trembling.

After a moment, Paul realized he just couldn't leave without finding out what had gotten into Eastman. He took the stairs down, found a guard at the doorway they had entered, asked if he could see his colleague, and was escorted down two more flights of stairs, into a basement space. It was poorly lit down here, no sunlight coming in and only an occasional lantern hanging from hooks in the ceiling. The guard took him to a large metal cage. Paul found Eastman inside this, sitting on a metal bench, elbows on his knees and his head in his hands. The guard pulled up a stool for Paul to sit on just outside the cage and left them to talk in private.

Paul didn't know how to begin. "Elder, I don't understand what just happened."

Eastman looked up at Paul with an unreadable expression. "I just took the blame for you."

So, he knew. Paul didn't bother denying it.

"But why? Why would you do this for me? I thought you detested me."

"Oh, I do. I find you utterly loathsome. This latest turn of events has only confirmed my initial impressions of a spoiled, cocky young man, and a fraud at that."

"I—I don't…"

"I opposed your assignment on this journey right from the start. I had several other church officials in mind. I wasn't given a choice. I was told you were the top student in your class and a rising leader. That, to me, meant you were probably in a high caste, being groomed for a big position. While I, having been unlucky enough to have been born into the Fifth Caste, am constantly being told that my talents are best served in something aligned with my station in life. I was supposed to help train you to surpass me. Help you learn about the world that you already so easily fit into, just by sheer luck. And then I met you, and my worst suspicions were realized. You are vain, arrogant, accustomed to getting your way, and your faith is weak if not non-existent."

Paul had never been upbraided like this before. He felt like he was standing naked.

"I'm sorry, Elder. I never meant to treat you with disrespect."

"Maybe you didn't mean to, but you did. Oh, I don't blame you personally. You're just a product of your upbringing and privilege. You don't know any better. You're a fool. But your contempt and superior attitude are impossible to hide."

"Why did you do it, then?"

"Very simple. I want leverage."

"What do you mean?"

"While it would be satisfying for me to see you thrown out of the Church and disgraced, it doesn't do much good, for me or for the Church. As much as it pains me to say this, I do see why they're grooming you for leadership. You're from the right caste. You're reasonably smart and charismatic. And the leadership of the Church is pathetic and needs new blood."

"All during this trip, you scolded me for even questioning the Church leadership…"

"Be quiet. I'm not done yet. You're on your way up. You have enough capability to make it. And that boy you saved— I heard what he said. 'Are you the Supreme Elder?' he asked. I was appalled. But I've been thinking about it ever since. What if he was right? What if this bratty, spoiled Assistant Elder is going to be in a position of power some-day? It's possible. Likely, even, given our pitiful state."

"So, you're trying to curry favor with me?"

"No, I'm going to be blackmailing you."

Paul swallowed nervously. "I don't understand what I could pos-sibly give you. You may think Caste 3 people are all rich, but we're not…"

"I don't want your money," he spat. "If I had wanted that, I would have pilfered money out of the Church coffers, like so many of the High Elders do when they think nobody is looking."

"Then what is it you want?"

"I am going to demand something from you. If you agree, we will keep this little story quiet. I will marry this whelp and take care of her and your lovechild. It's probably good that I am seen as 'normal' in that way. If you don't fulfill my demand, the secret comes out, and your career is ruined."

"Why would my career be ruined and not yours?"

"Because we are at different stages in our careers. Oh, I will cer-tainly be fined—they love to extract money from people—and very likely sent off to some undesirable posting in the hinterlands. But they need me. They know I know too much. I know where all the skeletons are hidden around here. They'll quietly let me resume my position in a suitable amount of time. But you? No, this is definitely a career-ending event for someone just starting out."

"But if I just left the Church and pursued another career…"

"You can't. There's no position in the KGL that doesn't come under the scrutiny of the Church. You would not be welcomed in any kind of job with a black mark like this on your record."

"I could leave the KGL."

Eastman snorted. "You wouldn't survive one day out there, not without our guides."

Paul felt like he was in the cage, not Elder Eastman.

"What is your demand?"

"Simple: once you become Supreme Elder, or something close to it, you will officially separate the Church from government."

"What? How can I possibly do that?"

"If you have enough power, you can do anything you want to."

"I don't understand why you would want this. You seem like a dedicated Church man. Why would you want to see it lose power like this?"

"Because it's corrupting. It's corrosive. People enter the Church because of the potential for power, not to serve God. People like you, in fact. The Church is so distracted with the business of running the country, it's lost sight of what's important. We can do more good if we are no longer fixated on temporal, mundane goals. I have a vision for the Church that is stronger than the compromised, self-indulgent mess that it is now."

"You expect me to snap my fingers and make everybody agree to change the very structure of our government and society?"

"Of course not. I'm not a fool. I know it will take time. You will have eighteen years, until the child comes of age. If you haven't set the wheels in motion by then, your cover is blown. A scandal like that will take you down, right when you can least afford it."

"But that's just the thing. I'm Third Caste, not First. This whole scheme of yours is predicated on the notion that I can leapfrog up the ranks and into high position. But you yourself just revealed that it's impossible to break through these barriers."

"It usually is. And it would be, for someone as far down as me. But the Third Caste is close enough. The First Caste, in case you haven't noticed, is full of inbred morons. They're idiots, and they're dying out. Their numbers are shrinking, and their women cannot get pregnant anymore. The Second Caste isn't much better. Someone like you can work your way up more easily than you might think."

Paul shook his head doubtfully. "I think you overestimate me."

"Probably, I do. It doesn't matter to me. Either you achieve this, or you don't."

"And until then, I am essentially your hostage."

"That is correct."

Paul walked up the stairs and out of the Black Pyramid, dizzy. He felt like a feather being blown by a breeze, in control of nothing. He was still finding it hard to believe everything that had happened to him, all in a matter of hours.

The weather was warm outside, just a hint of the dryness of autumn in the air. He didn't like feeling like he had no choices. Of course, his situation was a hell of a lot better than the situation for that poor, nameless nun, who will be paying a greater price than she can possibly imagine, all for sharing momentary pleasure with him. He closed his eyes as a wave of shame washed over him. *Maybe there's a way I can make it right for her, someday.*

But maybe, just maybe, this would work out okay for him—even if not for her. If all this was true—a big if, of course—if he was somehow destined for a position of power, maybe he could actually do some good with it. Helping this nun would be a start.

As it happened, and surprising to Paul, he was in full agreement with Eastman's demand. He agreed that the Church should be separated from the government. It would be healthier for both. And maybe Paul was the one to do it.

And didn't the Seer see some of the last great emperor in Paul?

Maybe this scheme wasn't so ludicrous after all.

"Paul!"

He looked up, his reverie broken. He had turned the corner to the front of the Black Pyramid, and there was his mother, standing with the two servants, all three of them grinning widely. He ran to her as fast as he could in his weakened condition and embraced her warmly. For a moment, at least, all was well in his world.

Donald C. Meyer, Professor of Music at Lake Forest College in Illinois, is a composer and music historian. As a musicologist, his research has focused on American music. As a composer, he is most active writing original music for independent films and for movies from the silent era. He has also collaborated with visual artists, choreographers, and other artists. Among the albums he has produced is a collection of souvenir music from the Chicago World's Columbian Exposition of 1893. In 2018, he co-authored the science fiction novel *Cold Shoulder* with Michael Pickard. He lives in Highland Park, Illinois, with his wife and daughter. For more information, please visit donmeyer.net.